HEAVENLY VISION

A star-studded sky enclosed Tony, yet he felt a brewing storm. His weary neck gave out and his head fell back. His eyes fluttered close. Soon he felt something sweetly hot and soothing against his skin. He opened his eyes and found himself looking up at a woman's face.

Eyes dark as Apache tears stared down at him. A sheet of pure silky white hair framed her high, prominent cheekbones, accentuating the narrow chin and full round lips. Her strong long-fingered hands stroked the taut muscles of his back.

"Tony," she sighed, her voice husky with desire.

Tony kissed the curve of her jaw, filled with overwhelming tenderness, irresistible need. She shuddered deliciously. Her hand movements quickened to a frenzy, driving him wild. He lifted his head abruptly and claimed her mouth in a rapturous kiss. She returned it just as passionately.

"Lily," he whispered. "Oh, my sweet Lily. How I love you. . . ."

Shadow of the Wolf

Connie Flynn

A TOPAZ BOOK

TOPAZ
Published by the Penguin Group
Penguin Putnam Inc., 375 Hudson Street,
New York, New York 10014, U.S.A.
Penguin Books Ltd, 27 Wrights Lane,
London W8 5TZ, England
Penguin Books Australia Ltd, Ringwood,
Victoria, Australia
Penguin Books Canada Ltd, 10 Alcorn Avenue,
Toronto, Ontario, Canada M4V 3B2
Penguin Books (N.Z.) Ltd, 182–190 Wairau Road,
Auckland 10, New Zealand

Penguin Books Ltd, Registered Offices:
Harmondsworth, Middlesex, England

First published by Topaz, an imprint of Dutton Signet,
a member of Penguin Putnam Inc.

First Printing, January, 1998
10 9 8 7 6 5 4 3 2 1

PUBLISHER'S NOTE
This is a work of fiction. Names, characters, places, and incidents either are the product of the author's imagination or are used fictitiously, and any resemblance to actual persons, living or dead, events, or locales is entirely coincidental.

To Brian Henry

Who taught me more about writing than he knows.
Thank you.

FOREWORD

Ebony Canyon, Quakahla, the Dawn People, and White Wolf Woman are totally the product of my admittedly quirky imagination. Students of Native American spirituality may notice discrepancies in my depiction of the Dawn People. I've given the Toltec/Aztec king Quetzalcoatl a much larger role than he actually played in any reference I found of him. Nor have I attempted to remain faithful to the traditions of specific tribes or even Native American beliefs in general. I've mingled them all, thrown in some Wiccan lore, and even a sprinkling of Eastern philosophy for good measure.

The pronunciation of Quetzalcoatl is "ket-sal-*kwat*-el." Quakahla is pronounced "kay-*kal*-la."

Prologue

Sienna Doe Becomes White Wolf Woman

Sienna Doe wept inside the wild forest and after a time her sobs reached the ears of Quetzalcoatl. Appearing in the guise of a feathered serpent, he coiled in front of her and asked, "Daughter, why are you so unhappy?"

Sienna Doe regarded him with sad brown eyes. "A wolf has eaten my mate, Great One."

"And this is why your heart is heavy?"

"It is so unfair! The deer have no defense against the sharp-teethed ones." As she spoke, Sienna Doe's tears began to fade. A glimmer of hope brightened her eyes. "Oh, Great One, I implore you . . . Turn me into a wolf so I might protect my relations and keep others from suffering as I am."

"All creatures are your relations, Sienna Doe."

The deer shook her lovely head. "Squirrel and Turtle, Hare and Mouse, these are my brethren. But not the flesh-eaters with their sharp claws and cruel fangs."

"And you believe you can be true to your deer spirit though you dwell in the body of a wolf?"

"I do, Great One."

"Then you shall have your wish."

With a flick of his serpent tongue, he changed her into a large she-wolf.

Several months later, Quetzalcoatl returned to the wild forest and came across Sienna Doe, who was bent over a fallen creature.

"Sienna Doe," he called. "Why do you eat your brethren? Was it not your purpose to protect them?"

Sienna Doe lifted her great white head, her muzzle dripping with the blood of her kill, and gave a wolfish grin. "Would you have me do otherwise, Great One? Am I not now White Wolf Woman, just as you made me? I am hungry, and the deer is my natural prey."

"It is ever so," replied Quetzalcoatl. With another flick of his tongue, he vanished into a part of the kingdom that did indeed require his help.

"You called me back from the hunt to tell me a children's story?" Tony White Hawk asked, not even waiting for Riva to open her eyes after the telling.

Slowly lifting her lids, Riva Star Dancer, High Shaman of the Dawn People, gazed at Tony in mild rebuke for his breech of protocol, but Tony met her eyes without apology and waited for his answer.

They stood inside a large cave. On the far wall flashed a pulsing egg-shaped light that was taller than a good-sized man and over four feet wide. Behind it lay Quakahla, the promised land of the Dawn People, and a place Tony always considered a metaphor until the pulsing gate had opened on the last full moon, heralding the fulfillment of the ancient legend.

Now, as he waited for Riva's reply, the gate flared and she turned toward it, her ageless profile silhouetted by the brilliance. "The night of the dark moon is little more than three weeks away," she reminded him.

"Old news. And it doesn't answer my question."

"Time is growing short and something is left undone. Look." She waved her arm in a graceful arc as the gate flared anew. "Look how creatures stay true to their own natures."

Tony's gaze followed the movement of Riva's arm, and he stared into a brilliance so intense it should have blinded him, but didn't. Shadows undulated inside the light, taking the form of a petite woman. Long silver hair flowed around a heart-shaped face. Dark haunted eyes beckoned him.

"Lily," he growled, tightening his hands into fists, and casting Riva a bitter glance. "What does the werewolf queen have to do with the legend of White Wolf Woman?"

"You already know, Tony. A werewolf has one nature. A haughty mortal woman stripped of her powers has another. So which nature does *this* creature have? Cleanse your heart. What do you see?"

Tony crossed his arms in front of his chest, meeting Riva's golden eyes, which were much the color of his own, but clearer, so much clearer, and he knew it was his hatred for Lily that kept his own eyes clouded. Yet he clung to it stubbornly, refusing to look again at the vision despite Riva's urging and his own conflicted feelings.

"Tajaya has been gone almost five years," she reminded him softly.

"Eons could pass and it wouldn't erase what the she-wolf did. My wife is dead. Nothing will bring her back. Although it isn't the way of the shaman, my heart cries out for vengeance."

"This is your opportunity to wash it away. The she-wolf must stand before the Tribunal, and you've been chosen to bring her back. This must be done before the dark moon—"

"—or The People will remain in Ebony Canyon for another thousand years," Tony finished for her.

"No, Tony," Riva answered with unusual urgency. "The People will not remain. The mechanical world encroaches and will soon absorb us. Our culture will die. If we do not pass now, we never will."

"I, uh—You've just received this information?"

Riva nodded. "The council met while you were on the hunt. We regretted meeting in your absence, but the message came and we couldn't do otherwise."

Unsettled by this unwelcome news, Tony resisted the urge to shift on his feet. He knew the tales as well as Riva did, though without her deep understanding and remembered that the story of The People's return to Quakahla was proceeded by a Tribunal. The accused had not been named—at least not in that story. Now it seemed the legend's fulfillment depended on him. . . .

"All the more reason to choose another warrior," he

finally replied. "I am too filled with hatred for such a vital task."

"Do not judge yourself so harshly. The Universe doesn't." She directed his attention back to the pulsing gate. "Look, Tony. See a future that is already done."

A white creature arose with a shriek, long powerful wings rippling as it glided behind the silver-haired woman. Glancing anxiously at the hawk, she started toward Tony with outstretched hands. Moved as always by her deceptively fragile shape, he found himself wanting to take her hands in his. As if responding to this desire, the hawk swooped down, cradled the woman in his sharp talons, then soared into the clouds.

"Enough," Tony said sharply. "I will do it!"

"So it was foretold."

Tony spun on his heels. At the mouth of the cave, he paused and looked back at Riva. "I make no promises to bring the she-wolf back alive."

"Do what you can, Tony."

Without further words, the High Shaman stepped through the flashing light and disappeared into Quakahla.

Chapter One

Lily Angelica DeLaVega woke up screaming.

Blood! Blood! Smeared on her hands. Spattered on the dolls and stuffed animals crammed into the shelves lining her darkened bedroom. Streaming down the damask-papered walls, dripping from the lace canopy of her four-poster bed. A warm, coppery tang filled her mouth, a once-thrilling taste that now repulsed her.

She shot upright and clutched her blankets to her chest, barely able to breathe. Just a dream. A familiar dream that visited almost every time she slept . . .

So why was she still screaming?

Smothering her cries, she doubled over, heart pounding. Not that it mattered if her screams carried. No one would hear or come rushing to check on her welfare. Her bedroom was located next to the long-vacated nursery which her parents had deliberately placed far from their suite to make certain no outraged wail or delighted shriek of the child she'd once been would disturb their sleep.

Although they often disturbed hers. Even this far away, she could hear their thoughts. Doris, her thin, almost emaciated mother was dreaming about chocolate and cream sauces again, indulgences long ago foregone by day, but which still haunted her by night.

Beside her, Lily's father slept deeply as usual, unaware of his spouse's nocturnal binge. Vincent, a partner in a prestigious brokerage firm, seldom dreamed. When he did, it was of bar charts and price/earnings ratios, with the occasional nightmare about being prosecuted for insider trading.

Now he snored loudly and fell deeper into slumber. As his noise escalated, Doris gobbled yet another calorie-free truffle.

The foray into her parents' minds eased the aftermath of Lily's nightmare, and she found herself breathing more freely. Soon her pulse returned to normal. She knew she wouldn't sleep again even though day was only beginning.

Central Park at dawn. If anything could ease her disquiet that was it. The New York City sidewalks would still be empty, the air not yet fouled by exhaust fumes or the discord of honking horns and neighing horses. She got up and went to the French doors that led to a balcony off her room, opening the fractionally parted shutters wider.

Was the bird still there? For three days now it had

perched on the railing, watching her with quick golden eyes. The last time she'd stepped out, it had given a banshee's shriek, then circled above her like a buzzard waiting for its prey's final gasp.

She shook her head impatiently. Although unusually large, it was still only a bird. Since when did a Lupine queen allow an animal to decide what she would do?

She swung open the doors, ready to inhale the morning air. Before she could take a single step, the hawk gave a shrill cry and soared into the room.

"Out, you filthy bird! Get out of my room!"

Grabbing a silk decorator pillow from her bed, she swung it above her head and leaped up toward the flying hawk. One swing caught a flapping wing and unbalanced it, giving her only brief satisfaction as she saw it quickly regain control. Gliding to the topmost shelf of a bookcase, it landed with a flutter of wings that sent a Neiman-Marcus teddy bear tumbling to the floor.

"Get out!" Lily cried again, frustrated that the loathsome creature was now well beyond her reach.

The hawk cocked its head, holding her in its gaze, and squawked with such heavy malice that Lily felt as if she'd been punched in the stomach. She stared up, recalling the night she'd worked so hard to forget. A white hawk, screeching from the rim of a smoldering fire pit . . . A tall shaman who had monitored her and Jorje's every action in Ebony Canyon.

Was the shaman coming for her? Absurd! This was New York, nearly three thousand miles from Ebony

Canyon. Though hawks were rare in New York City, that didn't mean she'd been followed. Dismissing the rush of fear, she hurled the pillow at the feathered intruder.

The bird rose gracefully to the ceiling, evading her shot, but the pillow struck the bookcase, and several dolls fell from the topmost shelf.

Porcelain heads ripped loose from their bodies and shattered. Arms and legs splintered. Rolling, the china broke into smaller pieces. An eye here, a nose there, a piece of an ear, a tiny finger . . . Fragile body parts littered the cherry-wood floor.

The sight made Lily's stomach lurch. Memories stirred; she pushed them back in a fit of rage. Practically flying herself, she waved her arms at the creature, shrieking at it to leave. One of her flailing hands closed briefly around a scaly leg. The bird teetered, sinking close to the floor before it soared out the open balcony doors to roost on the railing. Lily slammed the doors shut on its raucous cries.

Had the creature left its foul droppings, or a even a smelly feather that she'd have to flush away? Livid at the intrusion, Lily looked around.

Narrow streams of morning sun filtered through the slats of the shutters and cast muted striped shadows onto the flocked fleur-de-lis of the pale blue wallpaper, across the bland, accepting faces of the toys. Except for the china fragments on the floor, everything looked just the way it had before the bird arrived.

She turned away, strangely unable to look at the battered porcelain bodies. She'd clean them up later, before the maid came. But for now, she'd have her walk. Her parents would be up soon, preparing for the vacation Doris so "badly needed." By being out of the house when they left, she'd spare them all the discomfort of insincere farewells. No bothersome bird would interfere with her schedule.

With that decision, she went into her bathroom to cleanse herself of the encounter. Just as she turned the gilded faucets of the shower, she felt a malevolent presence. She shivered under the spray of warm water, supposing that since the day had started with an evil omen, she shouldn't be surprised.

Sebastian had found her. She didn't wonder how. Of all werewolves, his psychic powers were the most prodigious. He could discern another's thoughts across continents.

She'd known he'd come eventually. He wouldn't leave such a flagrant violation of Lupine Law unpunished. And killing another werewolf was the most flagrant of them all.

The queasiness in her stomach returned as it often did when she thought of Jorje, but she dismissed it and blocked Sebastian's probe, feeling a not-unexpected quiver of anger as her connection with him snapped. Her new concern left no room for dwelling on the bird, and she searched for a way to protect herself. She had no desire to learn what Sebastian had in store for her, but she couldn't escape him. So she'd . . .

Have to kill him, she supposed. And she knew just the way to do that. After all, wasn't she a werewolf queen?

Was a queen, came the psychic response.

Am a queen, she responded hotly. *Powers or not, I'm still a queen. Nothing can take that away.* Then, with an irate burst of energy, she severed their connection a second time.

Yes, she would have to kill Sebastian. But for now, she'd finish her shower, dress carefully, and leave the house looking like the queen she was.

This time the response came from her own mind: *Like the queen I used to be.*

Whenever Lily rose early to stroll the depths of Central Park, she was filled with animal energy. The mild blow of the wind, the leaves drifting around her feet, the cool, fresh morning air renewed her ties to the feral world. This particular morning the feeling lasted longer than usual.

She was elated with the prospect of returning to an empty apartment and knowing she'd have it to herself for weeks. Or maybe the battle with the hawk had revived her hunter's spirit. Even Sebastian's appearance was invigorating. She'd been waiting for months; now he was here and she could plan her next step.

She didn't spend much time pondering the reason. The morning was too clear, the solitude too refreshing.

She traveled alone for several hours, arms swinging, head held high, confident of her place in the world despite the feathered threat on her balcony and the furred one lurking in wait. The sun rose higher as she walked, filtering through the trees. Sounds grew nearer, more frequent.

As she turned a curve in the path, she met an approaching man—a bodybuilder type with limbs so pumped with muscles they strained his pants and shirt. Although she caught his lascivious leer, she gave him little notice as they passed.

Then she felt his lingering attention. Her hand-tailored jeans fit her flawlessly, and she could sense his eyes ogling the sway of her hips beneath the hem of her Dior jacket. She glanced over her shoulder and met the man's eyes. He stopped, then turned and strutted toward her, smiling cockily. Thinking she once could have eaten three of his kind for breakfast, she scowled regally and sent him a psychic warning: *Back off, foolish omega.*

His leering expression instantly transformed to fear. All swagger gone, he turned awkwardly and almost ran away.

Lily smiled. These foolish mortals hadn't the courtesy of the Lupine race. Not a single one of them dared treat another with such disrespect. Instantly, reality dawned. She couldn't have followed through on her mental threat. The man wasn't a lowly werewolf omega pup and she wasn't a powerful queen. He actually could have hurt her.

For twelve years she'd lived a life of power and invincibility, free from the fears and struggles of the human race. Now she was one of them again, vulnerable, in a world that had no place for her.

Her former burst of energy draining, Lily drifted to a bench and stared into a Chinese garden. The trouble with having once been a werewolf, she thought sadly, was that no one believed you. In fact they thought you were nuts. The Orientals might believe—and the primitive ones who dwelled in Ebony Canyon certainly did believe. But these cynical people of the West . . . ? No, not one of them believed.

When Doris and Vincent had come to the small-town Arizona hospital to reluctantly claim her, she'd been scratched, bruised, and hysterically babbling about lost powers, Dana and Morgan, and poor, poor Jorje. Her horrified parents had promptly swept her back to New York City. Pleading with the doctors to make her stop telling such outlandish and humiliating tales, they'd placed her in a discreet hospital catering to those whom they euphemistically labeled as "distressed."

The staff fed her drugs, told her she was hallucinating and clinging to her delusions as a defense against the horror of witnessing her friend's brutal death. She hadn't killed him. No one her size could have possibly broken a grown man's neck. This trauma, they further explained, had brought her emotionally barren childhood crashing down on her, making everyone around her seem like beasts. She was safe. No one was after her seeking revenge. Eventually Jorge's killer would be caught.

At first she denied it all. She was Queen Lily of the Lupine race, proud, invincible, ageless. Eventually, as the initial horror of her unwilling transformation back to human form waned, she realized the hospital would never release her if she clung to the truth. She stopped insisting and feigned a few sessions filled with weeping. Finally they let her go.

A sudden sound made Lily jump in alarm. She looked up and caught a flash of white. Her sight and hearing were extremely keen—a fact that had amazed the hospital staff—but even with this advantage she wasn't sure of what she'd seen. Not noticing any further movement, she soon became tired of looking and settled back on the bench to stare into the face of a smiling stone Buddha.

What was happening to her? No werewolf jumped at unexpected sounds or feared a posturing man. How would she deal with these insecurities and, even more important, what would she do with the rest of her life? Remain with Doris and Vincent, who could barely stand the sight of her? Go to work in some greasy fast-food restaurant and rent a cheap apartment with her meager earnings? And what of Sebastian? If she dropped her psychic guard she could feel him out there. Lurking, waiting, in no hurry. Unhampered by the short years allotted humans, he basked in the luxury of knowing he'd get her eventually.

Unless she got him first.

Lily shifted on the bench, deciding to make a stop before she returned to the mercifully empty house. Few things could kill a werewolf, but holy water was one of them. She shuddered involuntarily at the idea of even touching the stuff, but knew she had to overcome this unseemly cowardice. Her future, her very life, depended upon it.

While she shored up her determination, people began walking past her. A group gathered by the Buddha, half listening to a tour guide. A couple meandered down the leafy path, hand in hand. Such ordinary lives they led. Pale and colorless, especially when compared to the glory of roaming the great cities and forests of the world, feared and fearless. Ordinary, so ordinary. Still, these fainthearted humans somehow managed, didn't they? Despite the threats around them, they laughed, held hands, and found some enjoyment in their meager existences.

Just then a small girl broke away from the group, whooping gleefully. Looking back mischievously at her pursuing mother, she pedaled her chubby little legs as fast as she could. What fun, her smiling little face said. What fun. She came straight toward Lily's outstretched feet.

Although Lily hastily pulled them back, she wasn't quick enough, and the girl tripped anyway. Lily caught her before she hit the ground and met a pair of impish eyes, a sparkling smile. Flooded with warmth, she smiled back, then handed the child to her apologetic and grateful mother.

The pair returned to the group, but the girl still had her attention on Lily and delivered several quick grins from behind her mother's legs.

Lily could hear the girl breathe, hear her smothered little titters over the drone of the guide's voice. But she couldn't hear the blood, she realized, that soft and constant thrumming through those tiny veins. Nor did she feel its irresistible lure.

Lost powers, just two among countless others. Many of them she missed—the freedom, the invincibility, the sheer vitality of such massive brute force. But not the hunger.

No, she didn't miss the hunger at all.

On another bench about a half mile away, Tony White Hawk honed his link with the hawk perched in the high branches of the tree above Lily's head. Seeing what it saw, hearing what it heard, Tony maintained the careful watch he'd kept on the she-wolf since she'd slipped from the apartment. When the child careened toward her, he'd flinched, thinking of the daughter he'd left in the safety of the canyon, painfully aware he was putting her and all the others at risk by bringing back the monster.

Of course those slender fingers bore no claws these days, nor did her smile reveal deadly fangs. But those tilted eyes still held the menace of the wolf, as the man who'd so unwisely tried to intimidate her quickly discovered.

Lily Angelica DeLaVega hadn't lost her fight. She wouldn't easily fall into his hands, and if he didn't soon master the shape-shifting skill Riva assured him would come when he needed it. . . .

Don't just ride with the thought-form, she'd counseled during their last meeting before he left the canyon. *Become it.* Then, when it took him where he wanted to go, all he had to do was return to being himself.

Simple. Straight-forward.

Too simple.

Why couldn't the Dawn People's magic contain spells and rituals that worked without fail once they were learned? Why did they rely on the soul of the user? Becoming the hawk required incredible concentration, and whenever he thought he'd almost achieved it, he lost it all in a swirl of malice toward the she-wolf.

He'd flown into Lily's room that morning with intense concentration, sure he'd succeed this time. But the moment he'd seen her in that tiny top and skimpy bottom, her small curved body glowing with health, he thought only of Tajaya, who would never again dwell in such a womanly form.

Not only hadn't he shifted into human form, he'd tried to terrorize her. Not the shaman's way. Not even the warrior's way. Worse, she'd almost gotten the best of him. He thanked everything sacred that Riva hadn't seen his shame.

No, he hadn't needed to see her encounter with the man to know she still retained her fighting spirit.

A gentle trill from the hawk interrupted his reflections. Lily was on the move again. He melded his mind with his thought-form, sending it rising into the gray sky, and soon felt wings flex, the rise and fall of gentle air currents.

Although a product of Tony's mind, the hawk was real enough in every sense. Its beak and claws could shred both bark and skin with equal ease. Its cries resounded in the ears of men. Yet its winged body still felt as light and insubstantial as the puffy clouds above. Tony sank into its sway and rode the currents.

Below, he saw Lily detour off the street next to the park and hurry through the city, making several turns until she stopped at a house of worship. A Catholic cathedral, if Tony's memory served him. Soon she came out, lowering her head against a rising wind, her pockets bulging from something she must have gathered inside.

What could a church offer such a profane one? he wondered, dismissing the obvious answer. He glided after her, careful not to swoop too low as they approached the building where she lived with the indifferent ones who'd spawned her.

The wind blew in eddies along the curbs, tumbling leaves, tugging at the lapels of the she-wolf's lightweight jacket, rippling through strands of her silver-white hair. Not for the first time, Tony wondered how such a graceful, beautiful creature could be so evil.

His fury simmered again.

Below, Lily hesitated as if sensing his hatred. Pulling her jacket closer, she headed for the door of her gargoyle-infested dwelling, gave a tight little smile to the waiting doorman and ducked into the entry.

White Hawk sent the hawk to roost on the railing and waited. Another opportunity would arise. This time rancor wouldn't interfere with duty to the tribal council.

Still, despite this vow, he couldn't shake his conviction that the council had put their faith in the wrong man.

Chapter Two

Holy Water. Noxious to a werewolf's eyes and lungs. Fire to the skin. Fatal in large enough quantities. With trembling fingers, Lily opened one of the bottles she'd taken from the cathedral, chiding herself for her fearfulness. She was human now, the liquid should have no effect.

But still . . .

Smothering a tremulous gasp, she gingerly splashed a tiny drop on a finger. Cool. Wet. Only water. The gasp escaped as a relieved sigh.

She shifted on the velvet settee in the carpeted sitting area off her bedroom, then recorked the vial and put it back with the others in the pocket of her jacket. Now she had a weapon. She had no illusion that twelve bottles were enough to destroy Sebastian, but they would weaken him considerably, giving her an opportunity to drive a knife into his tender underbelly and wait for the blood to drain from his body.

Lily shuddered violently at the cruelly vivid picture the thought brought to mind. Sebastian had loved her, elevated her to heights she'd never dreamed of . . .

But no one loved her now. She had to take care of herself.

Her hands still unsteady, she stood up on equally unsteady legs, surveying her room. She hadn't realized how much she'd felt like a prisoner in these luxurious quarters. With Doris and Vincent gone, her mind was unburdened of their myriad and often conflicting thoughts, her keen ears were no longer assailed by their ceaseless noisy movements.

The maid had stopped by to say farewell and noticed the broken dolls on the floor, but Lily had told her to enjoy her rest; she'd clean up the mess herself. Though she'd always regarded the woman with a measure of sympathy for her frantic efforts to please Doris, she was grateful for the absence of swishing mops and feather dusters, of roaring vacuum cleaner.

For a time she would have some peace. She would rummage through the refrigerator for something to eat, maybe sit in the den, build a fire, watch soap operas or read an entertaining novel. But first she'd clean up the carnage left behind by the hawk.

Carnage, she thought as she picked up a waste basket and walked toward the mess. What an odd word to describe what was essentially broken pottery. But as she picked up a porcelain arm streaked with dozens of tiny cracks, her body tensed with dread.

As if sensing her mood, the hawk cried outside the balcony doors, its wide wings silhouetted behind the open shutters. She shivered and in that moment Sebastian's merciless animosity pierced the block she'd erected against him. Hastily reconstructing the block, she flung the cracked china body part into the trash can. It hit the bottom with a sick, dull thud.

She shivered again. All she wanted was peace. But peace was hard to come by.

It was after midnight when Lily heard the sound at her balcony doors. She sprang upright beneath her blankets, groping for the bottle she'd set on her bedside table, then enclosed it in her hand and cautiously got up.

Pressing against the wall next to the doors, she opened the shutters slightly, leaning forward to peek through the slats at glaring streetlights, at shifting shadows broken by flashes of restless white.

The omnipresent hawk. Although she knew the bird couldn't possibly see her through the narrow slits, it nonetheless darted numerous baleful glances at the door as it strutted along the railing. Annoyed that the damned creature had interrupted her sleep, Lily moved away from the window and wandered into the bathroom, the vial still in her hand. Putting it on the counter, she bent to wash her sleepy eyes.

Sufficiently revived, she turned to reach for a towel. It magically appeared in her hand. Her eyes snapped open and she met another pair of eyes—deep arctic blue and framed by a face covered with silver white hair.

"Sebastian!"

"You seem unhappy to see me, dear one." With a toss of his silver mane, Sebastian formed his muzzle into a grotesque smile. "I, too, am unhappy. It pains me to find you in such undignified circumstances."

Quickly squelching her instinctive thought of the vial of holy water before he could read it, Lily casually dried her face and hands, then gave Sebastian a mocking once-over.

Bending low to avoid the high ceiling, he supported his massive bulk on a gilded walking stick. Although at first glance he might appear to be an unusually tall and muscular human in his bright yellow topcoat with its matching bowler hat, a second glance would encompass his elongated muzzle and the thick white fur that covered every exposed part of his body.

He was indeed a werewolf—a man-wolf—and though he could shift from human to canine to man-wolf shape with ease, Lily knew he preferred the man-wolf form above all. And was flashy about it too.

Few werewolves could retain their clothing as they alchemized from wolf to man to werewolf, but Sebastian possessed this skill. As a royal member of the Lupine race, Lily had also mastered that ability, but she'd preferred a more subdued elegance and had frequently teased Sebastian about his garish tastes.

"You've outdone yourself," she gibed. "If work slaughtering humans gets scarce you might consider doubling as a fire hydrant."

He tipped his yellow bowler hat. "Always the

pepper-tongued one, an attribute undimmed by your mortal state."

"You're the best judge of that, my king," she retorted with a disdainful bow.

"Careful, Lily," he warned. "I have my limits."

"Of course you do." Arching her neck, she ran her fingers tauntingly down the center of her throat. "And I'm ready to die, Lord."

With a sharp rap of his walking stick, Sebastian shot forward and grabbed a handful of Lily's hair. Pulling her face within inches of his, he simultaneously pinned her left arm against his massive chest. "Do you pups never learn? Werewolves do not kill one another."

"This . . . is as much . . . your fault as . . . mine," Lily hissed though pain-clenched teeth. Sebastian's hold on her hair was merciless. Despite that, she pulled away, reaching back with her free hand for the vial. To block her intent from Sebastian's notice, and though it hurt even to talk, she forced out new accusations. "You just . . . just want to avoid . . . your own part in . . . in Jorje's death. A-admit it . . . oh . . . oh, High King . . ."

Sebastian gave several vicious pulls to her hair. "Do not address me with such insolence, pup!"

Agonized tears stung Lily's eyes as she groped for the vial, but finally she felt its smooth plastic surface. Palming the bottle and struggling to withstand Sebastian's excruciating tugs, she fumbled to free the stopper. It didn't budge and she decided her only recourse was to make Sebastian angry enough to release her.

Deliberately sagging forward, which relieved some of the pressure on her scalp, she fixed him with an accusing glare. "You know it's true! *You* chose Morgan as my mate. I never, never wanted him. Then you put me under orders to protect him. The wolfling was about to slay him. I regret—"

"Regret! Bah!" Sebastian slipped into the werewolf language. "Regret is for mortals."

He curled his lip, baring his gleaming canines. His breath hit her face—hot, reeking of fresh human blood—turning her stomach with stunning violence. But what surprised her most of all was that she'd understood him.

"But I forget," he added in a cooler tone, still speaking in the Lupine tongue. His apparent belief that she didn't comprehend a word he said reassured her that she'd successfully blocked his mind-reading abilities. "You are one of them now, are you not? A puny, sniveling mortal. Perhaps this is why you blame me for the law you violated, why you expected me to violate it also. No, dear one, I have other plans for you once you return to the pack."

"I'll never return!" she shot back, barely aware she'd instinctively replied in Lupinese.

Sebastian blinked in surprise. "You understand . . . Perhaps all is *not* lost . . ."

She started to speak again, but he raised his free hand. "Do not protest. You cannot avoid it. The next aspect of the moon and Pluto in the heavens is but days away. By then I will have persuaded you to endure the Song of Hades. Within a week you will be a Lupine again. But not as a queen." He chuckled darkly. "I have devised an exquisite sentence, and I am sure you above all can appreciate its subtlety. Imagine, if you will, your misery at spending the next century as the lowest of the low—an omega, destined to give your kills to alphas and"—another chuckle—"even the lesser betas. A fitting punishment for a murderess, and surely a warning to those who might deign to do likewise."

A chill crept up Lily's spine. Dear God, what hell he'd planned for her. Even life as an ordinary mortal living in a hovel was better than that. She faked a derisive laugh. "By Lupine Law, you cannot force me, Sebastian. And I'll never submit to the ceremony. Never!"

"You who breeched the Law so grievously dare quote it now?" With a frustrated groan, he released Lily's hair. The moment she'd been waiting for.

But before she could move to uncork the bottle, he put a finger on her cheek, grazing the skin lightly with his clawed finger. She hesitated, momentarily transfixed.

"How could you have done this, Lily? You were my upholder of the Law."

For an instant his eyes filled with sorrow. His hand moved to cup her chin. "Now my pack squabbles among themselves like common beasts. Only by your example can I restore my people's pride. You cannot escape."

His eyes flickered, narrowed hypnotically. Lily tried to wrench her head free, but he tightened his grip.

"Come to me, Lily," he crooned, beginning the werewolf spell.

Her arm now unfettered, Lily slipped it behind her, expecting her willpower to wane even before she attempted to open the vial. Although Sebastian's gaze bore deeply into her eyes, her desire to escape remained as strong as ever. His expression turned puzzled just as she yanked the stopper free.

With his realization dawning and no time left, she overcame her fear of wasting a single drop and wildly flung the water into his face.

"You foolish bitch," he roared. His hand fell from her cheek. Staggering on weakened legs, he reached out blindly, groping for balance. As he slumped to the floor, his claw snagged one of Lily's wrists.

Lily barely felt the skin tear. She hadn't injured him badly enough to give herself time for escape, and her only thought was to get another bottle of water from her jacket before Sebastian's superhuman healing powers restored his strength. Leaping over his writhing body, she dashed into the bedroom, trying to remember where she'd left the jacket.

There! There! Carelessly tossed over the back of a chair in the carpeted sitting area at the far end of the room. Blood seeped from her wrist, but it didn't matter. Only the jacket, the bottles, mattered. The jacket. The bottles. She dashed across the wooden floor, bare feet slipping on the smooth surface, her head growing strangely light.

Sebastian's moans filled her ears. "Noooo . . ." he cried and she heard him lumbering up, knew he'd read the purpose in her mind. But she was mere feet away now. The bottles were close, close . . .

A furred hand closed around her ankle and she plummeted to the white carpet.

"Do not fight me," she heard him rasp. "You cannot win."

Rolling, flailing, scooting on her belly and unwilling to waste energy on words, she inched toward the jacket, reaching out, less than a hand's span from the precious fluid. Blood trickled down her arm, leaving rivulets on her skin. Still she reached. Reached, reached, reaching . . . But unable . . .

Sebastian enclosed her legs and with a quick, jerky movement flipped her on her back. Suddenly pain more intense than Lily had ever experienced coursed through her body. As if in slow motion, she felt the skin on one thigh split, felt muscle coming apart, ripping, shredding. An agonized scream burst from her throat and her eyes shot wide open, searching for the source of her agony.

She saw Sebastian glaring up at her from the floor, his handsome wolf face ravaged almost beyond recognition, but the punishing throb in her leg dulled the shock of such a sight. Praying he'd injured her only slightly, she let her eyes drift to her leg . . .

Blood had once been her life—she should have been prepared—but the sight of the crimson geyser spurting from her thigh tore another scream from her throat.

Then Sebastian was above her, growling threats, swearing he'd make her an outcast for all her hundreds of remaining years. Her head swam, but still she struggled to reach the jacket. Her limbs were so heavy, though. She could barely lift her arm.

The jacket . . . it was almost within her grasp. Almost.

A screech filled the room. Initially thinking she'd cried out again, Lily strained to lift her head and saw the hawk soar through the open balcony doors, speeding toward Sebastian. Diving at the werewolf, the bird attacked with deadly beak and talons. Sebastian swatted back in rage.

The holy water had clearly taken its toll. Patches of blistered skin showed beneath his tattered, natty clothes, his melting fur. His blows became clumsy, often missing altogether. But one titanic lunge met its mark. He clamped a hand over the hawk's wing and hurled the bird toward the bed. Reeling, struggling for purchase on the flimsy canopy, ripping the fabric with its sagging weight, the bird finally managed to right itself. This gave Sebastian the time he needed. Before the bird regrouped to attack anew, he bellied toward the exit and slid out onto the balcony.

"Remember, Lily, you cannot escape," he threatened weakly. Seconds later, a soft thud resounded from the sidewalk below.

With one final angry cry, the hawk settled on top of the canopy. Then all was silent. How odd, Lily thought, that the creature who'd plagued her so horribly should now come to her rescue. Then the creature faded from her vision. She wondered where it was, and found she didn't care. Darkness had settled over her eyes and she didn't quite understand why.

She was safe, she supposed. Although for some reason safety no longer seemed important. Nothing could harm her. She was floating, wasn't she? An unusual feeling. Almost like being in a hot air balloon, rising, rising . . .

To where, she didn't know.

Suddenly a figure stood above her. A hard, angular, suntanned man with a sculptured face and unforgiving golden eyes.

The shaman, she realized hazily. The one who'd so sadly lost his wife. She stared up, and found herself untroubled by his presence, although she knew he shouldn't be there. Then her head fell to one side, and she stared blankly at the plush white carpet, saw stains, seeping stains, darkly red and indelible.

The last thought she had before closing her weighted eyelids was how horribly Doris would berate the poor maid for being unable to clean up the mess.

The last words she heard came from the shaman's lips. "You will not die, Lily," he said with chilling harshness, "At least not now."

Chapter Three

He should have let her die. Unconsciously flexing and unflexing his hands, Tony White Hawk gazed down at the unconscious woman in the lower berth. Beneath his feet, the train vibrated, its muted rumbles the only sound in the compartment.

Moaning gently, the woman stirred, arching her slender neck and giving Tony a view of her softly throbbing pulse. His hand dropped to the hunting knife sheathed at his waist and rested there.

He stared down reflectively for a long moment, then turned away to a desklike alcove and picked up a small basin and a box of bandages. Returning to his sleeping captive, he lifted one of her hands. Although he'd done his best to wash off the blood, the creases of her knuckles still contained dark flakes, and a dried trickle from beneath her bandage streaked her skin to the elbow.

As he stripped the old bandage from her wound, he found it hard to equate this fragile creature with the monster who had killed Tajaya. Pity speared his heart, angering him because it was so undeserved. The irony didn't escape him. For years he'd rued his hateful impulses toward the she-wolf, now he rued his lack of them.

He ripped off the bandage unnecessarily hard, and a pained grunt escaped Lily's throat. She flinched slightly, then settled back into slumber.

Beneath the bandage was a poultice, which Tony discarded. Running his finger along the closed gash, pleased with how well the Medicine had worked, he then dipped a eucalyptus leaf into the bowl and plastered it to the skin. Next he moved to her leg. This gash, the potentially fatal one, went deeper, but it was also healing well. She should have regained most of her strength by the time they reached Flagstaff.

He tended to her wound, still dazed by what had happened in Lily's room. No one would blame him for failing to save her from her werewolf lord. He'd have fulfilled his duty.

His thought-form had intervened instinctively, he told himself, roused by the sight of his charge's blood spilling on the white floor. Hawks were fighters to the core, and he could expect no less of this one, just because it was a product of his mind. But it wasn't the bird's ferocious protectiveness that shook him, it was what happened next.

One moment he'd been roosting on the frame of the frilly canopy watching the she-wolf's blood stain the carpet. The next moment he'd been in human form, standing over her, torn between the hawk's protectiveness and his own malice.

For years he'd struggled with shape-shifting, and though he'd had some minor successes before Tajaya's death, he'd had none since then. Yet the moment this unworthy creature needed him, he'd shape-shifted instantly, effortlessly.

Why had he been blessed with the gift to save this unholy one? He didn't understand.

Finished with the poultices, Tony put adhesive bandages on both wounds, then returned the bowl and package to the desk. A leather satchel leaned against the wall and he opened it to collect a smaller bag. From this he removed an abalone half shell, a packet of sage, and the feathered wing of an eagle. Crumbling some of the herb into the shell, he lit the leaves with a match. As spirals of smoke wafted up, he moved back to the berth.

Sweeping the wing across the shell and directing the healing smoke over Lily's body, he recited a prayer in the language of the Dawn People, thanking the Great Spirit for delivering Lily from death so she could face her crimes, and asking for relief from his shameful hatred.

And while one part of him delivered the words wholeheartedly, another part meant them not at all.

He should have let her die.

* * *

Lily felt a gentle sway, as if she were in a cradle or a womb. Her mind drifted through her life, moving from place to place, event to event, every scene so vivid she felt she was actually there.

Was she dead?

How odd she could hear a faint and rhythmic thump beneath her ear, or even be aware she had an ear. She wiggled her toes, amazed to find them working just as she remembered.

Then her thoughts went adrift again. She found herself in the distant past . . .

Paris, at seventeen, giggling near the entrance to the Eiffel Tower with her classmates. The sky above was slightly gray, promising another spring shower, and Lily was wearing her new Dior jacket.

"Have you ever seen one?" Jolene, always the boldest among her friends, was revealing the details of her first sexual encounter, secrets of experience glowing in her young eyes.

"No!" cried Christine. "And I never will. Not until I'm married."

"Only on the ceiling of the Sistine Chapel," Lily said with a half giggle. "Are they really that little?"

Christine's head whipped in Lily's direction. "You didn't look at those parts! Not in the Sistine!"

Laughing at her friend's shock, Lily twirled around. Just as she was about to turn back, she saw him. Dressed in a dramatic black cloak lined with crimson that flapped around the legs of his white suit, he had an aura of power about him. His hair was silver, but his face was unlined, youthful, and cruelly handsome.

Emboldened by her voyeur's journey into sexuality, Lily returned his stare and instantly felt a powerful tug on her psyche.

Should she approach him?

As soon as the thought crossed her mind, the man nodded.

Lily took a couple of steps forward.

"Where are you going?" asked Jolene, clearly annoyed by Lily's straying attention.

"That man . . ."

Lily moved dreamily toward him. When she came to stand before him, she felt his startling blue eyes caress her. With a flourish of his arm, he bowed. *"Bon jour, mon petite.* Sebastian at your service."

Although it normally would have felt silly, Lily curtsied without self-consciousness. *"Bonjour, mon ami."*

"Ah. You are fluent in French."

"Not really."

"So what is your name, dear one?" He touched both her temples. "No, don't tell me," he said, closing his eyes theatrically. Freed momentarily from his compelling gaze, Lily viewed him objectively. Everything about him was larger than life. His height, which towered better than a foot above her five-foot body. His movements, which were large and sweeping.

"Your name is Lily." He opened his eyes, holding her in his sight again. "Lily Angelica DeLaVega. Both your Christian names denote purity. You must possess it in abundance."

Lily's eyes widened. "How did you know?"

"Just by chance."

And though his uncanny guess made her slightly nervous, she felt drawn to him anyway. During the many lonely days and nights in her parents' home, she'd dreamed of her destiny. Somehow this man made her feel he'd help her find it.

"Come, dear one." He slipped a hand beneath her elbow. "Let me treat you to an ice."

They drifted away from the shadow of the Eiffel Tower, Lily barely hearing Jolene and Christine's loud objections, to search for a vendor. Afterward they strolled around the plaza, and Lily lapped up a raspberry ice that tasted better than any she'd ever had. Throughout their walk he treated her with an old-world courtesy that contained no hint of lasciviousness. By the end Lily felt she'd found the doting father she'd always dreamed of. Completely without shyness she turned to tell him this.

Suddenly the raspberry flavor on her tongue turned pungent and bitter. Reluctantly, she opened her eyes.

"Drink," said a harsh voice from somewhere outside her dream.

A large hand supported her head, the touch rough and uncaring. Although she wanted to spit out the liquid, Lily swallowed, more out of surprise than obedience.

"White Hawk," she said weakly, certain she hadn't died. Even the Devil wouldn't be so cruel as to deliver her into this man's hands.

She saw she was in a kind of three-sided box. White Hawk was outlined in light, and his wide shoulders blocked everything behind him. Her body felt leaden, and painful throbs came from her wrist and her leg. She wanted to seek the source of the pain but her captor was already forcing another sip of the fluid past her lips.

She swallowed involuntarily. "This tastes like hell. What is it?"

"A tonic." He tilted the cup again, silencing her for the moment. "It rebuilds the blood and will make you strong for traveling."

Downing the dose quickly, she raised her hand against the next one. "Where are we?"

Holding the plastic cup just a few inches from her mouth, White Hawk hesitated. When the silence continued, she repeated her question.

"On a train to Arizona. I'm taking you back to Ebony Mountain."

"Nooo!" Lily levered up on her elbows. Her head instantly spun. Spots danced before her face. "Sebastian . . ."

". . . cannot help you. Don't even hope for it."

"You fool . . ." Too tired to manage more than a whisper, she made one last effort to warn him. She supposed she owed him that at least. "You'll only . . . draw more danger . . . to your people."

He stared at her a moment with narrowed eyes, then moved the cup back to her lips. "Take another sip."

He didn't understand, and she was too weak to make him. Nor did she truly care that much. After taking her last dose of bitter medicine, she collapsed onto the bed and returned to her dreams.

She lost all track of where she was. Between her

sojourns to the past, White Hawk poured the bitter brew down her throat. On a few occasions he urged her to eat a bite of pear or peach, once a banana. Then Lily would drift off again, remembering . . .

The day of Gwen's tearful departure finally woke her. Such a small transgression, really, buying Lily yet another dress that her mother thought was too frilly and flashy. But Doris had fired her. Later, when Lily stared up at Gwen in the luggage-cluttered entry foyer and listened to her teary-eyed explanation of why they wouldn't be together anymore, she only knew she was losing the one person who'd ever made her feel wanted.

Although her parents often told Lily she was too big for tantrums, she'd thrown one anyway. It had done no good. Gwen was gone for good. The hard-faced Mrs. Preston arrived the next day.

Lily had been five, and the morning Gwen left was the last time she'd ever been held with love.

Now feeling the pain as acutely as she had that day, she lurched upright, a sob caught in her throat.

"Are you in pain?"

"What?" Lily asked, startled by the unexpected voice.

"I asked if you were in pain." On a bench opposite her bunk sat White Hawk, holding a newspaper in his hand. His loathing tone added to her misery, and when he got up and reached for her hand, she flinched.

"Don't!" She shoved her arm beneath her covers.

"The wounds may need more tending."

"I'm fine! I had a bad dream, that's all."

"I see." His warm golden eyes held more ice than

Sebastian's cool blue ones. "I imagine your kind have many."

"Yes." She arched one of her brows and returned his cold stare. "A favorite of mine is about plucking the feathers off a large white bird. One by one. A hawk, I believe."

A muscle twitched in his jaw, giving her a moment's satisfaction that was quickly dimmed by the realization she was trapped in this small room with him. Glancing around, she saw they were in a compartment of a train.

"How did I get here?" she asked in a more civil tone.

"I brought you."

"Can you even imagine it? I actually figured that part out myself. *How* did you do it?"

"It's unimportant, but if you must know I put you in a wheelchair and claimed you were very ill." He smiled grimly. "The porters were very helpful."

He returned to the bench, picked up the newspaper and resumed reading.

Lily combed her fingers through her tangled hair, which was twisted uncomfortably around her body. She felt stronger. Maybe strong enough to stand. She tentatively swung her feet to the floor.

Her blanket fell away, revealing the thin cotton camisole and thong panties she'd been wearing when Sebastian showed up. She looked at her legs, which dangled over the edge of her berth, bare to the waist. The toes of one foot almost touched White Hawk's rough leather boots, and when he saw how close their feet were, he drew his away.

"Did you enjoy the peep show?" Lily asked mockingly.

He gave her a scathing look, then inclined his head toward a small open closet. "Your clothing."

She saw her Dior jacket on a hanger. Underneath was one of her Hermes suitcases. "You think of everything, don't you?"

As though she hadn't spoken, he gestured to a narrow door next to the divan. "Change in there. It has a shower."

Pulling the blanket free from the berth, Lily wrapped it around her and got up to collect her things. The faint wobble of the floor made her steps unsteady, and as she neared him, White Hawk pulled in his other foot. She glanced down at it pointedly, gathered the blanket closer, then picked up the suitcase and entered the small bathroom.

Inside, she leaned against the closed door and stared down at her bandaged wrist. Her hand moved easily, with minimal discomfort. Cautiously, she peeled the edge of the bandage free, finding a leaf plastered onto the skin. She pulled that off too, then gaped in surprise.

She knew what damage a slashing werewolf claw inflicted, and the wound should still have been red and raw. So why did only a thin, healing crust remain? Lifting the bandage from the gash in her leg, she found only a thick, dark scab. Dear God, she'd seen that wound herself, knew it had gone to the bone.

How many days had she been unconscious?

Only White Hawk could answer that, but she didn't care to talk to him at the moment. Dismissing her questions, she stripped off both bandages and stepped into the shower, turning on the water full force. She took her time showering, scrubbing off every last remnant of dried blood as if it were toxic. When she got out, she toweled off the water, then went to face herself in the mirror. She still felt like death and wondered if she looked like it too.

Her image rippled unappealingly in the cheap mirror, and the flourescent light made a grating hum. From beneath her feet came the annoying clack-a-clack-clack of the train speeding along the rails. The swaying motion she'd found so soothing in the berth was now disorientating and made her slightly dizzy.

If not for the hostile man outside, she would have bled to death. Thanks to him, she remained in this world of sights, sounds, and senses, although the ones she now faced were none too pleasing.

She sank onto the lid of the toilet until the dizziness passed, then bent to get a comb from her suitcase. White Hawk had forgotten nothing. As she combed her tangled hair, she wondered why he'd gone to so much trouble. Surely he was planning to kill her. Why hadn't he simply let her die by Sebastian's hand?

Shrugging with more bravado than she really felt, she decided he must want to avenge his wife by administering the final blow himself.

What was he waiting for?

Shrugging again, Lily applied herself to unsnarling a particularly difficult tangle. White Hawk's reasons meant nothing to her, she told herself. If vengeance was what he sought, he'd find it very hard to come by.

Chapter Four

Arlan Ravenheart walked softly to avoid stirring the heavy dust on the ground in the village center. Although the air was thick with monsoon dampness, the Great Spirit had seen fit to delay rain. Even now lines of people in the fields passed huge cauldrons of water from the dwindling river to maintain their food supply.

Taking in the hogans, wickiups, and occasional teepees that haphazardly occupied the space surrounding the central longhouse, Ravenheart frowned. It was nothing short of blasphemy to let those who hadn't originally come from Quakahla to contaminate the tribe with their customs. Instead of properly rejecting the foreign ways of the latecomers, councils through the years had embraced them and integrated their customs until the traditions of the first Dawn People were all but lost. Even now, the High Shaman was carrying this odious practice into their true home inside Quakahla.

When he became High Shaman he'd put an end to it. The People dwelled in pueblos, not in unsightly structures of stick, clay, and animal skin. His first act would be to burn every wickiup, hogan, and teepee—even the longhouse—and declare pueblos the only fit dwellings.

The thought of all those messy shelters going up in flames brought a pleased smile to his lips. He banished it quickly, well aware it would be unwise to reveal his ambitions so early. Although even now Star Dancer was supervising the construction of a new longhouse, and was undeserving of such respect from him, he would still meet her with such dignified humility she couldn't help but realize that his right to be the next High Shaman far surpassed White Hawk's. She'd invite him to join the council and begin teaching him her secrets.

Ravenheart quickened his step and entered a narrow canyon to the left of the cliff that held the pueblos. Traveling over a path littered with wobbling rocks, he reached a cave that emitted a glow bright enough to be seen from outside, even though the sun blazed above his head.

Ravenheart stepped inside the cave. The walls and ceiling gleamed with reflected light from the pulsing oval on the far back wall. The gate to Quakahla. Soon it would flare, inviting him to pass through to the dimension on the other side.

The flash came. Squelching a familiar reluctance, he moved forward. The promise of returning home filled him with immense joy, but he hated this gate, hated the purity of its brilliance, hated the uncertainty about his worthiness that always arose in that moment of passing.

But less than three phases of the moon remained—nineteen days by the latecomers' counting. Then the Dawn People would file through this gate, one by one, and he'd never have to endure this uncertainty again.

With a prayer to the spirits for protection, he crossed quickly, fighting back overwhelming memories of his self-serving moments, his acts of cruelty, his lack of concern for the weak and sick. Once on the other side, the memories vanished, and he renewed his conviction that he was meant to rule here.

Several hundred yards from the gate stood Star Dancer, her back to him as she directed the workers constructing the new longhouse.

"Ravenheart . . ." She turned in his direction, although he hadn't made a sound. She always knew when another approached, a skill he hadn't yet developed, and he felt a surge of envy.

"You wish to speak, warrior?" A mild breeze blew at her rich chestnut hair and pushed her broomstick skirt around her strong, firm body. Such a display of health did not please Ravenheart. A long life for her only delayed his ascension in the ranks.

He hurried forward, wanting none of the others to hear his words. "Star Dancer," he said in an oily tone when he reached her side. "I'm still dismayed you did not select me to retrieve the she-wolf."

"So you have often said." She raised her eyebrows gently. "You have a new complaint?"

"A lack of understanding. Haven't I pursued my training rigorously? Although I'm not yet twenty-one winters, I am already a skilled warrior. I'm mastering thought-forms and soon shall conquer shape-shifting."

"And what of healing? How comes the healing?"

Ravenheart hesitated. Despite his best attempts, his healings had been weak and ineffectual. If not for White Hawk's intervention, old Frieda would have succumbed to the fever that spring, and he knew Star Dancer was aware of this.

"I still work on perfecting my skills." He bowed his head in false humility. "But I haven't come to talk of that."

"Then speak your truth."

"White Hawk's heart is poisoned toward the she-wolf, while mine is not. Since you didn't see fit to send me for her, I ask to be her advocate before the Tribunal."

Star Dancer glanced toward the busy workers, letting her eyes rest a moment on the fields beyond. "I've given little thought to her defense, Ravenheart. Quakahla has taken most of my attention. Isn't it magnificent?"

Indeed it was, and he could hardly wait to live there. Golden fields of wheat danced in the breeze. Beyond them, dark stalks of corn stood against the pure blue horizon like sentinels, guarding the endless herd of buffalo that grazed on the plains. The rushing of a thick and swollen river somewhere in the distance created a melody that added to the perfection.

Quakahla. It would be good to rule in Quakahla, far from the encroaching eyes of the white man. He was the rightful leader, a trueborn of the Dawn People, with a lineage he could trace back to the beginning. But this latecomer standing in front of him had somehow risen to claim their highest title. Still vital and in the prime of life, she'd be in his way for some time to come.

He could handle that, if not for White Hawk. Ravenheart had many winters ahead of him. But with another shaman in his way . . . Bringing the she-wolf to her rightful retribution would do much to further his cause.

"What of my request, Riva?"

She turned displeased eyes toward him. None except a peer addressed a shaman by given name.

"Star Dancer," he hastily recanted, cursing her for noticing his misstep. "I apologize for my breech."

"Don't think of it again," Star Dancer replied, her eyes filling with compassion. "Now about your request . . ."

Ravenheart's chest leaped in anticipation.

"The defense of the she-wolf must be administered with a loving heart," she said, "not for the gain of personal power. Before you are fit for such an undertaking, you must first conquer your pride."

Unnerved by the answer, he felt a subtle jerk in his jaw. He knew she saw it. Did she miss nothing?

"Consider taking a vision quest to ponder these

matters, Ravenheart . . . I know you hoped for a different answer, but I can't give it to you, not at this time."

"When does the Tribunal convene?"

"I don't know. I wait for the omen." She looked over her shoulder at two men by the longhouse who were heatedly disagreeing over the placement of a board. Although obviously feeling needed there, she returned her attention to him. "Do you wish to take the vision quest?"

"If that's what I need to prepare for the Tribunal, I'll do it. We'll speak again, after my return."

"Good. Go now and walk in beauty."

Then she turned toward the quarreling men, Ravenheart's concerns dismissed. He watched her bitterly as she smoothly eased the tension between the workers, knowing she would choose the favored one as surely as Quetzalcoatl brought the sun each morning. As matters stood, Ravenheart would be a feeble, useless old man before his days as High Shaman arrived.

No! He wouldn't let that happen.

This thought burning in his mind, he again surveyed the fertile grounds of Quakahla. This was his kingdom, he vowed, and though he had no vision of how it might come about, when the dark moon passed and the pulsing thruway closed forever, he'd make sure White Hawk remained on the other side.

"How long have we been on the train?" Lily asked, closing the bathroom door behind her.

Perusing the newspaper as if he hadn't seen one in

years, White Hawk didn't give her as much as a glance. "Since Sunday morning."

"And today is. . . ?"

He looked up. "Tuesday evening."

She gazed in confusion at her bandages.

Tony sensed her unspoken question. "The medicine of the Dawn People is powerful. I used all of it at my disposal. We'll reach Flagstaff in the morning and you need to be strong enough to—"

"Flagstaff?" She fixed him with a look of scorn. "You really think I'm going back to the mountain with you?"

"You will." He turned his eyes to the paper. "By all that is sacred, you will."

Ignoring the repulsed expression her nearness brought to his face, she sat down beside him. "You'll only bring more werewolves to Ebony Canyon."

"If you think you're frightening me, think again."

"Frighten a great warrior such as yourself? It never crossed my mind. But not all your people are as powerful as you."

With a heavy sigh, he slapped the paper closed and rose to his feet. "It's dinnertime and you haven't had a full meal for days. Since you're well enough to be so sarcastic, I assume you're able to walk to the dining car."

"Quite able."

Although Lily wasn't truly hungry, the prospect of escaping close quarters with him appealed to her very much. She stood up, waiting somewhat impatiently as Tony took a belt holding a sheathed knife from the closet. He buckled the belt around his waist, slipped on a gray wool blazer, then pulled out Lily's linen jacket and handed it to her.

"Put this on. They keep the cars very cold with their artificial air, and you'll be susceptible to a chill until your blood rebuilds."

"How thoughtful," she replied acidly, shrugging into the jacket as she followed him out the door.

They walked single file through the narrow aisles of the Pullman car and Lily couldn't help notice how well White Hawk blended into his surroundings. Not only was he wearing black-dyed denims, a tan shirt of soft cotton, and the blazer, but he'd knotted his hair at the nape of his neck, concealing its length.

Anyone encountering them would assume they were a pair of business people in comfortable traveling attire. In the absence of the leather leggings and fur cape he'd usually worn in the canyon, she wondered if she would even have recognized him if they passed in the halls.

But wasn't that the Dawn People's way? To blend with their environment, much like chameleons. It had made them difficult quarry in Ebony Canyon, which was why she and Jorje so frequently turned to outside hikers to feed the hunger.

An oddly distressing shiver shot up her spine. An aftermath of her injuries, she told herself, deciding to concentrate on the food she might order for dinner. A Caesar salad, perhaps.

The dining car had muted lights and candles, white tablecloths, fresh rosebuds in crystal vases. A romantic setting. Unless, of course, you were with your future executioner.

A liveried maître d' showed them to a window table for two, and when the waiter appeared shortly thereafter Lily requested the salad.

"Order something with meat," White Hawk directed. "Your body needs protein and iron."

Meat? She rarely ate it these days. "Not now. It feels much too heavy."

Ignoring her protests, he told the waiter she'd have poached trout. She interrupted defiantly, ordered her own potato and vegetable, and asked for a fruit bowl on the side, but didn't bother canceling White Hawk's main-course order.

Now she took an indifferent bite of trout, mainly to keep White Hawk from pressuring her. It tasted dry and unpalatable, and she poked at the filet with her fork, then reached for another slice of apple.

"Eat more of the fish," White Hawk directed, never taking his gaze from the blurred scenery outside the window. The dark glass reflected like a mirror, and in it Lily saw his golden eyes burning. Slanted somewhat over his prominent cheekbones, they reminded her of a large cat.

And they simmered with intense hatred.

She couldn't blame him. If not for her, his lovely wife would still be with him. But since when did a queen pay attention to the loathing of mere men? She'd been used to the hatred of her prey, as well as the envy of lower werewolves.

Her reassurances weren't helping her withstand the

assault of his animosity, which further dulled her appetite. Why had he saved her life just to torment her? Deciding his reason might prove valuable, she reached out her psyche to probe his thoughts. He'd shielded his mind well, so she expanded her probe, taking in the entirety of the train.

You cannot escape, Lily.

The mental message came from nearby, and Lily jerked her head, searching for its source. She saw nothing, although she hadn't expected to. Sebastian could be anywhere, but one fact was clear. He'd already found her and was probably on the train.

Just then, White Hawk looked back at her. "Eat your fish."

"I don't care for it." She reached for a slice of hot chunky bread.

With one fluid movement, he turned from the window and stilled her hand. "Eat," he said coldly. "We're not leaving until you finish."

"You sound like Mrs. Preston . . . but not quite as mean." She eyed him thoughtfully. Thinking of the blade he wore at his belt, she lifted a knife that had come with the fruit. Small, but keen and sharp enough to make a serious gash in the knife arm of a shaman—or the tender belly of a werewolf.

But escape would not necessarily benefit her with Sebastian so near. While White Hawk had his own plans for her, he was a much less formidable opponent. And he'd almost as much as assured her safety, at least until they reached Ebony Mountain.

She'd spent five years roaming the canyon that

housed the Dawn People and had never found her way through the maze that led to their village. She doubted Sebastian would fare any better. It looked as if the village was not just her best refuge, it was her only one.

To appease White Hawk, she speared a scrap of fish, pausing before she put it in her mouth. "Your concern for my well-being touches me," she said dryly, "but it makes no sense. You could have let me die and saved yourself the trouble."

His jaws flickered almost imperceptibly, but he remained silent and took a mouthful of half-raw steak. Lily chewed on her fish and waited.

"So why didn't you let me die? I know it would have given you satisfaction."

"You don't know how much," he replied grimly, the candles casting a dark shadow on his face, emphasizing the hard set of his mouth. "But it wasn't for me to decide. You must face the Tribunal."

She laughed suddenly. "Let me get this straight. I'm being pursued by the king of werewolves, who'll surely punish me more than you could ever dream. Do you think I fear any puny Tribunal your people could put together?"

Tony stared at her stonily. The thump of wheels on rails and the low murmurs of the other diners filled the ensuing silence. Then his gaze drifted to a spot behind her. Lily turned to follow it, but saw nothing.

"A female of the genus *homo lupus*," he suddenly intoned in a radically altered voice, "shall appear to The People cloaked in silver . . ."

His face seemed to grow more hawklike, sharp and menacing, and his tone brought back the night in the Clearing of the Black Hands. Dana Gibbs, robed in white and so obscenely pure. Morgan Wilder, fighting near to death for his love. Jorje, lying limp and lifeless near a snowy bank. And then the cries—hawk and dogs—screeching, howling, baying, as her werewolf heritage drained away. For the first time since being discharged from the hospital she felt the full horror of it.

"Although her names bespeak purity," he continued, "her heart is foul, and she shall answer to the Tribunal for her crimes . . ."

Lily's hands fluttered weakly, but she forced iron into her voice. "What the hell does that mean?"

White Hawk cocked his head with the same rapid movements of his namesake. Then his eyes cleared and firmly claimed hers.

"It is not for you to know yet," he said in a normal tone. "Now finish your meal."

Still somewhat shaken, Lily scooped another piece of fish onto her fork. "I take it back," she said with forced bravado. "You're meaner than Mrs. Preston."

"Who's Mrs. Preston?" White Hawk asked, seeming half surprised the question had left his lips.

She smiled wickedly. "My last nanny. I drove her mad. After that, no one would take the job."

White Hawk responded with a small sound, then looked back out the window.

As soon as Lily was certain his attention was on the darkly fleeing scenery and not on her reflection in the window, she snaked out her hand and closed a napkin around the fruit knife. After dabbing her mouth delicately, she lowered the linen to her lap, dropped the knife into the pocket of her jacket, and felt it settle among the plastic vials.

As she returned to her meal she wondered if she really had seen a smile tugging at the corners of White Hawk's mouth before he turned away.

Chapter Five

Tony guided Lily onto the debarking platform of the Flagstaff train station at dawn the next morning, keeping a possessive hand on her arm.

"You're treating me like baggage!" Lily irritably shook off his arm, dropped her suitcase, and refused to move until he let go.

"If you're thinking about escape, forget it."

"Never crossed my mind." He saw false sweetness in her smile, and her dark almond-shaped eyes gleamed like the wolf she'd once been.

But she was no longer fleet of foot. If she tried to run, he could easily catch her, so he didn't attempt to reclaim her arm. Picking up her fallen bag, he scanned the parking lot outside the open-air platform, seeking the vehicle he'd been promised would be there.

When he saw a squirrel's tail flying from an antenna, he heaved a relieved sigh. Delmar hadn't let him down.

"This way," he told Lily. "To our car." She accompanied him without objection, and as they approached the old boatlike vehicle, Tony saw her take in the seriously crumpled fender, the rust eating at the edges of the faded white paint.

"Our accommodations grow ever more luxurious."

Startled that her remark brought Dana Gibbs to his mind, Tony glanced at her sharply. It was not her comment that stirred the recollection, but her attitude. She wasn't complaining, simply making a rather accurate observation. Nor did she complain about the cold, although she hugged her linen jacket tight against the brisk mountain breeze.

He admired her spirit, one warrior for another. Although her cause was hopeless, she refused to bow to it. From the vantage point of her terrace railing, he'd seen the coldness inside that richly appointed mausoleum her parents called home. His heritage held such reverence for family; he could barely comprehend her uncaring parents or what harm such an upbringing might do to a child, but even that loveless childhood hadn't broken her spirit. Recalling her comment about the nanny almost made him smile again.

Then he thought of Tajaya's corpse, and his moment of sympathy evaporated. True, he found it hard to equate this small woman with the powerful beast who had taken his wife, but they *were* one and the same. Someday he might find forgiveness within his heart, but such was not yet in him and he wouldn't pretend it was. That wasn't the warrior's way.

At the car, he opened the passenger door. "Sit here," he said gruffly, wanting her out of his way. "You'll be warmer."

She gestured at the seat. "What would you like me to do with those?"

Several candy bar wrappers and a partly filled bag of potato chips were on the seat. A crumpled twelve-pack carton was on the floor. For the first time since he'd left Ebony Canyon to bring back Lily, Tony actually did grin. His father, it seemed, had partied long and hard the night before. Some things always remained the same.

Lily allowed him little time for fond memories. She stooped to gather up the rubbish. "Fortunately, the vandal managed to miss your seat."

Arms filled, she turned toward a nearby trash barrel. Keeping her in his line of sight, Tony went to the trunk, where Delmar had promised to leave some supplies. They would descend over eight thousand feet from the canyon's rim to the floor, where the Dawn People dwelled. There, the cloying heat of the monsoon season would be at its peak, so he'd taken only light clothing from Lily's closet. But first they must travel up the mountain to face temperatures even colder than it was in Flagstaff.

As promised, there were two parkas, a pair of sleeping bags, and a large hard-framed backpack crammed in amid several tire irons and a blown-out radial. Tony checked the parkas for size, picked up the smaller one, and turned toward Lily.

She still stood by the trash barrel, looking far into the distance, head tilted as if she were listening.

"Lily!" he called sharply.

She glanced his way, then came toward him.

"Here." He shoved the thick parka into her hands, trying not to look at her as he began jostling the items in the trunk to make room for his satchel and her bags. "Wait in the car."

"Thanks," she said softly, shrugging into the coat and zippering it against the cold.

He grunted an acknowledgment, and when he finally managed to crowd the bags into the overstuffed trunk, he slammed the lid and started for the driver's door.

A short while later, after filling the almost empty gas tank, Tony parked in front of a drugstore.

"Get out," he said to Lily. "We're going inside."

She complied without comment, staying by his side as they walked to the store. Tony had expected her to attempt escape, and even though she hadn't tried so far he had no intention of relaxing his vigil. When they went inside, he firmly took her hand in his.

"How tender," she remarked, nodding at a lunch counter at one end of the store. "Shall we share a soda afterward?"

Tony ignored her and headed for the aisle he knew displayed the merchandise he needed. This was an old-fashioned drugstore, not one of the chains, and they stocked items in bulk, carrying medicines and tonics that had long fallen out of common use.

He found what he needed and picked up two cartons.

"Smelling salts?" Lily asked, arching her eyebrows. "It's flattering that you consider me so formidable, White Hawk, but in case you haven't heard, I'm not a werewolf anymore. Or are you planning to choke me to death with the fumes?"

"Cut the crap, Lily," White Hawk replied sharply. He'd had about enough of this woman's acid tongue, nor was he pleased that some of her quips actually amused him. "You think I haven't noticed how you keep looking around? Your leader's out there somewhere, isn't he?"

Lily shrugged. "I told you he'd come, but you weren't in a listening mood."

She seemed calm enough, which puzzled Tony. "I'd think he'd be the last person you'd want to see, Lily. He tried to kill you."

Lily hesitated, her sarcastic expression fading. She shook her head. "The holy water made him clumsy, and he accidentally scraped my skin. Human skin is fragile, you know—"

"No, I don't know," he replied harshly, "but I'm sure you do."

She regarded him a moment. "You see us as such evil creatures, don't you?"

"Evil is too *soft* a word."

"Ah," she murmured. "We're merely hunters, like yourself. I wonder how the cow would treat you should you suddenly become a member of its herd? Much as you're treating me, I imagine."

Jarred by her logic, which too closely paralleled Riva's teachings, Tony stared into her large dark eyes. Still shadowed underneath by her recent loss of blood, they gazed back intelligently, implacably, waiting for his answer.

"We've a long journey ahead," he finally said. "Let's pay for these and get on with it."

Still holding her hand, he dragged her none too gently to the cash register, and didn't let go of her until he deposited her back inside the car. A knowing grin covered her face the entire time.

Trying his best to ignore it, Tony pulled onto the highway and headed east. They had several hours of rough roads ahead and another couple of hours of hiking before they reached the canyon's rim. Putting a heavy foot on the gas pedal, he kept his eyes straight ahead.

He wondered if Lily was up to the hike. Although her wounds were healing, she'd lost considerable blood and the prospect of carrying her down to the canyon floor didn't please him. Bad enough he'd been sent on this unholy mission, but to hold the wolf woman against his heart for hours on end . . . it didn't bear thinking about.

For the most part, Lily looked out the window. Once she let out a small gasp as he took a particularly sharp turn, and now and then she glanced over her shoulder out the rear window. He wondered what she expected to find? Was her werewolf king already in pursuit? Despite her defense of him, Tony doubted she'd welcome Sebastian's appearance, which would explain why she hadn't tried to escape.

It amused him darkly to think she might consider him her protector. Less amusing, he realized, was that he actually was. He'd saved her from a certain and well-deserved death, and was treating her more like a small ward than the evil-minded creature he knew her to be. This thought fed his bitterness, and he nourished it, unwilling to betray Tajaya's memory in the smallest way.

Lily shifted suddenly in her seat, interrupting his thoughts. They'd left the highway and were careening faster than White Hawk knew was safe toward Ebony Mountain. The morning sun streamed through the windshield, providing only marginal warmth, and an icy wind billowed through the open passenger window.

Pulling up the hood of her parka, Lily reached for the window's handle and turned it. Nothing happened. She gave it a hard yank, then another. The handle came off in her hand.

"Throw it in the backseat," White Hawk offered, and she heard him choke back a laugh.

She gave the handle a cavalier toss over her shoulder. It landed with a thud. "Finally I've discovered your scheme. Death by freezing."

"It's an easy death they say," he replied, his amusement fading as quickly as it had come. "Better than you deserve."

"Do you really believe I'll let you kill me?" Lily

asked softly, not really caring about his answer, just wanting to hear a voice. She'd grown weary of the silence.

"It is already done."

Already done. Those words did not come lightly from a shaman, and they sparked the same tremor Lily had felt in the dining car. They weren't so different, really, the Dawn People and the Lupines. While Western civilization worshiped timetables and science, both their kind followed a primal connection to the seasons, the tides, the moons. Signs and visions signaled coming events, which, thus indicated, could not be reversed.

Refusing to let him see her fear, she said, "Don't rely on your superstitions to protect you."

"I rely on nothing. This act is Star Dancer's decision and you're only alive at her mercy."

"Who, pray tell, is this person with the whimsical name?"

"You'll find out soon enough."

"How soon is that?"

"We'll reach the rim of the canyon a short while before the sun reaches the top of the heavens."

"Why don't you just say around eleven o'clock?" Lily suddenly felt cross. What did she care about this peasant shaman's convictions, or of whether or not he spoke to her? "You obviously understand clocks well enough to abide by a railroad timetable."

"There are no clocks in Ebony Canyon." He glanced over at her scornfully. "You of all people should know that."

Yes, Lily thought, but she'd already forgotten. How

odd that she'd retained some abilities, yet not others. Even now, if she tuned in, she could discern squirrels chattering softly in the thick fir trees. A wren alighted in the dark branches overhead. Somewhere, not far away, a brook rushed over a stony bed, gurgling softly. And though White Hawk kept his thoughts carefully guarded, she could feel his loathing so acutely it seemed like a physical force.

But she no longer retained the rhythm of the wild. The scents and sounds around her seemed alien, making her almost long for exhaust fumes and honking horns. That she'd survived—no, thrived—for years in this raw country seemed suddenly incomprehensible.

Tony made a sharp turn that sent her lurching toward him. Quickly righting herself, she saw they'd turned onto a rutted road lined with towering pines. Her seat was bathed in shadow, stealing away her only heat. Her teeth began chattering, and even the thick parka couldn't keep her from shivering.

Tony looked over at her. "You'll find blankets in the back."

She'd have preferred to deliver a sarcastic retort, but was too cold to expend the energy. Scrambling to her knees, she reached over the seat for a rough wool blanket, refraining from comment even when dried grass and stones tumbled out. Draping the blanket over her head and shoulders, she settled back into the seat, weary of the battle and weary of the cold.

Tony tapped the accelerator, which forced her deeper into the warming covers. "Sleep," he instructed. "We'll be there soon and you'll need your strength for the journey."

The sun was heading for its apex when they reached the canyon rim.

"We'll stop here to eat," Tony told Lily as they skirted the skeleton of Morgan Wilder's burned-out cabin.

Lily would have preferred not to sit in the shadow that reminded her of her folly, but they'd hiked countless miles since parking the car and she needed rest. She let White Hawk remove the steel-framed backpack from her shoulders, then sank gratefully to the ground.

The dense forest surrounding the clearing mercifully restrained the wind, and the sun felt blessedly warm. Lily untied the bindings of her parka as White Hawk removed his own burdens.

At his insistence, she'd put on heavy socks and hiking boots. They pinched miserably, so she bent to loosen the laces. When she was more comfortable, she swiveled around to look toward the canyon, wanting to avoid the memories revived by seeing Morgan's cabin.

Although she'd often tried, she hadn't forgotten this place, and knew very well what she'd find if she roamed the western rim. If she went deep inside the forest several miles to the south, she'd come across her old den. Were her tapestries and lush rugs still there, she wondered, or had they been taken by hikers or eaten by rodents? She preferred occupying her mind with this question to remembering that visiting her den would require passing the Clearing of the Black Hands. The site of the Indians' ancient rituals, it was also the place where she'd lost her powers, and the memory made her shiver. To avoid her distasteful feelings, she turned her attention to the rim.

Not far to their north was a path leading to the bottom of Ebony Canyon, which she assumed was the one they'd take. Less than two miles down; eight thousand feet at the most. A short distance really, especially compared to the hike they'd undertaken to get to the top. On flatland such a trek could be easily completed in about an hour. But the floor of the canyon was almost straight down, and the twists and turns would make the descent so arduous she doubted they'd get to the bottom much before dark.

When she first came to Arizona the contrast between the cool green mountain peaks and the hot shallow desert valleys amazed her. It wasn't uncommon to find people in one part of the state shoveling snow while those in lower elevations sunbathed, and here in Ebony Canyon the contrast was extreme.

A gust of wind swept up a cluster of fallen leaves, spiraling them in the air not far from where Lily sat, as if reminding her that winter was coming to the rim. She hugged her parka closer, knowing it would soon become a burden. The temperature would rise at least five degrees for every thousand feet they descended. At the bottom they'd find the tail-end of summer. Ninety degrees—if they were lucky—but possibly warmer.

"How are you feeling?"

Lily jerked her head in White Hawk's direction and felt an unpleasant crick in the cold stiff muscles of her neck. "Are you asking from curiosity, or do you really want to know?"

"It's still a long hike down," he replied evenly. "Your injuries were severe. I don't relish the idea of having to carry you."

"Nor do I. Don't concern yourself. I'm fine."

Drawn to the charred skeleton that had once housed her former lover, Lily barely registered his curt nod. "What happened to the cabin?"

"I burned it at Morgan's request."

"You were friends then, you and he?"

"Yes . . ." He paused, and she felt him adding fuel to his hatred. "And Dana was also my friend."

"I see."

Her eyes were still riveted on the cabin and she pried them away in time to see White Hawk walking toward her. He handed her a leaf-wrapped loaf and several dark sticks of dried meat along with a small leather flask.

"More of the tonic," he informed her. "Drink it."

"I'm not taking another drop of that vile stuff."

"Drink it," he repeated in a gentler tone. "I have a pear in my sack that will wash away the aftertaste."

She fixed him with an obstinate look.

"I promise."

Lily met his gaze. Although the gash on her leg hadn't hurt through the difficult hike upward, and her wrist didn't pain her, she felt light-headed. From the altitude, she'd told herself, unwilling to believe her once invulnerable body felt any aftereffects from Sebastian's attack. But even sitting wasn't restoring her energy the way it should. The medicine had helped before . . .

"One more dose can't hurt." She downed it swiftly.

White Hawk promptly produced the pear, and she bit into it eagerly, mildly surprised to learn he'd been telling the truth. She found she was hungrier than she'd thought, and she gobbled up the fruit, then began unwrapping the loaf.

Giving it a suspicious look, she tore off a small piece and popped it into her mouth. Grainy with cornmeal, it had a slightly sweet flavor that was delicious. Soon it was gone. All that remained were the slices of meat jerky.

She lifted one to her lips, feeling a wave of revulsion. She didn't understand it, but meat did this to her every time. Lowering the slice, she placed it beside the others. Some animal would eat them later. Better it than her.

White Hawk hadn't noticed. He'd arranged his satchel into a roll under his head and now reclined on the ground, basking in the afternoon sun.

The silence felt oppressive. Occasionally a jay cawed from the forest, and if she cared to pay attention Lily knew she'd hear the scurrying of mice in the drying grasses surrounding the remains of Morgan's cabin. Rain had not graced these lands in quite some time, she realized, and the very dryness made the hulk of the blackened building all the more ominous.

Yealanay cawfanay nayfanay may.
Yealanay cawfanay nayfanay may.

The opening words of the Shadow of Venus came unbidden to Lily's mind, bringing a chill. She wrapped her arms around herself, trying to banish the refrain. But it continued, and she tore her eyes from the burned-out structure, believing it had stirred the memory.

The act didn't help.

Yealanay cawfanay nayfanay may.
Yealanay cawfanay nayfanay may.

Again without willing it, she translated the words into English: Spirits of light, hear our plea.

How could such a ceremony have worked its magic on her? Sebastian taught that one never pleaded with the spirits, one commanded them. Yet Dana Gibb's words, meant for Morgan Wilder, not for her, had somehow stripped her of the werewolf gift.

She lowered her head to her knees, willing her mind to be still. Finally the repetitive verse ceased, but her soul still felt battered. For Morgan's sake, she'd been robbed of her superhuman powers. For Morgan's sake, she'd killed Jorje and violated Lupine Law.

Sebastian's angry face appeared in her mind as it had just days before in her luxurious bathroom. By his order, she'd followed Morgan to this canyon. She'd begged Sebastian not to make her go, but he had remained immovable in his demands.

Now he blamed her for Jorje's death. The wolfling had been about to break the Law himself! If he hadn't tried to kill Morgan, he'd be alive today. How dare Sebastian put this all on her head?

Yes, she'd done it, but she'd already suffered for her crime. Now she belonged to no one, belonged nowhere. What good was a werewolf queen who had no werewolf powers?

The jay cried out again and Lily looked up, then dropped her gaze to the meat strips on the ground beside her. Warmed by their time in the sun, they gleamed with heavy grease.

Lily's stomach rolled and she snatched up the pieces, hurling them in the direction of the canyon. What foolishness, she thought, as she watched them flying through the air. What was done was done. She couldn't undo it.

She got to her feet and looked over at White Hawk, who was still relaxing and clearly unprepared to leave.

"Come on," she said. "I'm ready to travel again."

Chapter Six

Ravenheart had chosen a particularly rigorous vision quest, foregoing even water as he stoically carried Stone People from the surrounding area up the steep slopes of the mesa to the sweat lodge. He stacked the small boulders beside the deep pit outside the door to the lodge, where he would later build a fire and heat the rocks until they glowed like coals.

He had stopped sweating long ago, and he planned to wait for the hottest part of the day to build the fire. Strenuous testing of the body sharpened the mind and brought the visions faster.

This sweat ceremony would bring his answers, he felt sure. He'd have a sign so magnificent even Star Dancer could not refute it. He had no doubt it would come. He was a trueborn, with unbroken lineage, and his power was now arising, preparing him for the years of rulership ahead.

For hours he'd collected rocks, more than he needed, stacking them high beside the deep hole in the ground. Father Sun blazed down on his head, scorching his face and his almost naked limbs. He'd soon shed even the loincloth and entered the lodge where the spirits would visit. His guides would come, unveiling their plan for how he'd assume his rightful place.

Around him, the Four-Leggeds rustled, the Winged Ones roosted in the scant shade of rain-starved chaparral, not even wasting energy to chirp. But he could endure the heat, the cloying dampness that refused to return to Sister Cloud and drop its moisture on the earth.

Soon the sun hurled its greatest heat, and Ravenheart knew the time had come. He gathered rotting corpses of fallen cacti, picked up broken twigs and crackling dried grasses, again performing the tedious task without thought to his own discomfort.

Later he bent beside the firepit and took a box of matches from a small sack belted around his waist. Lost in his own heady arrogance, and momentarily forgetting that matches were not the way of the original Dawn People whose traditions he'd so sanctimoniously sworn to restore, he struck the match against a rock. Dropping it, he lit another, and another.

The fuel exploded in flames, spewing sparks that drifted to his hairless skin, singeing it. Of this he took no heed. Instead he moved closer, allowing the searing heat to purify him, wipe out all thoughts of weakness and bodily needs.

Lifting his hands to Grandfather Sky, staring boldly into the scorching eye of Father Sun, he stood silhouetted on the mesa against the spitting fire. A triumphant laugh rose from his throat and he allowed it to escape, sending cactus wren fluttering in alarm from their shady roosts.

The Spirits would bless him this time. And woe to any who might stand in his way.

Lily leaned into the crook of a paloverde tree and gingerly peeled her hiking boot away from her shin. She could hardly breathe, the air was so thick and heavy, yet the parched landscape through which they were traveling begged for water. Even the towering, long-fingered cacti looked shriveled and limp amid the barren rocks. Her fears had been realized. Just hours before, she'd been shivering in the mountain air and now she was sweltering. Ninety degrees? Yes. And ninety percent humidity with it, or so it seemed.

Looking behind her, she tilted back her head and gazed up at the rim of the canyon, taking in the once-sharp edges that had now blurred into muted shades of red, gold, gray, and green. They must be close to the bottom. Surely they were. They'd been hiking down for eons.

At a grueling pace too, and the minute White Hawk suggested they take a rest at this sparsely shaded spot, Lily had dropped the hiking pack off her back without reply.

White Hawk had also foregone words, and now he knelt beside a narrow stream, filling lightweight gourds with water. Having changed into loose-fitting lightweight pants and a shapeless hemp shirt lightly decorated with beadwork, he now looked more like the Indian he was than the traveling businessman he'd appeared to be on the train.

A surge of resentment flashed through Lily, provoked, she supposed, by the moment of abject gratitude she'd experienced when he'd said they could stop. Except for the occasional touch of a hand to steady her when she found it hard to keep her footing, he'd ignored her throughout the entire slippery descent. Gratitude was the last thing he deserved.

What right did he have to drag her here? She held no fond memories of Ebony Canyon, had certainly never entertained a desire to return.

She was sunburned and aching. Every nerve and muscle of her body groaned from hunger and fatigue. And her leg hurt like hell. Not from the rapidly fading welt on her thigh left by Sebastian's attack, but from the damned boots her captor had made her wear.

Peering into the gap between her boot and shin, she examined an angry blister.

White Hawk returned from the river with the gourds slung over his shoulder. He hung them from the tree against which Lily rested, but she paid him no attention as she gently prodded the tender skin beneath the tongue of her boot.

"No wonder you've blistered," he said umsympathetically. "Those are a poor excuse for hiking shoes."

"You're the one who packed them!" she countered. "Couldn't you see they're fashion boots? While they're all the rage in the city, I'm sure Doris never dreamed I'd put them to this kind of use when she ordered them for me." She looked up at him crossly. "Do you by any chance have more of those Band-Aids in your bag?"

"Who's Doris?" White Hawk bent down to search through his deerskin satchel.

"My mother," she replied, unlacing the boot.

"You call your mother by her first name?"

"Not to her face." She paused in the unlacing and looked up again. "Why do you ask? As I remember, your people often call their parents by first name."

He shrugged, lifted out the box, then moved toward her. "They aren't very warm people are they?"

"Who aren't?"

"Your parents."

Lily let out a strangled laugh. "You haven't said anything to me but 'eat' and 'walk' since we started. Now you're suddenly interested in my parents?"

For a second, his face had softened, but now his mouth tightened into a hard line. Bending to help her unlace the boot, he coldly said, "Not really."

Lily swatted his hands. "I don't want your help!"

Although the line of his lips grew even harder, he ignored the slap and continued unlacing her boot.

"Why do you care if I'm blistered anyway?"

"I don't." Slipping off her boot, he met her eyes coldly, then shimmied her sock to her ankle. "But it's a long journey. You'll never make it if this gets any worse."

Dropping to his knees, he dragged his satchel closer and took out a small ceramic bottle and a leather packet. Lily continued grumbling, but watched with interest as he opened the packet, took out an irregular circle-shaped leaf, then untied a strip around the bottle, releasing a stopper that reminded Lily of an animal's bladder. After pouring the murky liquid onto the leaf, he applied it to her shin.

When the sharp menthol odor drifted up to her nose, Lily stopped complaining. She recognized the smell from the shower, when she'd stripped the poultice off her miraculously healed wounds.

It was then she noticed his gentle touch. His hands, now exceedingly warm, rested over the blistered area, syphoning away the sting. His face no longer looked harsh. He closed his eyes languidly, speaking in a language Lily didn't understand, but recognized as belonging to his people. White Hawk, the shaman, had replaced White Hawk, the warrior.

"What are you saying?" she asked.

He shook his head, a mute request for silence, and Lily obeyed. This man might be her captor, but he still possessed a healing touch. Leaning back against the tree branch, she closed her eyes.

"You can start complaining again whenever you like," he said after a time. Lily lifted her lids to see him plastering a Band-Aid over the poultice.

"Herbs and adhesive bandages," she remarked. "What century are you from?"

"The People use what works." He climbed to his feet and picked up a sleeping bag, which he began unrolling. "I took a pair of sandals from your closet." He inclined his head in the direction of the backpack. "We'll stay here until the worst of the heat passes, so you might as well put them on and give that leg a rest."

Lily nodded. She'd transferred the sandals from the Hermes suitcase into the backpack herself before they left the meager shelter of the rattle-trap car. When she'd finished, White Hawk had tossed the exquisite bag aside, murmuring something about "leaving gifts by the side of the road." Although she knew she had bigger challenges ahead than protecting her belongings, and actually cared little if sparrows made a nest inside the damned thing, she'd asserted herself anyway, needing some illusion that she still had control.

As was growing common, her protest went unheeded. But she'd won one battle that day. As they descended deeper into the bowels of the canyon, the heat became insufferable. White Hawk discarded their parkas and blankets, then directed her to change into shorts. She'd eagerly complied. The jeans had been sticking to her skin, making the steep trail even harder to handle. But then he insisted she leave the jeans with the other items, and she'd adamantly refused to give up her last warm piece of clothing. Who knew if she might get an opportunity to escape?

Now she shoved the still-damp jeans aside, searching for the sandals, feeling a delicious relief as she slipped out of the heavy boots. Life did hold its simple pleasures, she thought cynically, wandering over to one of the sleeping bags White Hawk had unfurled on the ground. She sat down, casting a sharp eye about for ants or scorpions.

White Hawk handed her another leaf-wrapped loaf. "Eat again. We'll sleep until the heat passes, but the night journey will still be arduous."

She unwrapped the loaf hastily, remembering its pleasing flavor. As she was chewing, White Hawk placed several strips of jerky in her empty hand.

"I don't care much for meat," she said, attempting to give them back.

His sharp look conveyed immense disbelief. "Eat it anyway."

She had every intention of defying him, but when she finished the loaf, her stomach still felt empty. Torn between her desire for autonomy and her hunger, she eventually gave in to the latter. The strip was firm and leathery, but she gnawed at it greedily, especially appreciating the salty taste that seemed to ease the aches in her muscles. When the first one was gone, she attacked another.

"Sienna Doe becomes White Wolf Woman," White Hawk said.

"What?"

"Nothing. A legend." Then he lay down on his bed roll, folded his arms behind his head, and closed his eyes.

When Lily finished her last strip of jerky, she did the same, troubled that she couldn't get White Hawk's remark out of her mind.

* * *

Ravenheart could barely hold up his head. In the corner of the lodge, inside another pit, the Stone People gave off their intense heat but he refused to succumb to the lure of the cooler floor. He dropped another ladleful of water on the fiery rocks. Steam filled the lodge. He lost track of time and tried not to think of how much more comfortable he'd be on the floor.

The vision would come. It would come.

But why was it taking so long? Hadn't his first quest been rewarded quickly with the appearance of the Raven, whose name he now bore? The spirits had blessed him with the sign of magic, yet that obstinate female shaman had not seen fit to take proper notice.

She'd greeted his announcement calmly, then remarked that his quest had taken an unusually short time. Was he certain his true animal guide had appeared? Was Coyote, the Trickster, at work here? Ravenheart had hidden his outrage and had refrained from asserting that he'd been hand-chosen by the spirits. Star Dancer, he knew, would interpret his truth as excessive pride. But was it prideful to claim one's rightful place?

No! A chosen one could never be denied. It was written.

Then, despite his strong will, Ravenheart's head lolled on his neck. He toppled slowly toward the floor. He floated up to the miserly clouds, caught in their mist, tortured by the moisture they promised but refused to bestow.

Curling up, sightless to all around him, he keened a

vision quest chant. The spirits had deserted him, he knew it now, and he was dying. None denied themselves fluids during a monsoon sweat, yet he had, and it would be the end of him.

The spirits had deserted him.

A low growl broke through his slurred chants. He lifted his weak neck and saw a figure walking through the fog. A silver muzzle dripping with blood emerged, followed by eyes as blue as the sweltering Ebony Canyon sky and so piercing that Ravenheart groaned and looked away.

"Brother Raven," said a silky voice.

A long-fingered hand touched his shoulder and he felt the bite of claws. His limbs grew stiff with terror, but he forced himself to remain still. The sign had come at last; he would not quail before it.

"You shall have your rightful place," the voice continued. "And we ask little in return. Meet my eyes, brother. I am the guide you sought."

Ravenheart did as the creature asked. The mist had settled, revealing a monumental figure of such magnificence he scrambled to his knees and bowed.

"White Wolf Woman," he murmured. "You have come to aid me."

A brutal laugh rose from the wolf's sleek throat. "Do not confuse me with that one. I am Walking Wolf, teacher of those with claims to power. You are such a one, are you not?"

"Yes, yes." Ravenheart raised his arms beseechingly. "You have seen. I knew you would."

The blue eyes gleamed approvingly. "Yes, Brother, I have seen. Again I say to you, we ask little in return for bestowing your rightful place. Are you prepared to hear my request?"

Warnings flashed through Ravenheart's heat-baked mind. Animal guides never requested gifts from those they served. But he quickly dismissed the warning and nodded eagerly.

"A woman shall come. Though she appears frail, evil is her path, and she shall bring much harm upon your people. Seek her out, Ravenheart, and deliver her to me. In return, you shall rule forever."

Forever. The long-awaited promise rang sweetly in Ravenheart's ears. But again a warning came. Mornings spent with other young followers of the warrior's way at Star Dancer's knee: A guide who lured a seeker with pledges of power was a false guide. Turn away, the teachings advised, turn away now and seek a higher guide.

"Forever," Walking Wolf repeated.

"Yes. Yes, Lord." Ravenheart stretched up, clawing toward heaven, pierced by the ecstasy of his certain triumph, barely aware he'd addressed as Lord the one who should have been his servant. "I will deliver her. I swear it."

"Go now and do that which you have sworn."

Instantly, Ravenheart sank into the clouds, falling, falling, faster and faster toward the sweat lodge. Before he smashed against the baked earth floor, his awareness splintered into a million fragments.

When he awoke, the rocks in the corner pit were dull, devoid of heat. As he rolled shakily to his feet, feeling weaker than ever before, he tried to forget that the dying of the Stone People before a vision quest ended was a bad omen.

Chapter Seven

Although sweat trickled down Lily's neck, she woke up shivering, a cold, malicious presence creeping through her mind.

So Sebastian was already behind them. She never doubted he would come or that he'd bring others. She expanded her psyche to explore the extent of his entourage, being careful to shield her mind from a return probe. There were eight with him, among them the envious Beryl, who must even now be crowing over taking her place beside Sebastian as his prince. She also found Philippe, a young French wolfling. The rest she didn't know.

Sebastian had come prepared, she thought, smiling grimly. Seven wolves for the ceremony of the Song of Hades, and one in reserve for emergency. How like him to provide for all contingencies.

She sat up and looked around. While the chirp of crickets grated on her ears, at least the scorching sun was leaving. The last rays shimmered off the leaves of chaparral and dying grasses and, behind the lip of the canyon, clouds rolled by, kissed with crimson and gold, flamingo pink and dusty orange.

She glanced over at the shaman, who appeared to still be sleeping. Should she warn him? Although his hatred of her simmered constantly between them, he'd refrained from brutality. She knew his heart had been pierced by the death of his wife, and she supposed she owed him a small favor before she escaped.

Remembering his scornful reply when she'd tried to warn him on the train, she decided against it. He'd learn of Sebastian's presence soon enough, and the Dawn People had their hidden village to protect them.

A laugh bubbled in her throat, and she choked it back. She hadn't thought far enough ahead. The hidden village would protect her too, but only for a time. She'd have to escape before they scheduled her execution. But escape to what? Sebastian's waiting arms.

She could work that out later. For the moment, a more immediate threat loomed. She could hear faint quarrels among Sebastian's underlings and grumbles about traveling in daylight, acts unheard of in her time with him. They hadn't reached the rim of the canyon yet, but if he should catch scent of them or somehow connect with Lily's thoughts, Sebastian would quicken the pace. Their safety depended on reaching the village before that happened. They must hurry.

"It's getting dark," she called to White Hawk. "Shouldn't we start now?"

Apparently wide awake, White Hawk rolled to a sitting position, then stood up. "Your eagerness surprises me."

"Anything's preferable to sleeping on this bug-infested ground," she groused.

Bending to roll up his bedroll, White Hawk told her to put on her boots and tend to her sleeping bag. Lily chose to wear the sandals and she slipped her feet into them, then kicked her bedding into a haphazard square pile. What did a person do with these things, she wondered, when finished sleeping on them?

White Hawk came to her side with a small square of lamb's wool. "Use this to protect the blister. The sandals are more comfortable, but you'll have better luck with the jumping cactus if your feet are covered." He chuckled darkly as he turned away. "The scorpions too."

"Scorpions," Lily repeated dully. She scanned the darkening landscape. Nebulous shapes crept among stands of eucalyptus. Somewhere far away, a coyote cried. A burro brayed. Behind them came Sebastian with his twisted schemes and obedient followers.

She'd never cared for the sterile canyon floor, and had usually managed to avoid it. Scaly things abounded here, creeping and slithering creatures that caught one unaware. A faint tremor of distaste trilled through her body. She saw White Hawk regarding her, his golden eyes reflecting the soft hues of the sunset.

Lily returned his look with a haughty glance. "You aren't scaring me, if that's what you think."

"Of course not," he said insincerely, stepping into his own boots.

Not caring for his tone, she busied herself by kicking off the sandals and donning her boots, giving the area around the blister a generous padding of lamb's wool. Then she knelt to roll up her bedding. After a struggle, she managed to crush it into a lopsided ball, fumbling for the cords, which barely met and left no room for tying. Rocking back on her heels, she tugged at the ties with all her might. One of them slipped out of her hand.

She toppled backward, landing on her behind with a jarring thud. An annoyed grunt left her mouth, followed by another sound that hadn't come from her. She shot a startled glance over her shoulder to see White Hawk with his head thrown back, laughing insufferably.

She wanted to leap up and pummel him until he stopped. Then she looked down at herself. With her legs spread awkwardly, her hands splayed to hold her bottom off the rocky ground, and the sleeping bag slowly unrolling, she truly was a comical sight. A giggle bubbled in her throat.

Just as quickly as it began, White Hawk's laughter ended. He came over and hoisted her to her feet.

"You're not good for much, are you?" he asked gruffly, picking up the sleeping bag. "I'll take care of this."

The sharp stab in Lily's stomach startled her. How many unkind things had he already said with little effect? Yet this one struck too close to home. What was she good for? Pampered as a child, then transformed to a life of ease and invulnerability, she'd never had to lift a finger. Not cook a meal, wash a dish, or clean a room. And certainly not roll up ragged, sleepworn bedding.

"If you have business to attend to, do it now." White Hawk ordered. "It will be well past middle night before we reach the village and we must travel hard."

Orders and more orders. Insults and jibes. She walked regally away, telling herself she wasn't running from his scorn. This peasant was unworthy of her attention and she'd given him far too much already.

She returned to find him arranging the bedrolls and provisions on his back. While he was thus occupied, she went to the backpack which was outside his line of sight and rummaged for her linen jacket. When she found it, she flinched, realizing it was rumpled beyond repair. But the bottles in the pocket were what counted. As she reached for one, she sensed White Hawk's eyes on her. Turning away, she scrambled toward her sandals. "Just putting these away," she explained, lifting them up. "Is there anything else left to go in?"

He lobbed over his moccasins, which she stuffed inside the pack along with the sandals, pausing only to palm a bottle of water. Then she turned to face him, concealing the vial as she slipped her arms through the straps of the backpack. "Buckle them for me?" she asked.

With a puzzled frown she attributed to surprise at her unusual meekness, he walked behind her. By the time he'd finished securing the pack, she'd slipped the bottle into the pocket of her shorts.

"Come on," he said, moving toward the rough trail. "It's a long hike and the tribe waits for us."

Lily fell in behind him, watching the rhythmic sway of his shoulders as he swiftly covered the ground before them. Moving at night was easier, especially since her keen eyesight let her see the treacherous spots. Soon she adjusted to his pace, only occasionally patting the bottle in her pocket. If Sebastian showed up, she had her protection. And the shaman? Well, he could take care of himself.

White Hawk hadn't deceived her. It was a long hike, and after the first ten miles or so Lily slipped into a daze, stumbling occasionally from lack of paying attention. She wondered how White Hawk did it. Although he lacked her sensitive sight, never once had he faltered.

So far she hadn't felt Sebastian's presence again. Perhaps he'd taken pity on his squabbling pack and allowed them to rest. But, just in case, Lily checked the bottle in her pocket for the hundredth time.

They descended from the harsh desert terrain into an area of lush growth. From somewhere nearby she heard gently flowing water, and the trail soon twisted beneath huge cottonwoods and sycamores that were so thick with leaves they sometimes blocked out the moon. At these times White Hawk would give her directions to turn this way or that, but otherwise he never spoke.

After what seemed like endless hours of silent hiking, broken only by the scuttles and chitters of nighttime desert dwellers, Lily heard a frog chirrup. Something splashed, the frog quieted, then sang again.

"Stop here," White Hawk commanded.

Ahead of them Lily saw an oasis. More cottonwoods, and ancient sycamore too, their curving trunks showing mottled gleams of white in the faint illumination of the moon. Chaparral and mesquite clustered tightly together. Scrub oak, shrubs, and waist-high grasses filled every space between them.

"Papa!" A child's voice called out from the dense vegetation. White Hawk's face broke into a delighted smile.

A small girl flew forward, slim brown legs whirring, and threw herself at White Hawk. "Papa! Papa! Papa!"

With a whoop, he swept her off the ground, buried his chin in her neck, and made funny little growls.

"I missed you," she cried, peppering his cheek with kisses. "I missed you so much."

"I missed you too, little one."

Lily watched, feeling an odd tickle in her throat. A few minutes later White Hawk told her they were moving on. He shifted his daughter's weight to let her rest in the crook of his arm, then resumed walking. As Lily started to follow she heard the girl whisper a question.

"Who's that?"

White Hawk didn't bother to whisper. "No one you want to know."

Again, his remark slithered through her defenses, pricking briefly, but sharply. Lily paused. Despite the poultice and padding, her blister pained her every step. But that wasn't what made her lag behind.

The Dawn People kept a close eye on their children. If White Hawk's daughter was running free, the village must be near. Safety lay just ahead. So why did she want to droop and let her feet shuffle wearily across the ground?

Fatigue, perhaps. Surely she didn't fear the contempt of these simple people? Of course not. Forcing steel into her spine, she lifted her aching legs briskly and held her chin up high.

They continued through a mazelike trail. She remembered trying to wind her way through this area once, finally howling in frustration over the many dead ends and giving up entirely. But White Hawk obviously knew where they were going.

Suddenly he was no longer in front of her. For an instant, Lily felt a surge of panic. Dear God, she'd been unable to traverse this maze even as a werewolf. How would she cope if he left her?

"Lily!"

Stifling the relieved cry that wanted to escape her mouth, she squared her shoulders and walked forward, finding White Hawk standing near an almost invisible split in the undergrowth. The girl was no longer with him.

He stared at her darkly, then removed the backpack from her shoulders. "The tribe awaits your arrival, so listen carefully. When we go through the village, you must walk behind me. Keep your head bowed, your hands clasped in front of you. Don't look at anyone."

Lily stared back just as darkly. "Are your people afraid of my evil eye?"

"That has nothing to do with it. You're merely unworthy to gaze upon their faces."

Despite the steaming heat, Lily felt cold. Very cold. And so alone. She tilted her chin up defiantly, then quickly snatched the backpack from White Hawk's hand. With a pivot that made her blister scream, she started marching in the direction from which they'd come.

"You won't find your way out, Lily. You'll end up starving to death in there."

Or falling into Sebastian's hands, she thought, ruing the impulsive act. Forcing her chin to remain high, she returned.

"Very well," she said, as if this was all her own idea.

"Wise decision. Let's go on in. And remember the instructions I gave you."

He turned his back on her and started forward. Lily glared at him hotly as she followed him through the narrow leafy passage.

The change came abruptly. One second they were surrounded by foliage, the next moment they entered a clearing that was enclosed by high cliffs on all sides but the one from which they'd entered. A hawk perched on an overhead branch, crying out, as if to announce her entrance.

Chapter Eight

The clearing was dotted with dancing fires and filled with chanting people. Lined up on the right, lined up on the left, of all shapes, sizes, and ages, their bodies formed a wide path that ended at the cliffs. Plump women with round faces stood beside squat men with square jaws and flat cheeks. Tall slender women with aquiline noses leaned into taller muscled men with sharp profiles and fierce gazes. Wise old men and wise old women. Children peering from behind the legs of their elders.

Continuing to chant as Lily followed White Hawk between the two lines of people, they stared at her as if she were a horse being led into a show ring . . . or a prisoner going to execution.

Lily planted her hands on her hips and stared back.

Each person she passed quickly turned away. Children shrank deeper into their mother's skirts. One gawky boy, apparently bolder than the rest, returned her gaze. Lily bared her teeth. A grandfather swept the boy behind him, glaring back. Lily clicked her teeth together, gratified to see him flinch.

A bent wizened woman came forward, leaning heavily on a walking stick, and spit at Lily.

"Frieda, no!" a young woman shouted, bravely hurling herself between them. Lily merely snarled and kept on walking.

White Hawk glanced over his shoulder and scowled, which Lily acknowledged with a feline smile. His scowl deepened. With the smooth grace of a predator he dropped behind her and wrapped his arms around her body, then pushed her hands toward her midsection. Lily struggled, but she was unwilling to squirm like a snared rabbit in front of this censuring audience, and White Hawk easily managed to trap her wrists with a leather thong.

Her stride interrupted, Lily faltered, causing White Hawk's chest to strike her back. His hemp tunic scraped lightly across her bare sunburned shoulders, but instead of stinging as she'd expected, the touch soothed the burn. His presence almost seemed to draw the heat from her sticky, sunbaked flesh, and she realized with a shock that she didn't want him to move away.

"You can complete this journey like a lady," he whispered, his breath cool against her skin, "or I can tie your hands together and force your head down. It's your choice."

More shaken by her reaction to his nearness than his threat, she nodded her head. He let go of her hands and backed off, taking away the thong and his soothing touch with it. But he remained behind her, and she felt his wary gaze piercing into her.

The rest of the short walk was the most interminable journey of Lily's life. They passed a long log building, where more people were gathered to watch her pass.

And always they chanted. At times monotonous, then rising to a sweet crescendo, only to return to monotony.

Finally they reached the cliffs. Lily dared a glance up, and saw windows and doorways carved into the stone. Crude wooden ladders and narrow ledges gave the people access to their homes.

White Hawk nudged her. "Climb."

"Are you taking me to my cell?" Lily asked as she put a foot on the bottom rung.

He waited until she'd climbed several rungs, then he moved to follow. When they were many feet above the ground, he answered, "If you're asking if you'll be locked up, no. The desert is a much more unforgiving jail than we could ever devise."

She didn't doubt him. If she'd found this place inhospitable as a werewolf, her mortal shell would find it abhorrent. Deadly.

But she glanced down at him anyway, startled to see they were already about three stories above the ground. The height made her momentarily dizzy. She paused, clinging to the polished rung, and squeaked, "How much farther?"

"The next plateau."

"Umm, good." Reluctantly she released one rung, clutched another, then another. Soon they reached the plateau and she scrambled off the ladder and waited for White Hawk to join her.

He led her along the walkway—which was much wider than it had appeared from the ground—until they reached the farthest door.

"These will be your quarters until you face the Tribunal."

"And then what?"

Hostility flashed in his eyes. "I can't say."

"Won't, you mean."

"Whatever you choose to think."

She turned from him and went into the pueblo. A clay lantern hung from the ceiling and held several lit candles that flickered across the spacious room. Lily had expected a cave of sorts. Instead, she found the room quite pleasant, almost as comfortable as the den she'd shared with Jorje. A platform built of reeds and branches, and covered with several layers of sheepskin, occupied one end. A well-crafted table sat against the adjacent wall and held a brightly painted basin, a pitcher and a cup. Several cloths hung on a rail beneath it.

She heard White Hawk drop the backpack and then release the burdens on his back. A sleeping bag flew over her shoulder, landing on the platform. Glancing back, she saw him kneel to remove his few belongings from the pack.

"Take off your boots," he said, standing and walking toward the platform with the now-familiar packet and bottle in hand. "I'll tend that blister."

Lily almost groaned. He'd ignored, insulted, and humiliated her. Now he wanted to be her nursemaid again. Too tired to protest, she did as he asked. The blister was driving her crazy, and his voodoo medicine did seem to help.

When she lowered herself onto the bed, sinking into its incredible softness, she realized how deep her weariness ran. It almost seemed to take too much effort to bend over and remove her shoes. As if sensing her fatigue, White Hawk began unlacing the boot on the blistered leg.

"Star Dancer will call for you at dawn," he said, stripping down her sock. "Rest while you can."

Needing no encouragement, Lily fell back. As her overworked muscles sighed in relief, White Hawk removed the boot and sock from the other foot, then began massaging both her arches.

"White Hawk," she said drowsily, her eyelids feeling like weights. "Why are you being so nice? I know you hate me for what happened to your wife."

His hands stop moving, and she felt them flex ever so slightly. "You're weak from your injuries and the difficult journey," he finally said. "The Tribunal needs you healthy for the inquisition."

"Inquisition," she echoed softly. "Oh what a pleasant thought to carry into my dreams." Then as White

Hawk's strong fingers stroked her aching feet, she fell fast asleep.

"Lady? Lady?"

The tentative feminine voice stirred Lily from her dreamless sleep. Reluctantly opening her eyes, she saw a young girl peering shyly at her.

"Yes?" Her parched throat made her voice raspy, and the girl didn't respond immediately, so Lily repeated herself.

"It's dawn time, lady. Star Dancer has sent for you."

Right on schedule, Lily thought, wondering how these people did it without clocks. She elbowed herself into a sitting position and a lightweight blanket fell to her waist.

White Hawk must have covered her before he left, she thought, running her hands through her tangled hair and feeling somewhat like a calf being pampered for the kill. She glanced over at the girl, who looked terribly frightened.

"Couldn't your tribe spare a warrior?"

"I don't understand, lady."

"Never mind." Lily climbed off the platform. She still wore her dust-encrusted clothing and dirt streaked her arms and legs. She imagined her face didn't look much better.

She turned to the girl, who had her eyes firmly affixed to the floor, and asked, "Can I wash first?"

"Oh yes. That's why I'm here. To help you dress for the meeting."

"In a ceremonial robe I suppose."

The girl's brows knitted together, but she still didn't meet Lily's gaze. "Robe? No, lady. You may wear what you will."

Now that her mind was clearing, Lily realized the poor frightened child had nothing to do with her misery, and while she wasn't exactly being cruel, she wasn't being kind either. "My name's Lily," she said more gently. "What is yours?"

"I am Shala White Hawk, daughter of Tajaya and Tony," the child replied in a proud voice, bobbing her head.

Instantly Lily recognized her from the night before. As the girl spoke, her dark hair bounced around her face, falling back to form a flawless chin-length cap, and though her face was still childishly round she had White Hawk's prominent cheekbones.

In her bobbing, Shala's eyes met Lily's for a fraction of a second. She quickly directed them back at the floor. This gave Lily just enough time to see their clear blue shade and the lapis-hued striations that made them seem like cracked glass.

The child has her mother's eyes, Lily thought, suddenly feeling a little sick.

"Does your father know you're here?" she asked, certain White Hawk would never want his daughter within miles of her.

Shala chanced another glance. "Star Dancer said I could come, lady."

"I see." Lily wanted to walk over and give the girl a pat, maybe a hug, but knew she'd only frighten her, so she simply added, "Lily, sweetheart, not lady. Call me Lily."

"Yes, Lily. Would you like me to pour water for washing? Later, after you meet with Star Dancer, we can go to the river for a real bath."

A nice way to tell me I'm filthy, Lily thought. The girl moved to the table and stood on her tiptoes to reach the pitcher. She solemnly filled the basin, then bent and took a small painted box from a shelf. Lily watched her precise movement, wondering how old she was. Six perhaps, eight at the most, and despite her trepidations she was poised and articulate beyond her years.

Now that the bowl was filled, Shala turned to her, holding out the box.

"Items for your cleansing." After Lily took the box the girl pointed to a large pot on the lower shelf. "That's for, well, other necessities. You may empty it each morning into the pit at the other end of the walkway."

During the entire explanation, Shala kept her head turned away, and Lily smiled wryly, knowing the reason.

"I can't enchant you with my eyes, Shala."

"Yes, la—Lily." But she kept her eyes averted nonetheless.

Supposing reassurances from a werewolf weren't really very reassuring, Lily opened the box. It held a small mirror, which she took out and put on the table, not wanting to see herself until she'd washed. Underneath the mirror was a large-toothed comb and a rectangular bar wrapped in some kind of polished bark. With a small start, Lily noted the comb was plastic, and when she removed the bark she discovered a new bar of soap etched with the word Ivory.

Ivory soap? And there were also a toothbrush and a tube of Crest.

"I thought the Dawn People never left the canyon," she said as she bent to splash the wonderfully cool water on her face. "Where do you get these things?"

"Oh, some of our warriors, both men and women, go to the mechanical world. They bring back that which we can use." Lily slanted a glance at her as she washed her face, and saw the child dare a quick return look. "Have you ever uh, ever seen the Disney lands?"

"Disneyland. Yes, yes, Shala, I have."

"Are there truly monsters? And high, high rolling carts that fall down mountains very fast?" Her soft voice quickened and Lily could see excitement on her face.

"Yes, there are, but they're only make-believe. You're always safe. It's a fun place to visit."

"Oh, I knew it!" Shala clapped her hands to her chest. "And are there big longhouses where people watch moving images that tell stories? And carts that move without horses or donkeys?"

Lily nodded. "How did you learn of these things?"

"We small ones hear the warriors talking." Shala dipped down, snagged a cloth from beneath the table, and gave it to Lily.

The cloth was soft and absorbent against Lily's sunburned skin, even moreso than the expensive towels she'd used most of her life. When her face was dry, she placed it back on the table, then began washing her arms.

"Was it a long walk from the top of the canyon?" Shala asked.

"Very long."

"Too long for a little girl, I bet. And are the Disney lands far away?"

"Very far," Lily answered gravely, bending over to tend to her grimy legs. "Especially if you're walking."

"Maybe Papa will take me there. I'd so much like to see it before we return to Quakahla."

Lily lifted her head questioningly. "What is Quakahla?"

"When the nights grow longer and the dark moon rises, The People will pass over into—"

"Shala!"

They both jerked their heads toward the door, where a scowling White Hawk was holding back the drape. Today he wore cut-off denims and a Jerry Garcia T-shirt. It figured he'd be a Deadhead, Lily thought irritably.

"I didn't think he'd like you being here," she whispered to the wide-eyed child.

White Hawk scowled at Lily, but his face softened as he looked at his daughter.

"What are you doing here?" he asked gently.

"Star Dancer said I could come."

"She did, did she?"

"She asked me to wake the lady and bring her to the longhouse."

"A very fine job you've done of it too, but I'll take over from here. You may go now. Your friends are waiting."

"Yes, Papa." Shala looked disappointed, but she went out the door as asked.

When she was gone, White Hawk dropped the curtain and stepped into the pueblo.

"Stay away from her, Lily."

Lily indolently returned to drying her legs, then peeled off the adhesive bandage, only mildly surprised to find the blister had completely healed. She glanced up at White Hawk, but felt in no mood to thank him. "Do you think I'll eat her? If you recall, I rarely indulge in meat these days."

"That doesn't change what you did to her mother. If she becomes fond of you . . ." Lily could feel him suppress a shudder. "It would break her heart should she ever find out."

"Oh that." Tossing the towel back onto the table, Lily turned toward the backpack. "Well, don't you worry, White Hawk. It's unlikely she'd ever grow fond of a monster such as me, isn't it?"

A quizzical expression crossed his face. As usual his thoughts were guarded and Lily couldn't read the source of his emotion, but he radiated far less animosity. Probably from lack of energy, she concluded. It had been a long hike for him too.

"Hurry," he said bruskly. "Star Dancer is waiting." When Lily didn't move, he added, "Now."

She gave him a pointed stare, but got no reaction.

"Do you mind?" She glanced at the door. "I have to change clothes."

White Hawk backed out of the door and pulled the curtain shut. Going to the high windows, Lily stretched up and drew the coverings closed, then dropped her clothes and washed the remainder of her body.

She took her time, running the comb through her dirty tangled locks and longing for the bath in the river Shala had mentioned. Outside, she could hear White Hawk's moccasins making soft rapid taps on the walkway.

Let him wait, she thought, moving to the backpack. She opened it and rummaged through the contents. After slipping into underwear, she pulled out a filmy Armani blouse and almost smiled. One day in this environment would leave it sweat-stained and tattered beyond repair.

"What's taking so long?" White Hawk called.

Lily didn't answer. Not caring what the weather would do to it, she put on the blouse, then chose a pair of raw silk shorts that wouldn't hold up much better. If she was about to face her judge, she would damn well look her best.

Chapter Nine

"Coffee?"

Although Lily didn't know exactly what she'd expected, this woman definitely wasn't it. Her tall, regal, and ageless bearing wasn't surprising, nor was the loosely braided black hair that fell to her waist. What came as a shock was the gray T-shirt with a large fiery orange basketball and the words GO SUNS that somehow blended naturally with her ankle-length broomstick skirt.

The coffee, which Lily accepted appreciatively, also came as a shock.

"How do you like it?"

"With cream?" she replied hopefully.

Star Dancer turned to a metal stove where a small clay pot wafted a rich coffee aroma, and nodded to a small jar. "Will powdered do?"

Despite her apprehension, Lily laughed. Star Dancer looked at her with twinkling eyes. "I said something funny?"

"All those years . . . Well, I assumed your tribe survived off the land." Lily shook her head in bemusement. "Ivory Soap, Crest, toothbrushes, and plastic combs . . . coffee and Cremora? I almost feel I'm home."

The High Shaman smiled.

"It's our weakness. We've grown attached to the comforts of the mechanical world. Fortunately many of our brave ones are willing to venture out to bring them back." Star Dancer's grin widened. "Although at times I think they don't find it much of a hardship."

Lily relaxed under the wattage of Star Dancer's smile. She'd entered the longhouse expecting judgment. But from the moment she'd met those eyes that were much the shade of White Hawk's, she knew they were different. Unlike her captor, this woman's eyes radiated only kindness.

Star Dancer came forward, holding two brightly painted cups, and handed one to Lily, then turned to a cupboard beside the stove. In a moment she gave Lily a spoonlike utensil, lovingly crafted from silver. "For the creamer," she explained.

As Lily spooned the powder into her steaming coffee, she said, "White Hawk wasn't happy that Shala came to get me."

"He has implied as much." Star Dancer stepped onto a dais at the end of the building and lowered herself to a sheepskin rug, sitting cross-legged. She gestured to a nearby stool. "You may sit there if you wish."

"The rug is fine." Lily found herself unable to emulate the woman's graceful descending movements, but she finally made herself comfortable and took a sip of coffee.

"The child has much curiosity about you," Star Dancer said, as though their conversation hadn't been interrupted. "She is wise well beyond her winters and has a destiny as a shaman. White Hawk knows he must respect her free will."

Lily nodded sagely as if she actually understood the philosophy behind the woman's words. "A lovely girl."

"Delightful. As is this delicious brew." Star Dancer sipped her own coffee, swallowed, and then made a noise of appreciation. "Now ask me what you will, Lily. You must have many questions."

Astounded by the directness, Lily laughed again. "Many? Oh, yes, many questions. I don't even know where to begin."

"Begin with what's at the forefront of your mind."

"What will you do with me?"

"Yes, yes, that's good. You will face the Tribunal, Lily, to answer for your crimes against The People."

The reply wasn't unexpected. Hadn't White Hawk already told her that? Yet, though she'd never known a quarry's fear before, she felt it now and recognized it for exactly what it was.

"That's all you wish to know?" Star Dancer asked gently when Lily remained silent.

To deal with her panic, she assumed the business-like tone she might have once used with an attorney. "Am I to be executed?"

Star Dancer took another sip of coffee, swallowing appreciatively. Finally she answered.

"Most likely you won't survive."

"Are you saying I could?"

"Only if you meet the Tribunal with an open heart, Lily. Acknowledge and own up to the evil and pride in your deeds—the evil and pride that is in all of us. By doing this you will prevail. Denial. Blaming others. These will bring your downfall."

At a loss for words, Lily took another sip of coffee.

Star Dancer patted her knee. "I've offered prayers in your behalf to the Great Spirit."

Lily's eyes widened. "Your people don't want me dead?"

"Some do. But all is as it should be and they will come to understand that. Finish your coffee now, Lily, then you may go. You're free to roam the village. Eat when you're hungry, go where you like, talk to whomever you wish. But don't be surprised if most do not reply."

She wouldn't be surprised at all. They wouldn't even look at her. As she quietly sipped her coffee, Star Dancer rose and went to a long simple table in the middle of the platform, where she lit a slim stick and placed it upright in a block of clay. In a few minutes, a sweet, pleasing fragrance filled the longhouse.

When she'd drained the cup, Lily put it on the floor

and got up too, in no hurry to leave but well aware the audience had ended. As she passed Star Dancer, the woman gave her a gentle smile, but didn't speak.

Lily continued to the door. When she reached it, she looked back over her shoulder. "When is the inquisition?"

"The time hasn't yet come. I wait for the sign and will let you know when I receive it."

Although it was no answer at all, Lily simply nodded and left the longhouse.

Shala was waiting for her, a straw basket in one hand and some thin blankets draped over her shoulder. "I came to see if you would like to bathe now, lady."

"Lily," she corrected absently, glancing toward the ladder leading to her room. A long climb, and she wasn't sure she was ready for it.

Apparently noticing Lily's reluctance, Shala tapped the basket. "I got clean clothes for you from your room."

"Clothes, hmm?" Lily peered at the goods Shala toted. "What else do you have? Shampoo, maybe? How about conditioner?"

Riva was sitting in front of her loom when Tony entered the longhouse. She looked up when the door opened.

"Welcome home, Tony. You've done well."

"Thank you, but the praise is undeserved."

"Oh, you've earned it unquestionably. Despite your

personal feelings you brought Lily safely to us. I suspect you also had some success with shape-shifting. Am I right?"

Tony pulled up a nearby chair, sat down, then put his elbows on his knees to rest his chin on his folded hands. "My last success was before Tajaya's death," he said. "Now this. I don't understand." He went on to tell her of what had happened in Lily's room. "And when I saw her life's blood gushing out . . ." Tony glanced away, remembering the intense alarm that had compelled him to save her. "I've wanted this woman dead for years, Riva. I can't comprehend why I was able to shape-shift then . . . and for that reason."

"Didn't I tell you it would come when needed? Don't question the Universe's gifts. You'll understand in due time."

Tony gave her a frustrated glance. "You came from the outside too, Riva. How do you reconcile your faith with what you learned out there?"

Riva laughed gently. "Ah, Tony, I didn't have logic drummed into me the same way you did. I had the advantage of not being college-educated."

Grinning, he replied, "But you can't program a computer either."

"Since we have none here"—she laughed again—"I don't feel the loss."

Tony rubbed the back of his neck, taking his eyes from Riva's smiling face. "We need to talk about Shala and the she-wolf."

"I wondered when the subject would arise." Riva

paused, clearly weighing her next words. "You must keep in mind that Lily isn't a werewolf anymore."

"Not in form. But in her heart. Wickedness does not die with the form."

Riva's luminous golden eyes clouded. "You're twisting the truth, Tony, and you know it . . . here." She tapped her heart. Her eyelids began fluttering. Soon they closed, and in a radically deeper voice, she started talking.

A herd of deer surrounded White Wolf Woman, and several stags lowered their thick necks, aiming their pointed racks at her exposed belly. The does behind them squealed encouragement.

"Kill the traitor!" they urged. "Kill her!"

Suddenly Quetzalcoatl appeared. "Deer People, what are you doing to my daughter?"

Jeshra, the largest stag, stepped forward, lifting his antlers proudly. "Though Sienna Doe swore to protect us, she has betrayed us grievously. One of our sisters lies dead in the clearing beyond, slain by her fangs. We seek only justice, Great One."

"By betraying yourself?" asked Quetzalcoatl. "Do Deer feed on Four-Leggeds? Nay. By doing violence on this one, you do violence only to yourselves. Do you question the creatures I make, the natures I give them?"

"Jeshra lowered his proud head and the herd backed away," Tony mumbled, completing the story and shamed by the truth it revealed. He couldn't meet Riva's now-open eyes, but still felt compelled to defend himself.

"You're right. I can't know what changes have come

over Lily. Yet she shows no remorse about killing Tajaya, and her pride is insufferable. I'm worried about Shala's safety. How can that be wrong?"

"Shala is of you, Tony, but doesn't belong to you. You can't shield her from life for fear she'll suffer Tajaya's fate. She expressed interest in Lily, which I've permitted her to explore." Riva turned back to her weaving, signaling that their talk was over. "She'll soon tire of the woman."

"I wish I were as convinced," he replied uneasily, rising and moving to the door.

"Walk in beauty," Riva said absently, without replying to his remark.

But then he hadn't expected her to.

Restless and uneasy, Tony wandered aimlessly around the village center for a while, stopping at a hearth for a nibble, chatting briefly with Kessa, the fire tender. As he started back to his wickiup, he realized he wasn't behaving like the warrior and shaman he proclaimed himself to be.

Since when did a warrior wallow in his conflicted conscience? From his first days at Riva's knee, he'd been taught to face such turmoil head-on.

He checked first on Shala, learning from Kessa, who delivered the news with a frown, that his daughter had accompanied Lily to the woman's pool. Tempted to go after them, he wavered, remembering Riva's counsel.

His daughter had her own will; he must allow her to use it. And the woman's pool was safe enough with so many other bathers there. He smiled grimly, thinking the she-wolf had no idea of the snubbing she would receive. Mothers mourning their lost sons and daughters were the most vengeful of them all.

Not true. His own vengeance ran far deeper. And he knew he must come to terms with it, knew exactly where to go to do that.

The air had grown still by the time he reached the glen, and Tony's T-shirt clung to his sweating body. Accustomed to the harsh summer heat, he barely noticed. He came often to this place where he'd scattered Tajaya's ashes—to speak to her, to listen. At first she appeared every time he called her—either in memory or in a vision—but this last year she'd often failed to come.

She'd moved on, he'd told himself, renewing the Circle of Life within All That Is. But his grief had remained, twisting, growing darker, until it turned into a warped loathing for her slayer. Although it violated everything he believed, Tony clung to his hatred.

He settled under the shade of a mesquite, plucked a moist blade of grass from the ground, and chewed on the tender end.

Tajaya had been his light, his beacon. Through her, he'd learned the mysteries of love and finally the mysteries of the Universe.

And now he was betraying her.

The thought startled him. Betray? What had he done? The question was answered quickly with images of Lily. Her saucy remark on the train about her nanny, and his barely suppressed amusement. The admiration he'd felt for her strength upon debarking the train in Flagstaff. Worse yet had been the laughter they'd shared when she'd tumbled during her clumsy struggle with the sleeping bag. And he'd almost enjoyed that tender moment when he'd massaged her aching feet.

Sharing laughter and tenderness with his wife's killer? He hadn't just betrayed Tajaya's memory, he'd defiled it!

His misery couldn't have been more intense, and he lowered his head to his knees, seeking some word, some sign that his wife's spirit still abided here. Only she could ease his torment.

He almost knew what she'd say. He'd first caught sight of her when he was still a string bean of a boy hiking in the forests on the canyon rim. From that first day he'd recognized her gentleness. She'd taught him to respect the Creepy-Crawlers, to kill no more of the Four-Leggeds and Finned-Ones than his family could eat, and she followed the shaman's way without fail.

A cactus wren twittered and Tony looked up. Removing the chewed-up grass from his mouth, he waited for a vision. The wren grew silent and he slumped back against the tree.

Yes, he knew what she would say. All creatures had their place in the Great Spirit's domain. The Circle of Life rolled on and shamans used all at their disposal, never complaining when they themselves were used.

No! He wouldn't accept that! And wishing that his thoughts had come from Tajaya's spirit, he affirmed to himself that a shaman's life should not be plucked just before her final rites. A daughter should not be robbed of her mother, a husband of his loving wife.

He clung to her memory furiously, fearing if he stopped, she'd be gone forever. If this fueled his hate and anger all the more, so be it. Bless it, in fact. He would not let Tajaya's spirit die!

With this, he flung the grass blade on the ground and sprang to his feet. The wolf woman had robbed him of his wife and he'd be damned by all that was sacred before he'd let her steal his daughter.

Chapter Ten

"Tell me more about the mechanical world," Shala begged, splashing water as she swam in the secluded grotto.

Luxuriating in the silky feel of the milky substance Shala had given her to use as a shampoo, Lily massaged it into her scalp. The girl stared at her with avid interest, having obviously forgotten sometime during their walk that she shouldn't look Lily in the eyes.

"What would you like to know?"

"Everything!"

Lily laughed. "All at once?"

"Hmm. Guess that would be hard." Shala scrunched up her pert little nose. "I know! Tell me about the superbig markets where you pick whatever you want from shelves! Are there really such miracles?"

A short distance away a group of women also bathed. They'd been laughing and talking when the two of them arrived, using an odd combination of English and their own language, but had immediately lapsed into silence when Shala and Lily had entered the water. Now they glanced over surreptitiously, all ears.

Realizing that interest in the mechanical world wasn't limited to children, Lily was half tempted to change the subject, but Shala was waiting so eagerly. . . .

"It's not a real miracle, Shala. Many people work very hard to put food on those shelves. When others take something, they must give money for it."

"What's money?"

Having never been around children before, Lily had no experience with these kinds of questions. At a loss for how to answer, she said she had to rinse her hair and dipped beneath the water. Feeling marginally better prepared, she broke the surface of the water with a big splash, sending drops flying as she shook her head. Shala squealed when the spray hit her face, and the carefree sound wormed its way into Lily's heart. She smiled broadly and Shala smiled back.

"Still want to know about money?"

Shala nodded excitedly.

"Well, it's complicated. People have been trying to explain money for years. Instead of trading—you know, like giving fur for corn or baskets for venison—we print up paper which we get when we work and give back when we take things."

"This is really confusing, isn't it?" Shala took a quick

dunk under the water. When she bobbed back up, she said, "I've never heard of this trading either, Lily."

"Don't your people trade?"

Shala shook her head.

"I mean, if one family has a farm, don't they get gifts from those who take their food?"

"Oh!" Shala's face brightened. "Some of the late-comers do that at first, but after a time they stop."

Now it was Lily's turn to frown. "If you don't trade, how do you exchange what you make?"

"Everyone does what is needed, and everyone takes what they need. Is that wrong?"

"No. Just different." She turned around, wanting to drop the difficult subject. "Would you wash my back?"

"Sure." Grabbing the soap, Shala paddled closer and lifted a spongelike scrubber hanging from a cord around her neck. She started running it gently up and down Lily's peeling sunburned back. Although Lily had foreseen possibly three or four strokes before Shala lost interest, the girl scrubbed with amazing patience.

"Shala," Lily said, rolling her arm so the girl could reach a particularly itchy spot beneath her shoulder blade, "who are the latecomers?"

"Most of us are born here." Shala dribbled water down Lily's back. "But some come from the mechanical world after they grow up.

"From the beginning of our time," she continued, her tone and words making Lily think she was reciting something she'd heard many times before, "others joined the Dawn People—the Utes and the Pawnee, the Cherokee and the Apache, the Navajo and Cree, and many more. Some sought refuge from drought or famine or ma-ma . . ."

Glad Shala couldn't see her face, Lily smiled at the stutter.

"Marauders," Shala said with sudden certainty, having finally tamed the word. "And some came just to live by the old traditions, but each brought the customs of their own tribe. And still they come, now in greater numbers as the days outside Quakahla draw to an end."

Apparently tiring of reciting a school lesson, she added more perkily, "Papa is a latecomer. So is Star Dancer."

"But they're both shamans," Lily responded in surprise.

"Oh that doesn't matter. Shamans are sent by the Great Spirit. Mama was a shaman too, and she was a trueborn from the line that came from Quakahla. She returned to the spirits when I was very small . . ."

Lily heard a small hitch in Shala's voice, which made her heart twist. What thought had she ever given to the pain her werewolf acts had caused? None. But here was the aftermath in the form of a small, sweet girl who was scrubbing her back in an aquamarine pool.

"Werewolves killed my mother, Lily." The sponge stopped moving and Shala's voice grew very soft. "Did you know that?"

"No, Shala," she lied.

"But you were a werewolf once, weren't you?"

Suddenly Lily wanted to sink under the water and swim away from the girl who asked impossible questions. She couldn't undo the past, and she had nothing to be ashamed of—all she'd done was survive according to her werewolf nature. But she wanted to ease Shala's misery, so she said what she knew the girl wanted to hear.

"Yes, but I know nothing about your mother."

"I didn't think so." Shala sounded relieved.

When Shala started stroking her back again, Lily looked over her shoulder, forcing a smile.

"You've done such a fine job on my back, I think you can stop now." They'd treaded water during their entire bath. Lily's legs were tiring, and she suspected Shala was also getting weary. "Think we're clean enough?"

Shala grinned impishly. "Very clean. Much of your skin is now in the water."

With a laugh, Lily headed toward a floating platform. The Dawn People valued modesty highly, and the women used lightweight blankets to cover themselves as they entered the water. These were then placed on the platform. As she and Shala retrieved their blankets, the other women shrank back, averting their gazes. Lily quelled a desire to snarl at them as she covered herself and waded out of the grotto after Shala.

Now at Shala's side, Lily realized she'd responded mostly from instinct because with this small girl beside her she didn't really much care what the women thought or did. Glancing down at the top of Shala's head, she ached to stroke the black water-sleek hair and smooth it around that impish little face.

Werewolves didn't bear children, at least not in the ordinary sense. They initiated other adults into their race, as she had done with Morgan and Jorje, teaching and nurturing them until they came into their full Lupine powers. But Lily had once dreamed of having a child—a girl much like Shala, on whom she could shower all her love. After she'd joined the Lupines, she sometimes felt regret over what would never be.

Shala renewed this half-forgotten dream.

"What a sweet one you are." Lily bent and impulsively kissed the top of Shala's head. "Thank you for scrubbing my back."

Shala slid her arms around Lily's neck and gave her a kiss on the cheek. "You're welcome."

Unexpectedly, Lily's eyes filled with tears. Forcing a small laugh, she patted the girl gently on the back, saying, "Go dress now."

As Shala scampered into the shelter of the shrubs and Lily turned for the place she'd left her own clothing, the tall cottonwoods came alive with birds. With raucous whistles and trills they rose as a group and flew away. A moment later a branch sagged and Lily saw a flash of white. She stared briefly then started forward.

White Hawk blocked her path.

"I told you to stay away from Shala."

Pulling the wet clingy blanket away from her body, Lily adjusted it before meeting White Hawk's glare. "I enjoy her company. Since she also enjoys mine, I don't intend to send her away."

"Do you think I care what you enjoy? I'm only interested in my daughter."

"Papa! What are you doing at the woman's pool?" Shala stood off to their right, her hands planted scoldingly on her hips.

Immediately White Hawk's expression softened. "I came to take you to your lessons. You're late, little one."

Shala glanced up at the sun. "Oh dear." She looked back at her father. "I'm sorry. But Lily and I were having such fun—"

"That you neglected your studies." He moved forward, reaching out his hand. "Now let's hurry. Star Dancer is waiting."

Shala took her father's hand and followed him to the trail leading back to the village. As they started to round a bend, she grinned over her shoulder and wagged her fingers good-bye.

Lily smiled back so hard her face almost hurt.

"The wolf appeared to me in exalted form."

Arlan Ravenheart kept expectant eyes on Star Dancer's face, his pulse racing. He knew what she would think—what he wanted her to think—yet he had cleverly avoided any falsehood.

She sipped from a cup, her expression guarded. Coveting his gift from the spirits, he concluded, and unwilling to admit he'd won them.

"White Wolf Woman came to you?" she finally asked.

"I was lifted to the clouds where the wolf came in human form. Coat of silver. Tall. Strong as many buffalo, yet gentle." He feigned a catch in his voice and looked humbly into the distance. "So heavy was my shame for my prideful thoughts, I wept. Then the creature said to me, 'Ravenheart, lift your head and go forth. You are cleansed.' "

He paused for several measured breaths, then looked directly at his teacher. "Can you tell me what this means, High Shaman?"

Star Dancer remained silent. Ravenheart heard sounds outside. The clunk of a utensil against a heavy pot. Children laughing. Frequent footsteps passing the longhouse door as workers headed for Quakahla.

Filled with impatience, he waited. For three days after the miracle on the clouds, he'd stayed near the mesa, determined to avoid any question about his early return. He snared a rabbit, then roasted it over the embers of the Stone People in the outside pit. Unable to wait until it was fully cooked, he ripped it from the spit and shoved pieces in his mouth, barely taking time to chew. When only bones remained, he gnawed them too, until he'd consumed even the marrow.

That morning he went to the stream below and bathed for his journey home. He washed and braided his hair, entwining feathers he found beneath the trees. As a final touch, he added the rabbit's foot.

Now, seated in all his finery before Star Dancer, he

breathed evenly, confident the spirit's powerful sign couldn't be denied even by this envious one. His next step on the shaman's way was assured.

Her words came, wrenching his heart.

"I must consult the council. Such momentous news will provoke much discussion. We'll let you know."

Ravenheart rocked forward. "You would deny my next step? After this?"

"No, merely a delay. These decisions mustn't be made hastily." She rose, cup still in her hand. "I'll call for you when we decide."

Hiding his outrage in a cloak of humility, he also rose. Her jealousy had prevailed again. Argument would be useless. Bowing his head respectfully, he stepped off the dias, said his parting words, and left the longhouse.

Star Dancer's response had so thoroughly doused his expectations that Ravenheart was almost surprised to find the sun still shining. He stared at the bleached-out sky, still reeling from the new obstacle she'd thrown onto his path. Again, she doubted him! Again!

He could, of course, continue the shaman's way without her blessing. Others had traveled the path without a High Shaman's guidance. But he would waste countless winters mastering what she could teach in a single moon, and though he scoffed at the thought, it nonetheless occurred to him that without her help he might never master the teachings at all.

As he headed for his pueblo, he realized he'd stepped into shadow. Looking up, he saw a gathering storm mass scudding toward the sun. Soon the village center turned bleakly gray.

Another omen? He turned away, refusing to doubt the great wolf's words. *You shall rule forever.* Yes, forever.

And by the time he'd reached the walkway to his quarters, Ravenheart almost believed he really had encountered White Wolf Woman.

"You are the werewolf?"

Lily looked up to see a man of probably twenty years or so regarding her with intense gray eyes. She'd been eating the evening meal by herself, sitting on a stone wall that surrounded the fire pit and trying to ignore the covert glances and murmurs of the other diners, all of whom stayed well away from her.

"No," she replied. "I'm not."

Lowering himself cross-legged to the ground in the smooth way all Dawn People seemed to possess, he leaned forward earnestly. "But you were a werewolf, isn't that true?"

"One might say that."

He inclined his head gravely and continued looking at Lily as she nibbled a piece of bubbly brown bread that had a delicious flavor. After four days of being ignored by everyone but Shala, it felt odd to be under such scrutiny.

"I am Arlan Ravenheart," he said after a time, giving his head a proud toss that sent the red feather and rabbit's foot in his hair flying. "I returned but yesterday from a vision quest and only now learned you were here. Otherwise, I would have sought you out before."

Lily looked up from her food. "Sought me out? I'm not exactly an honored guest."

"The wolf came to me in my vision. It bodes well to receive such a powerful guide, and I now wish to fully understand its ways."

Lily laughed. "By asking a *were*wolf? Would you learn about men by studying gorillas?"

Just then his sharp, beak-nosed face twisted in annoyance and he bellowed, "That is mine!"

Lily followed his livid gaze to find a gawky adolescent boy hovering over a plate on the hearth, a piece of pork halfway to his mouth. His hand froze at Arlan's shout and he quickly dropped the meat.

"Well, perhaps you might take that approach," Lily commented caustically as she watched the boy scurry away.

Arlan greeted her remark with a blank stare. "These young ones have no manners. As to your question about the gorilla, I see it differently. I believe this is more like learning of the spirits by studying men. We are all made in like image. As above, so below."

Lily gawked at Arlan, trying to decide if he was serious. She'd learned from White Hawk, Shala, and Star Dancer that these people possessed a keen and subtle sense of humor, but this grave face in front of her held no hint of amusement.

So far she hadn't been sure if she much cared for him, but now she knew she didn't. She supposed she couldn't afford to turn away a supporter, but on the other hand what difference did it make? Rocking forward, she made a move to leave.

"Wait," he implored. "It's important I learn all I can. I'm Star Dancer's apprentice in the shaman's way. Someday I will be High Shaman. It is already done."

Not so, Lily thought. Surprised to hear a shaman speak those words lightly, she gave in to her urge to goad him. "Really? I thought White Hawk had the job cinched."

Ravenheart sneered and rapped his chest. "White Hawk's heart is soft, like a woman's."

"I'm sure Star Dancer would be delighted to hear that opinion."

His eyes clouded with obvious confusion, but before he could respond the screams of a bird tore the air. A few seconds later a hawk dropped from the sky and landed in the village square. After several more cries it flew off.

"I will do much greater things," Ravenheart mumbled sullenly, then he climbed to his feet and walked away, leaving Lily to wonder what he meant by that.

A few minutes later she saw White Hawk emerge from a group sitting around one of the other fires. He stopped not far from where she sat, looked at her solemnly, then hurried toward the longhouse door.

Chapter Eleven

Delmar is dying, Riva," Tony said to Riva, stalking back and forth across the width of the longhouse. "I must go and make my peace with him. There's unfinished business in Quakahla, which I'll take care of in the morning. When the heat of the day has passed, I'll leave."

"This is an important time between you and your father," Riva replied, putting down her shuttle and turning to him.

"Two more requests . . ." Tony looked away. "Please forbid Shala to keep company with the she-wolf."

"Tony—"

"Lily already lied to Shala," he said heatedly. "She's denied her knowledge of Tajaya's death."

"That's not surprising."

"But Shala is growing fond of her." Tony glanced

beseechingly at the ceiling. "Although it defies my understanding. When the truth comes out—and it will—she'll be devastated. What father wouldn't want to prevent that?"

"Do you honestly think forbidding her to spend time with Lily will dim her—Please stop that pacing, Tony."

Riva patted the seat of a chair next to her. Tony grimaced sheepishly and sat down.

"Your desires are very human. But as you should know by now, you can't keep surrendering to them. What's more, defending your desires so ferociously only feeds them."

Although she hadn't said it in so many words, Riva clearly wasn't going to honor his wishes about Lily and Shala, and though her biting insights made Tony feel like squirming, he decided to put his second request on the table.

"I've tried to honor Lily's nature. Unsuccessfully, as you well know. It's time I took this to the spirits. I want to go on a vision quest before I return to the village."

"Will you also ask for help in releasing Tajaya's memory?" Riva asked. "And in permitting your daughter to seek her own path?"

Tony pressed his lips together. "I'll ask, but my heart isn't in it."

"It will be," Riva replied. "It will be. Your request is granted. Now let's sit and talk of other things until your heart is again at ease."

She rose and went to the cupboard to fill two cups

with tea. While Tony waited he thought how often they'd simply sat together, laughing, talking about inconsequential things—the pattern of Riva's latest weaving, the antics of one of the village children, a particularly fine meal at one of the hearths. But as he accepted the cup and sipped the liquid inside, he knew this wouldn't be one of those times. His heart would never be at ease again until Lily was gone from the canyon.

Or dead.

The next morning Lily carried her breakfast to a shallow ravine she'd discovered a few days earlier that had an enormous sycamore in the center. The ancient tree's trunk branched out into dozens of limbs that grew so tall Lily had to tilt her head to see their tops. She took a seat on one of the lower branches, enjoying the cooling effect of the shade beneath the gently swaying leaves.

It was just shortly after sunrise, but the sun was already warming the moist air, and her thin cotton top clung uncomfortably to her body. She shook the fabric to fan herself, then picked up a vegetable omelette that she'd wrapped inside a soft tortilla.

When she'd dished up her breakfast at the hearth, a few of the tribespeople sneaked looks her way, but most didn't give her a second glance. Apparently they were getting used to her.

They were a busy people, she decided, and happy too. They toiled in their fields, tended their sheep and pigs and goats, wove and constructed their clothing, made pots and baskets. But they never seemed in a hurry. . . .

Except when they were headed to and from the mysterious narrow canyon at the far end of the pueblo wall. What was so fascinating about that canyon? Quakahla maybe? She'd heard it mentioned again and again, and the gaily reverent tones made her believe it was some kind of holiday, probably occurring at the fall equinox on September twenty-third.

She vaguely recalled something significant about this year's equinox. Even though astrology played a large part in the Lupine culture, and as a queen she'd been well educated in it, she couldn't quite put her finger on why this one seemed particularly important. But there was no reason to renew that recollection. The equinox was over two weeks away and she'd be gone by then.

She just wished she felt more urgency about escaping. Lately she seldom thought about it. Her days with Shala, walking along the river as she explained the uses of various plants and told the ancient stories of her people, filled Lily with contentment.

Taking a bite of the omelette burrito, she realized she even liked the food. It was better than anything their maid had prepared, although the woman was an excellent cook.

A dragonfly buzzed overhead, and she observed it for a while, oddly fascinated by the iridescent tones of its wings. Then she shook her head. She had to make plans to leave the canyon. The Tribunal could convene at any time and though she'd pressed Star Dancer for a date on several occasions, the answer was always the same: "The sign hasn't come."

Exactly what *was* this sign? No answer to that one.

"Mind if I join you?"

Lily looked up to see Arlan Ravenheart entering the ravine. Without waiting for a reply, he sat down on the branch beside her. It sagged slightly from the additional weight, and Lily waited for it to settle down, then bit into her burrito again.

Ravenheart leaned forward, his gray eyes filled with eagerness. "I've come to learn more about werewolves."

Lily's appetite vanished. She put the burrito down. "I don't have anything to tell you."

"You must remember what it was like. How are your kind created, for instance?"

His question made Lily remember how much she'd once yearned to talk about her Lupine life. No one had been willing to listen. Until now. Although she found Ravenheart less than endearing, at least he believed her.

"A number of ways," she finally offered. "Certain flowers, when eaten, will bring about the transformation. Some rivers contain water with properties that will do the same. But both of these are rare and hard to find. The most common way is by ceremony."

He nodded, his expression turning reflective. Lily went back to her burrito.

"Can you make me into a werewolf?"

Lily's head jerked up involuntarily, and she stared at him darkly. "Do you know what you're asking? By the next day you'd be eating your people for breakfast"—she tapped her plate—"instead of one of these."

"Wolf came to me in a vision and revealed a destiny I plan to fulfill to its ultimate end."

"Ultimate. . . ?" Lily laughed incredulously. "How many of your people did my companion and I slaughter, Arlan?"

"Such impulses wouldn't enslave me. Wolf is my brother, not my master, as he is for you."

He was clearly unaware he'd insulted her, nor did he realize he'd displayed his arrogance. She gave him a scathing look. "Why would I do such a thing?"

"In repayment, I would grant your freedom."

Freedom . . . The word rang in Lily's ears. Freedom. Her eyes drifted beyond him, taking in the lush foliage of the shallow ravine. Near the entrance, two flourishing mesquites lifted their thin-leafed branches to the sky. She fixed her gaze on them, watching the nearly imperceptible motion of their leaves.

Freedom.

"You have the power to do that?" Not that she had the power to grant *his* wish, but she could deal with that later.

He nodded his head. "Tell Star Dancer you want me to be your advocate before the Tribunal. Instead of taking you to meet them, I'll lead you out—"

Torn between horror at the treasonous offer and her own desire to escape, Lily barely heard the rustle coming from behind the mesquites. Obviously Ravenheart heard, because his pause lengthened.

A second later Shala stood beneath the branches of

the trees. Her blue eyes grew large with apprehension when she saw Arlan glaring at her.

"Go away, girl," he ordered curtly.

Lily quickly intervened. Giving the man a look that commanded him to be civil, she pointedly asked, "Are we finished here?"

"For now. But we will speak more of this." Getting up with obvious reluctance, he gave Shala a resentful look, then disappeared behind the trees.

Shala hurried over, climbed up on the tree limb, and settled beside Lily. "I had a little time before my lessons, and thought you might want to hear the next White Wolf Woman legend."

"You thought that, did you?" Lily asked lightly, sensing Shala was holding something back. "All on your own? First thing in the morning?"

Shala looked away, plucked a piece of peeling bark from the tree's enormous trunk, and studied it intently. "Well, uh, Star Dancer said you might want to hear it."

So Star Dancer had sent Shala. Lily wondered what the High Shaman's purpose was—she knew the woman had one. Considering White Hawk's obvious disapproval of their friendship, she wondered why Star Dancer encouraged it. Overriding another's wishes didn't appear to be the Dawn People's way.

"Shala," she asked, "your father isn't very happy about us spending time together. Why doesn't he make Star Dancer stop sending you to see me?"

"She is my grandmother."

Lily's eyes widened in shock. "Your father's mother?"

"No, no. My mother's mother."

The news stunned Lily. Star Dancer treated her so kindly, and with so much understanding, yet she'd lost a daughter. . . .

A mystery better left unsolved, she thought, returning her attention to Shala. She particularly liked the stories about the deer who'd become a wolf and enjoyed listening to Shala telling them. Already the girl possessed an exquisite sense of timing, knowing when to pause and when to speed up for maximum drama.

"I'd love to hear your legend," she said.

Shala jumped off the branch, lowered herself to the ground with folded legs, and then let her eyelids drift half closed.

"White Wolf Woman was hungry again," she began in a high, sweet voice.

Since becoming a wolf it seemed she was always hungry. And this particular morning, she slunk through the forest, nose to the ground, sniffing for the scent of a young buck. This one was inexperienced in the way of the predator, and he sped into a ravine where there was only one escape. White Wolf Woman licked her greedy chops, already savoring his taste.

She followed the buck into the canyon. When he spied her, he leaped wildly against a rock wall, trying to climb out of the deep ravine. Young and tender he was, with his small rack of fuzzy antlers.

Jaws open and prepared for the kill, White Wolf Woman flew at the buck's tender throat. Just before she struck, he turned to look at her.

Here Shala paused, moving her slender arms in a graceful curve.

Although he'd been only a spotted fawn when Quetzalcoatl had granted Sienna Doe's request, White Wolf Woman recognized him immediately. This young buck was her son. She fell back in horror at what she'd almost done.

Her son was too young to remember, and when she retreated he gave a long warning call to his relations, then circled around her and ran away.

White Wolf Woman crumpled onto her haunches and howled. So loud and powerful was her cry, it reached the ears of Quetzalcoatl, who was in the Old World attending to some folly of the Two-Leggeds.

"Please, oh Great One," were the words he heard. "Please, oh Great One, return me to my people."

Suddenly a fiery ball sped down the narrow ravine. White Wolf Woman knew it would surely kill her, but so great was her sorrow, she did not run. If Quetzalcoatl willed her life to end, she would accept his decision.

The light struck like a thunderbolt, smashing her against the rocky soil. Her body and mind burst into thousands of bubbles.

When she finally awoke, the sun was setting. She climbed to her feet and looked down, confused. The ground was much farther away, and soft brown hide covered her long slender legs, though just a short time before she'd borne shaggy white fur. Her heart rejoiced, and she gave thanks for the miracle Quetzalcoatl had wrought.

As darkness fell on the ravine, her stomach growled, reminding her she still had not fed. Walking easily, lightly, glorying in the movements of her restored body, she moved to a cluster of grass and began to eat.

Shala stopped, and Lily waited for her to go on, thinking the pause was just for effect. But the child remained silent and opened her eyes.

"I'm not sure I get the point, Shala."

The girl's eyes widened in obvious surprise. "But it's so plain. All is as Quetzalcoatl makes it, Lily. When White Wolf Woman again becomes Sienna Doe, she forgets that just a short time before she'd wanted meat, not grass. That is the way of the universe."

Is it? Lily thought. "Maybe for the beasts, but people don't forget so easily."

"Star Dancer says we can if we choose to."

Lily wanted to ask if Shala had made the choice to forgive her mother's killer. She'd made a big mistake by lying when the subject first came up. But what else could she have done? She hadn't wanted to hurt the girl. That the lie would only add to Shala's pain if she ever learned the truth was something Lily preferred not to think about.

She hopped down from the tree branch and offered Shala her hand. "Teach me more about these marvelous plants of yours, sweetheart. I never get tired of them."

After another stolen hour with Lily, Shala went off to her lessons. At loose ends, Lily wandered around the village, wondering what to do with the rest of her day.

As usual, food was simmering over the fires, with the tenders periodically stoking the coals. Meals didn't seem to be an event here. People simply wandered in and out, taking food whenever they were hungry, although greater numbers gathered at midday and again at dusk. Right now, the stone benches were empty. Men and women toiled in the fields. She heard the giggles of children coming from the longhouse, joined by the richer, deeper laughter of Star Dancer. More laughter and excited voices came from the narrow canyon entrance to the left of the pueblos. For some reason all these high spirits made Lily more keenly aware of her own isolation.

At first she hadn't been bothered much by the Dawn People's disregard. If she'd given this any thought at all, she would have realized the treatment was so reminiscent of her childhood it seemed normal. But at the moment, her brush with loneliness made her long for Shala's company again.

The girl had so much warmth, yet she was unusually perceptive and confident for one so young. Clearly the product of gentle guidance and loving attention, she had everything Lily once wished for and never had.

Except a mother . . .

Despite the heat, Lily shivered. Turning her attention to the mouth of the canyon, she saw a woman come out carrying a basket overflowing with speckled ears of corn. Lily glanced at the fields where the rows of stalks were wilting, harvested long ago. So where had the woman found the corn?

Badly needing diversion, she strolled toward the canyon and looked in, finding a barren place filled with sharp amber-hued rocks that didn't invite one to walk on them. No one was there, and she concluded there must be an exit on the other end. Sensing the others wouldn't want her there, she glanced over her shoulder. No one had noticed her presence, so she moved quickly, hopping from one wobbly flat-topped stone to another until she saw a flash come from the mouth of a cave. Peering inside, she saw that the far wall pulsed with brilliance. Strangely, she could stare right into it without squinting.

What was this place? A site for sacred ceremonies? A burial ground?

She started to step in, but was stopped by a familiar shrill cry. Above her circled the large white raptor, nearly invisible against the harsh glare of the summer sky. Tony's messenger. Or so she'd assumed. Every time it showed up, he wasn't very far behind. Annoyed, she looked away and started into the cave.

"What do you think you're doing, wolf woman?"

Lily spun. Dark sunken eyes that were almost lost in folds of thick wrinkles stared at her menacingly, and Lily clearly read the woman's murderous thoughts.

"Who wants to know?" she asked haughtily.

"Frieda, mother and grandmother of warriors and shamans, and she demands an answer." The old woman weakly lifted a walking stick, slamming it down more from the weight of her teetering body than from the force she applied. How this fragile creature had navigated the rocks was beyond Lily's comprehension.

"I was just curious." Lily plastered a smile on her face. Although she recognized the old woman as the one who'd spit at her the night she'd arrived in the village, this wasn't a formidable foe and she was unwilling to berate her.

"Curious, eh? I thought curiosity was for the cat. You of the wolf lack the intelligence. Sleeping, quarreling, and eating, that is your way."

Images of a vital square-shouldered woman standing over her with a spear came from Frieda's mind. Probably a younger version of herself, Lily thought, able to do what the old woman no longer could.

But Frieda glared up at her as though she was unaware of this fact. Bending farther forward, leaning heavily on the walking stick, she curled her upper lip, revealing a mouth with very few teeth.

"See these," she croaked, tapping the black and yellow stubs. "My daughters now mince my food as I once did for them. Yet I would rather live with these than have the sharp, dripping fangs of your kind, or even those smooth pearls you show with your false smile."

Frieda suddenly reminded Lily of Mrs. Preston, and her polite smile vanished. "Why are you telling me this?"

"Two sons and a granddaughter I lost to werewolves. Retribution now comes. The Tribunal will prevail. Your time to walk this earth is ending, wolf woman." With great effort, Frieda straightened her bent back and again fixed her dark eyes on Lily. "Now leave my sight. You are not fit to be at the doors of Quakahla."

A small old woman, capable of harming no one, and yet the fury in the quaking voice shook Lily deeply. Struggling to maintain her dignity, she turned and hurried back up the narrow canyon, stumbling several times along the way. By the time she reemerged into the village, she'd almost convinced herself these people were more dangerous than Sebastian and all his underlings put together.

As she made the long climb to her quarters, the raptor cried out again. Lily had the spooky feeling it was laughing at her.

Chapter Twelve

Lily's skin crawled, and she felt suddenly dirtier than she'd ever felt before. Determined to wipe the encounter with the vile old woman from her mind, she hurried to her quarters, collected her bathing supplies, then climbed back down the ladder.

Some of the People were gathering about the fires now, while others still worked in the field, and with everyone thus occupied, she hoped to find the grotto empty.

It was, filling her with more relief than she cared to admit. Stripping off her clothes, she waded into the cool water.

For a time, she simply floated, allowing the buoyancy to rock away her troubles. Frogs croaked and crickets chirped. Pigeons cooed in the trees above. Occasionally she heard the hammering of a woodpecker. The place was a virtual paradise, and despite the open disdain of her jailers, she felt safe here.

What if she just stayed?

The idea startled her so badly she treaded water again. Reaching for the sweet-smelling goo Shala had given her to use as a shampoo, she rubbed some into her scalp and began sudsing her hair. Those disdainful people, she reminded herself, would eventually kill her. And if they didn't. . . ?

Well, Sebastian still lurked somewhere out there. Although she hadn't sensed him nearby since she and White Hawk hiked into the canyon, she knew he hadn't given up. Then, of course, there was Arlan Ravenheart, the would-be shaman who thought he could tame the werewolf power. Her best bet was to dupe him into believing she could deliver what he wanted, let him lead her through the maze.

Then what? Run from Sebastian the rest of her life?

None of these possible futures appealed to her and she decided to forget about them for the moment. She was alone now in a lovely grotto and wanted to enjoy this rare opportunity while it lasted. She drifted onto her back again, allowing the lapping water to rinse her hair, and enjoyed the slippery feel of Ivory against her skin as she soaped her body.

Wanting to take in the sky, she opened her eyes. Fluffy white clouds drifted lazily above. One looked like a giraffe. Another reminded her of a budding rose. And that one looked like a bird floating on wind currents.

Lily blinked hard. It was a bird! The hawk. How she

despised that creature. Whenever it showed up something unpleasant happened, usually appearing in the form of the shaman who hated her so much.

Her tranquil mood shattered, she sudsed up, wanting to make short work of the rest of her bath. The bar slid from her hand and she turned to retrieve it.

That's when she saw him.

"How long have you been standing there?" she inquired irritably, ducking for the cover of the water. "I got the impression this area was off limits to men."

"It is." White Hawk looked slightly dazed.

Lily stretched her mind to discern his mood and was puzzled by what she felt.

Desire?

No, she must be misreading him. This man despised her. She read it in his thoughts, if only hazily, and saw it in his subtle gestures, his facial expressions. "Then what are you doing here?" she asked demandingly.

"I'm leaving the village for a while, maybe a week, even longer." He crouched down next to the water, eyes downcast, uncharacteristically tense, and drew idle lines in the silt. "I'd like you to avoid Shala while I'm gone."

Of course. She should have known he'd ask again. It was a small thing, really, or at least it would seem so to him. She supposed she could tell him what he wanted to hear, but it would only be another lie.

"I can't." She said, her voice thickening.

"Why is that?"

"Because I . . . I'm—I just like being with her, okay?"

He lifted his head, leveling his golden eyes at her, which were now dark with concern. "No, Lily, it isn't okay. This is a dangerous game you're playing, and Shala's the one who'll get hurt."

As she listened to his plea, Lily realized that this man stood for something. Yes, she'd felt loathing seeping from him, and during their journey she knew he'd been sorely tempted to use that sharp blade of his to wreak vengeance for his wife's murder. But his reverence for justice had prevailed, and he'd delivered her unharmed into Star Dancer's hands.

Even now, as she saw hope flickering on his features at her extended silence, she felt his struggle. They were alone; he could easily dispose of her and tell the others she'd escaped. And yet he didn't. His principles meant more to him than personal gratification.

She'd stood for something once—Lupine Law. She'd believed in the Law, which had provided the rigid rules of conduct she'd longed for as a human child. They were simple, straightforward rules. Werewolves respected each other's territories, didn't harm another's underlings, and honored one's betters. Werewolves didn't kill each other. . . .

In one moment of rage and despair, she'd violated all she held dear.

Even now, knowing White Hawk was right, she couldn't make the sacrifice needed to protect Shala. Her loneliness ran too deep and the girl was the only person who cared at all for her.

"I can't," she repeated.

His hope vanished, immediately replaced by outrage. "You killed her mother, Lily!" he growled, springing to his feet. "Have you no pity?"

A gasp followed his question, then a small voice said, "Lily? But . . . but, you said . . ."

White Hawk's face sagged as he slowly turned toward his daughter. Lily dropped her gaze, saw her own agonized eyes staring back . . . watery . . . rippling with regret.

"You heard?" White Hawk asked dully, although the air was heavy with the answer.

Shala bobbed her head. Tears slid slowly over her lower lids and streaked down her face.

"Shala . . ." Lily swam toward the shore, reaching out, longing to say it wasn't true, wanting only to see Shala's eyes again sparkling with happiness.

"No!" Shala whirled and flung her arms around White Hawk's waist, clinging hard. Her small shoulders shuddered, and Lily knew she was crying even though she smothered her sobs. White Hawk put his large hand on her back, turned, and guided her away.

As they moved out of sight, Lily heard him say, "I didn't want you to find out this way."

"It's okay, Papa." Shala's voice sounded thin and teary. "I won't go near her anymore."

Lily pressed her hands against her heart. Over half a year ago, by her own unwise actions, she'd destroyed everything she valued. Then this gentle light named Shala had appeared in her life. But all too briefly, because now she was also gone.

Yes, Lily had stood for something once. But the

golden-eyed man who'd pleaded for his daughter's happiness still did.

And now Lily had destroyed that happiness too.

Tony approached the square cinder-block house his family had lived in since the government tore down their wickiup. The white Buick was parked crosswise in the dirt yard, a jack sitting beside one of its flat tires. Two equally large cars in even worse disrepair sat farther off.

Moving between rolling tumbleweeds, Tony tightened his collar against the chill wind. He'd sent the hawk to roost in a tree outside his father's bedroom and knew what he would find. Delmar's bed was surrounded by angel candles, crystals, and smudge pots. A crucifix graced one wall, the suffering Jesus gazing down on Delmar's wasted form. A dream catcher hung above the bed.

Although his father had long ago converted to Christianity, in his last hours he'd permitted Uncle Joseph to waft smoldering rosemary and chant Apache prayers for Delmar's place in the afterlife.

On the cement slab in front of the house, two boys and a girl raced radio-controlled cars. After speeding the distance, the cars careened onto the dirt, and the children ran to turn them over and begin the race again.

Watching them made Tony think of Shala. He'd left her with Star Dancer, and even though she had stopped crying long before he departed the prior evening, he knew her spirit ached.

If he'd kept his peace Shala would never have found out. No one else in the village would have told her—interference was not The People's way. But Lily should have avoided her like he'd asked. The recollection of her refusal strengthened his malice. She had killed the child's mother; now she'd broken her heart.

"Hey, cousin Tony," called out one of the boys, who was inspecting the underside of his vehicle for damage.

"Tony!" cried the other two children.

"Hey, kids," he called in return.

By the time he reached the patio a new race had started, and Tony watched until the little cars flew off the slab again.

"I won!" cried the oldest boy, scampering to get his car.

"If you slow them down, you can race them in a circle and they won't fall into the dirt."

The boy glanced up from his shiny blue racer. "We know."

Then he fell to his knees to line his car beside the others. Tony stood and watched them for a while, recognizing he'd once again butted in when events were progressing as they should.

When the race ended, the older boy said, "Mom and Dad are inside with Grandfather."

"Thanks." Tony opened the door and went in. The television was on with the volume turned down. Toys covered the carpet. An open, half-full Fritos bag lay on the sofa.

He found his aunt in the kitchen briskly flattening

dough between her hands. The sizzle and steam of bubbling fry bread came from the stove. A plate on the table held finished pieces. "I'm making it for Delmar," she said, turning to give him a smile. "It's his favorite."

She lifted a browned pastry from the fryer, put it on paper towels to drain, then dropped the next one into the fat. Tony reached out toward the table.

"You mind?"

Jenna shook her head. "Your father won't eat much anyway."

Tony ripped off a chunk of the bread. Nobody made fry bread like his Aunt Jenna and he savored the flavor. Soon his hawk spirit told him Joseph had finished the prayer. He finished the last of the bread, then went into the bedroom.

His uncle looked up from the sleeping man in the bed. "Delmar has been asking for you."

Joseph took a smudge pot and a bird wing to a battered chest and set them down, then led Tony as far from the bed as possible.

"He refuses to see the white doctors or go to their hospital," he said in a hushed tone.

"Is your medicine helping?"

"He sleeps, but the poison remains in his blood." Joseph leaned toward Tony's ear, lowering his voice further. "You must convince him he needs the white medicine. He'll listen to you."

"You want me to contradict his will?"

Joseph's eyes suddenly blazed. "He's your father, Tony! You nearly killed him when you abandoned your career and went off to join that wild tribe! Make up for it now by using your shaman's power!"

"Isn't that a contradiction, Uncle, using shaman medicine to convince him to submit to the white doctors?"

"We've done enough dancing and chanting. It isn't doing any good."

Tony saw his uncle's lined and worried face and felt his pain over the impending loss of his brother—and his disillusionment. "Let me sit with him. If his will to live is strong and this is not his time, he'll survive the crisis. But if his soul yearns to cross over, not you or I or the white medicine can save him. Don't you understand that?"

Joseph looked away. "Call me if there's a change."

He shuffled to the door and closed it softly behind him.

Tony crossed the room and sat in the chair beside the bed. Delmar snored softly and peacefully in the aftermath of Joseph's ritual, and Tony picked up his bony hand. When his father turned sixty that spring, Tony requested leave from the Dawn People to attend the celebration. Even then he'd felt this frailness. Years of hard living—too much rum and beer, too many cigarettes, fatty foods, and sugar—had brought Delmar to this place where liver damage and diabetes were slowly and painfully stealing his life essence.

Weary from the long trip, Tony leaned back and closed his eyes. Although he didn't doze, his thoughts drifted, eventually coming to rest on a childhood memory.

He'd been almost ten and Delmar had taken him

camping on Ebony Mountain. They'd driven in as far as possible in an old boat of a car, stopping when the rutted roads finally ended. After lighting yet another Camel cigarette, Delmar sat on the lip of the trunk, leaned in and ripped the wrapping off several twelve-packs of beer. As he began methodically stacking the cans inside a backpack, he caught Tony staring at them. "Nectar for the soul," he said. "But not for you until you're old enough."

He came to the last can, put it on the trunk floor and reached for the supply of Coke which he piled in on top of the beer. After adding food, he put the back-pack on the ground.

"Ready for the bags, Tony?"

He nodded eagerly. Since their first trip, taken shortly after the death of Tony's mother three years before, his father had assigned the sleeping bags to Tony. The task always made him feel he was doing his part.

Gazing into the forest while his father strapped on the bags, he saw a raven land in a tall pine.

"See that, Dad?" He pointed at the bird. "Uncle Joseph says Raven created the world."

"And his old teacher would tell you it was Turtle," Delmar replied with a laugh. "At least on Mondays. By Thursday he'd say it was Coyote. Those are just stories, Tony, and if your uncle had ever been born again into Jesus he'd know it."

"But Uncle Joseph talks to the spirits."

His father stood up, threw down his cigarette and crushed it on the ground. "Well I talk to Jesus, and Jesus talks to God." Picking up the backpack, he slipped his arms into the straps. "Enough talk of the old ways," he said. "Let's see what surprises nature has in store for us today."

Grabbing the beer from the trunk, he slammed the lid and cocked his head toward Tony. "Come on, son. It's a long hike to the creek."

With that he popped the top on the can, took a healthy swig, and started walking into the forest.

Still taking peeks at the raven, Tony followed, not knowing what to believe, as usual. The conversation was the first of many to follow, and eventually Tony rejected both his father's and his uncle's spirituality. He put his energy into doing well in school, playing football, and making the honor role. When he first encountered Tajaya in the mountains, he hadn't given thought to the subject of spiritualism in years.

He never dreamed meeting her would lead him to shamanism, and as he sat holding his father's hand the bitter irony didn't escape him. After years of discipline in the magic of healing, he possessed the skills to help his father live awhile longer, yet he knew such action would only violate nature's rhythm and prolong his father's suffering. Still, he could lessen the pain of the ulcerated leg.

Opening his heavy lids, he stood and lifted the blanket. Someone, probably Jenna, had elevated his father's leg and swaddled it in heavy bandages. Calling on the spirits, Tony felt the familiar electric sensation travel through his fingers as he placed his hands on Delmar's diseased flesh.

After a short time, Delmar's eyes fluttered open.

"Well, if it isn't my son the computer genius," he said in a cracking voice. "Come to see me off." Then a wide smile crossed his ravaged face. "I'm so glad to see you, Tony."

Delmar died peacefully in his sleep three days after Tony arrived. He had a Christian burial that included none of the old ways, and though Uncle Joseph lamented this decision, he stoically endured the service. Later, after Delmar had been cremated, he handed Tony the urn filled with ashes and asked him to speak to the Great Spirit in Delmar's behalf when he scattered them.

Tony embraced his uncle, gave his aunt a kiss, then left for Ebony Canyon. He'd been gone five days.

Now, passing Morgan Wilder's burned-out cabin, he paused, remembering the afternoon he'd set it afire at Morgan's request. The crumbling remains still seemed an affirmation to him of triumph over all that was unholy, and he stared at it awhile.

Instead of bringing thoughts of victory, however, it brought memories of Lily. Not the huge sleek werewolf with her groomed silver coat, but the naked, mud-covered woman he'd found in the forest bordering the Clearing of the Black Hands. She'd snarled and snapped at him, speaking in that unintelligible language that those creatures used. But she'd been human, slender, short of stature, and still fighting.

He'd also seen her genuine grief when she'd fallen

on the lifeless body that had once been her companion. Slain by her own hands, yet regretted by her heart.

Tony turned away impatiently. Why was he thinking such things? What remorse had Lily shown for the lost lives of his people?

Searching for more evidence of her evil nature, he walked to the rim of the canyon, where he planned to free his father's ashes, letting them drift into the canyon. His spirit had always been happy here.

The walk was short and he unlaced his satchel on the way, taking out the brass urn when he reached his destination. Lightning ripped across distant storm clouds. The air was heavy. And still. Although the clouds rushed across the mottled sky, not a breath of wind stirred the surrounding grass and trees. A monsoon would strike the canyon tonight. He hoped it brought rain, but past experience told him it might only bring Brother Wind.

He took the seal off the urn and lifted it up.

"Great Spirit," he mouthed, slowly tipping the urn. "Accept this gift. Absorb your child Delmar into the One from which he sprang. Let him sit by your side until he is renewed."

The ashes slid from the urn, slowly at first, then streaming down. Suddenly a breeze appeared, lifting the dark ash and swirling it into a funnel that weaved and danced as it made its way to the canyon floor.

Tony smiled, knowing Delmar had made an appearance. Fittingly dramatic for one who'd lived life so lustily.

He stood on the rim until the funnel disappeared into the scrub oak and cacti below, then moved toward the trail to the bottom.

He'd asked for a vision quest, and now that the time was at hand he felt unprepared. By concentrating on the way Lily had hurt Shala, he'd been fueling his hatred for her rather than trying to overcome it. Worse, he didn't want to let it go. His hatred had sustained him for almost five years—and bound him eternally to Tajaya.

But he was doubting the spirits. He'd chosen to do the sweat ceremony *because* he was unprepared, not in spite of it. When the time came, the appropriate guide would appear and show him the way to cleanse the stain from his soul.

They'd never failed him before. They wouldn't fail him now. And he was ready.

Reassured, Tony slung his satchel over his shoulder and took his first step down the steep trail. He *was* ready. Sure he was.

Chapter Thirteen

Lily had started scratching lines outside her pueblo door on her first day in the village. Since the encounter at the grotto, she'd added seven new ones.

Except to add the markings and empty her waste in the lime pits at the far end of her walkway, she seldom left her room. She lay around, sleeping, staring at the walls, sometimes braiding and unbraiding her hair for hours. Although she knew she should do something about it, the thought of escape seldom entered her mind. Occasionally she remembered Ravenheart's offer, but felt too listless to search him out.

Each mealtime, drink and food mysteriously appeared at her door, but she never saw who brought it. Nor did she care. On her single excursion, when the heat made her succumb to the lure of a cool bath, she learned she was the object of renewed interest, but no one allowed their eyes to linger or spoke to her.

Expecting Star Dancer to deliver news of the inquisition any day, she told herself the information would spur her into action. Finally, after a week of brooding without a word from the High Shaman, her restless spirit reemerged and she decided to end her self-imposed exile.

A pleasant breeze greeted her when she stepped on the walkway. It was nearly noon, but most people were in the fields and the village center was relatively empty. As she watched the miniature bodies strolling below, she had a devilish urge to drop the contents of the pot in her hands upon their scornful heads. She let it pass, and walked along the railing, staring below, feeling very isolated.

When she reached the catwalk that led to the lime pit, she hurried on, eager to dump her smelly burden. She leaned over, turned the pot upside down, and once it was emptied turned to go back to her room. That's when her eyes brushed the slanting cliff, and she wondered why she hadn't noticed how close it was to the catwalk wall before.

She glanced quickly down the walkway. Finding it empty, she climbed onto the wall.

A daunting drop lay below, but the distance between the wall and the cliff was an easy jump. A small scrub oak clung to the rocky soil and would give her something to grab at when she landed.

Footsteps sounded on the walkway, and she jumped from the wall, feeling more hopeful. Not that she could just take off. She needed food and water for the long hike back to civilization. Maybe, when no one was paying attention to her, she could sneak into White Hawk's wickiup and search for a parka.

It was time to find out exactly when the Tribunal would convene. Did she have weeks to prepare or only days?

But clouds were hiding the sun, and the humidity was still bearable. She'd eat a full meal, squirrel away some extra food, then take a walk and enjoy the unusually mild weather. After that, she'd seek out Star Dancer and possibly mention Ravenheart's offer to defend her.

But why? she asked herself. She didn't need his help, and her werewolf instincts made her scorn traitors. A pack only survived through loyalty. So did a tribe.

She returned to her quarters for something suitable to wear while facing the cold shoulders she knew were coming. The silk blouse had fared better than she expected, so she put that on, along with her denim jeans. Then she braided her hair again.

When her feet hit the ground after the long descent down the ladder, she inhaled the aromas from the hearths and her stomach growled. A woman wearing a beaded tunic stood beside the nearest fire pit, stirring something in a kettle hanging above the flames. Not far from her feet, a child of about two or three guided rocks along the ground, chortling at the clouds of dust they raised. People were gathering now, forming a line. Lily fell in behind them, trying not to notice their furtive looks.

When the fire tender served her the fragrant stew

with a tight-lipped expression, Lily gave her a haughty stare, then moved on to a piece of pork bubbling on the spit, thinking her body needed meat for the trek ahead, despite her aversion to it.

Hotter than she expected, it burned her hand. She dropped the meat on the plate and popped her fingers in her mouth. A man behind her chuckled. She turned, recognizing him as the grandfather who'd protected the rashly brave young boy. Since then she'd learned his name was Gerard, and that he was a member of the council. His status meant nothing to her, though, and she jutted out her chin, then clicked her teeth together. His amusement faded, and he fell back a few paces.

Her fingers stung like hell, but she refused to pay them any heed, and forced herself to finish filling her plate in a leisurely fashion despite the grumbles she heard from behind.

Just as she turned from the hearth to find a place where she could discretely plunge her fingers into cool water, the sound of whooping laughter filled the village. A herd of older children rolled a giant hoop with long sticks, each trying to gain mastery over it.

"Careful," Gerard warned. But they were too engrossed in their game. One of the bigger boys raced by the fire pit, jabbing his stick at the hoop. Suddenly, his foot struck a rock and he stumbled.

Arms whirling, he struggled to right himself by reaching for anything to ease his fall. His hand found the end of the spit; his fingers closed around it.

The weight of his body dislodged the spit from its supporting forks. With a doleful creak of splintering wood, it crashed into the fire. The heavy metal pot, which had been supported by the pole, wobbled, then tilted, sending the steaming contents rushing toward its lip. The toddler still happily moved his rock creatures along the dusty soil beneath.

Lily dropped her plate. Dipping low, she swooped the baby up just before the boiling stew spilled on the spot where he'd been playing.

Trembling, she clutched him to her chest. He touched her hair with his chubby brown hand, round eyes calmly unaware of the danger he'd just escaped.

"Pretty," he said, or at least that's what Lily thought she heard.

Then his mother tore the boy from Lily's arms.

"Joey, Joey," she babbled. Joey began to cry then, apparently sensing his mother's alarm, and she rocked him gently, crooning in her language. Lily heard the older boy beseeching a grandmother for forgiveness.

Rattled well beyond what the circumstances dictated, Lily looked down. Chunks of vegetable and meat lay on the ground, their juices already being sucked up by the dry soil. Her plate was upside down, it contents covered by yellow dust. She bent to scoop up the mess.

Somebody touched her shoulder. Flinching, she looked up, meeting Frieda's black-toothed scowl.

"Get up, wolf woman," she rasped. "We don't need your help."

A sarcastic retort sprang to Lily's lips, but something in the faded eyes made her stop. Lily had killed three of this woman's offspring, who'd once been like the plump, happy-faced baby she'd just held. Soft, accepting, defenseless—and so easy to love. Perhaps this ancient one had a right to her hate. Perhaps it was the only thing that sustained her. Perhaps . . .

Lily got up and walked to another hearth. No longer hungry, she sat on the stone bench, not sure what to do next. Trembling slightly, and unaccountably sad, she put her elbows on her knees and buried her hands in her hair. After a time, she saw a shadow fall upon her feet.

The baby's mother stood in front of her, a plate in one hand. "I am Kessa," she said, "mother of the boy you saved. You may eat at my hearth."

Distress lined Kessa's attractive face, as if she feared she'd fallen in with the devil, but Lily took the plate anyway and followed her back to her fire pit.

Lily had told herself she'd leave the hearth as soon as she finished eating and go seek out Star Dancer. But Kessa had taken a protective stance toward her, giving squelching looks to anyone who whispered about her or regarded her with curiosity. So Lily stayed, sipping a sweet-tasting tea and staring into the flames which drew her gaze hypnotically.

Memories lingered inside those red-orange fingers, and each time they flared, another emerged. She saw Dana Gibbs, arms stretched to the sky as she recited her deadly verse. The fire sputtered and flared anew. Another memory arose—Morgan Wilder, bleeding and half dead, crawling toward the sanctified ceremonial ring.

The licking flames subsided only to arise again, this

time bringing images of Jorje. Fangs bared, poised above Morgan's throat, growling murderous threats.

Repeatedly she'd told herself she'd slain Jorje only to protect Morgan. But had that been her only choice? She'd been stronger than the wolfling. Couldn't she have found another way?

Lily tore her eyes away, a mass lodged in her throat. All this second-guessing was wasted energy. It was done. No matter how wise a different course of action seemed when viewed after the fact, the past couldn't be changed.

To keep her mind off it, she turned her attention to the men, women, and children around her. Only a handful stayed by the hearth now, but they talked animatedly among themselves, joking, laughing, totally relaxing.

Such a happy people. The only time she ever saw fear or anger in their faces was when she somehow entered their awareness. Where they found their happiness, she didn't know. They led such a boring life. Working in the fields or with the livestock, eating, sleeping, protecting themselves against the elements. And so ordinary—no operas or plays or shopping at Harrod's and Neiman Marcus. Not even cinemas or Kmarts. No wonder some of them looked forward to their journeys to the outside.

But many, she noticed, seemed perfectly content to be where they were. With this thought she stood up, stretched her limbs, and went to the hearth. Giving her cup to Kessa, she thanked her for the meal and headed off to find Star Dancer.

She stopped abruptly.

Shala was coming her way. Lily didn't know if she'd been spotted yet, but she expected that when she was the girl would turn away. Their eyes met, but Shala didn't swerve. Although appearing small and frightened, she continued in Lily's direction.

Lily walked forward slowly, afraid to make any sudden moves.

"Were you coming to see me?" she asked when their paths met halfway between the hearth and the longhouse.

"Yes," Shala replied somberly. "Could we walk together for a time?"

"If you like."

Shala led her to the river, which was full of life. Evening was approaching and birds twittered excitedly. Insects made their various night songs. Even the river sang as it rushed between its shores.

But Lily felt like death. Obviously Shala had something important on her mind, which she wasn't sure she wanted to hear.

"Frieda Red Feather says you saved Joey's life this morning," Shala finally said, glancing down at her small intertwined hands.

"His life?" Lily replied, startled by the subject. "No, I didn't save his life. Although he probably would have been badly burned if I hadn't been there."

"No, no. The kettle was falling, Frieda says. It would have squashed him."

"It was? I didn't notice."

"Well, if Frieda says so, it must be true." Shala shot

a glance at Lily. "She doesn't like you very much, you know."

Lily laughed. "She hates me, Shala."

"That is true."

Shala bobbed her head again and looked back at her hands. As they continued walking, the sun danced on her blue-black hair, tempting Lily to try to capture one of the shimmering highlights.

Instead she probed the girl's thoughts, which were still open and unguarded. She caught fleeting memories. She doubted Shala herself was aware of some of them. One, at age three, particularly caught Lily's attention. She'd been playing with other children, and one by one they'd drifted to their mothers. Shala had turned to White Hawk, and though she loved her father she now understood he was the only one she had.

Even earlier—Shala, barely able to walk, screaming in terror on a floor of ancient pine needles. Lily plucked images from the baby's unformed mind—sharp teeth, blood, blurred and swiftly moving figures, a woman's piercing cry.

The cry was cut short. Baby Shala screamed again.

As the horror of that moment flooded Lily's mind, she suddenly felt Shala's love. Pure, undemanding, unwavering, and directed at her. At her.

Her eyes misted. She lifted her arm. Her fingers hovered just above Shala's shining hair.

"Did you kill my mama, Lily?"

Lily dropped her arm.

"Is that what your father told you?"

"Yes."

"Then you must believe him."

Shala turned her head and stared up, unshed tears covering her blue eyes. Her mother's eyes, Lily thought again, just as she had the day they'd met. *Because of me, this wonderful child will never know she has her mother's eyes.* Unable to stop herself, she reached for Shala's entwined hands.

"I'm sorry, Shala," she said quietly. "It happened a long time ago, and I would change it if I could."

"The past is gone," Shala replied sagely, letting the fingers of one hand curl around Lily's palm.

"That's right." She stared earnestly into Shala's solemn face. "But I can promise you this. I'll never hurt you, your father, or any of your people again. Do you believe me?"

"You lied to me once, Lily. The word of a liar . . ."

Lily looked away. "I was . . . I was afraid you'd stop liking me."

"Star Dancer said you might say that."

"And what do you say?"

"I say—" Shala's face twisted and she shook her head rapidly. "I don't know what to say."

She pulled her hands from Lily's and whirled away. "I'm going back to the village now. Maybe we'll talk again."

Then she broke into a run. Lily watched until Shala disappeared among the trees, her chest aching so badly she wanted to double over. For the first time in her life she truly loved another human being, and also truly regretted who and what she'd been.

Which was another first.

* * *

Something nudged Tony's face. Slowly he opened his eyes. The logical computer scientist side of his mind recoiled as he stared into round, dark eyes surrounded by a field of white. Impossible, he told himself, white bears didn't exist in the southwest. But his shaman nature reminded him that anything was possible during a vision quest.

The lodge was filled with mist. He vaguely remembered splashing chaparral water over the blazing Stone People, but that seemed so long ago. He had no idea how much time had passed, or whether he was even conscious.

"What brings you here, Brother Bear?" he asked weakly, not sure if he'd actually spoken the words or if they came from his mind.

"Wolf shall be your mate." The bear rocked back on its haunches, crossing one hind leg over the other as a man might do, and stroked its chin thoughtfully.

Although noticing the incongruous gestures, Tony was more occupied with the words. He should be repulsed by the very idea, for he knew of whom the bear spoke. But he felt only delicious anticipation.

"This is not right," he said, unwilling to accept his true feelings.

"She will nourish your offspring in ways you cannot and awaken a love in you that now seems impossible."

"Impossible," Tony repeated with a short derisive laugh. "She murdered my wife."

"Hatred hardens your heart. You think you keep it to honor your wife, Warrior, but you deceive yourself.

It serves only to conceal your doubts about your life among the Dawn People. If you do not face these doubts, monstrous events will occur.

"These forces are already in motion. Turn to her, Warrior. Her valiant spirit will support you in this task. Remember, the fish that insists on swimming upstream becomes dinner for the bear. Relax into the current and all will be well."

The mist swirled around the bear's great head. It inhaled sharply, forming great smoke rings on its exhaled breath. Tony stared up with glazed eyes, feeling the rings tugging at his spirit.

The bear chucked him under the chin. "We wait to see the glory of your surrender."

Then its form began to fade.

"Wait," Tony cried. "I . . . I have questions . . ."

Paler and paler it got, until nothing remained but a buttonlike nose and two large brown eyes.

"Call on me, Brother, in the hour of your greatest need."

Then it vanished, leaving only the rising rings in its wake. Their tug on Tony's spirit increased, pulling his awareness up and beyond. The heat of the sweat lodge disappeared, the roof no longer existed.

A star-studded sky enclosed him, yet he felt a brewing storm. His weary neck gave out and his head fell back. His eyes fluttered closed. Soon he felt something sweetly hot and soothing against his skin. He opened his eyes and found himself looking down at a woman's face.

Eyes dark as Apache tears and shadowed with sexual

hunger stared up at him. A sheet of pure silky white hair framed her high, prominent cheekbones, accentuating the narrow chin and full, round lips. Her strong long-fingered hands stroked the taut muscles of his back. Her thighs were sweetly parted, allowing him to press the fire between his legs against the beckoning moistness that promised to calm the flames.

"Tony." She sighed, her voice husky with need.

Tony kissed the curve of her jaw, filled with overwhelming tenderness, irresistible need. She shuddered deliciously. Her hand movements quickened to a frenzy, driving him wild. He lifted his head abruptly and claimed her mouth in a violent kiss. She returned it just as violently, bucking beneath him.

Slick she was, and hot, so, so hot, meeting and fanning the fire in his belly. Their tongues danced and their teeth clashed. He cried out as he claimed her, sliding his engorged self inside her.

The sky exploded with lightning. Thunder roared, and the night grew bright as day. She sighed and gasped beneath him, her cries mingling with the sky sounds. His convulsion came as suddenly and intensely as the lightning, and bordered on pain. But with such sweet and tender pain he found himself begging for more. Begging, begging . . .

"Lily," he groaned huskily. "Oh, my sweet Lily. How I love you."

Chapter Fourteen

Lily shot upright in her bed, wide awake and shivering violently. She heard thunder rumbling outside, the sound of wind rattling the roofs of the hogans and wickiups below. Flashes of lightning came through the window, and the air felt thick and heavy, and very warm. She shouldn't be shivering, she realized, clutching her light summer blanket to ward off the cold.

Something felt wrong, very wrong. Although the chill weakened her ability, she extended her hearing to take in the entire village. A sheep gave out a forlorn bleat. Some of the pigs grunted anxiously in their pens. People snored in their beds.

A spasmodic shudder raced through Lily's body. Springing from the bed, she raced through the curtained door to the edge of the walkway beyond. Holding back her whipping hair, she surveyed the village. From the churning sky, a three-quarter moon beamed a misty light onto the village. Banked fires glowed dully inside their pits. No one stirred around them or on the lower walkways. Apparently the sound of the animals hadn't disturbed anyone but her. She sniffed the air and caught a faint but distinctive odor.

They were out there. How they found their way through the maze, she didn't know, but they had.

A man came out of the shadow of the cliffs, walking through the village with his back to her. Suddenly how the werewolves got in wasn't important. The man was in terrible danger! Lily squinted, listened intently, drawing on all the powers she'd retained. Brush stirred at the entrance to the maze, moving against the wind, and in its shadows she heard the low rumblings of the Lupine language.

"Watch out!" she shouted, but too late. The man disappeared into the foliage. Lily held her breath, waiting for a scream, sickened that she'd brought this curse to the Dawn People. Lightning ripped through the clouds above, wind whistled, thunder echoed off the canyon walls, but the scream didn't come.

Then the man reappeared to stand by the maze entrance, looking back. Seconds later, two werewolves joined him. Their faces were shaded by the towering trees, but Lily recognized the taller wolf as Beryl. The subservient actions of the other told her it was an omega.

But who was the man hidden in the shadows, and why hadn't Beryl and his companion killed him? Then the man pointed to a hogan near the longhouse, and

Lily's hand flew to her mouth. He was pointing at Star Dancer's hogan!

Pivoting back and forth, momentarily paralyzed by fear, Lily finally got hold of herself and ran into her room. Her linen jacket hung on a peg, unworn and almost forgotten. She ripped it from the wall, shrugging into it as she slipped on her sandals. After patting the pocket to make sure the bottles and knife were still there, she made a dash for the ladder.

Just as she swung a leg over the edge, she saw Beryl enter the heart of the village.

"Shala," he crooned seductively. "Shaal-laa. Come to me. Come to me."

"No!" Lily scrambled onto the ladder as fast as she could. "Leave her alone, Beryl!"

At one time her order would have sent him scuttling back. The Queen had spoken. Now he lifted triumphant eyes toward her, showing his fangs in a wolfish smile.

Do not interfere, he warned telepathically.

Lily considered screaming for help. Drawing on her own psychic powers she entered the minds of the tribespeople. Beryl had enchanted their dreams, essentially drugging them into deep sleep. It was for the best, she decided. If she called on them, more would die in their attempts to subdue the werewolves.

The ground seemed even farther away than she remembered, and she quickened her descent. Thunder clapped again. Several fat raindrops fell on her head. About halfway down, her feet slipped. For a terrifying moment she hung several stories above the ground, supported only by her grasping hands. Finally she found a rung.

"Shala, Shala," Beryl continued calling. "Come to me, Shala."

Moving cautiously for fear of again losing footing, Lily dared a glance at the village. The door to Star Dancer's hogan opened. A small hand emerged. Shala's dreamy face appeared, and she stepped across the threshold.

"Shala, come . . . come to me, Shala."

Angry streaks of lightning tore through the night, illuminating Beryl and Shala like a spotlight. The girl's eyes looked vacant, unaware of anything but Beryl's voice. His eyes shone with satisfaction. The high winds whipped the surrounding trees, sent the kettles swaying on their spits. Flames spurted from the banked fires.

Dark hair billowing, Shala continued moving like a sleepwalker in response to Beryl's seductive call.

The ladder rattled and trembled. Although the rain had stopped as quickly as it had come, the rungs were now slippery. Lily could barely keep her hold, and the going was excruciatingly slow. By the time she reached solid ground, Shala was within a few feet of Beryl. Lily grabbed a bottle from her pocket and broke into a run.

The gusting wind slowed her down. Beryl laughed uproariously, then gave a great leap, landing beside Shala. He scooped her into his arms, and with another leap disappeared into the maze.

Lily dashed after him, racing along the twisting trail, ignoring the twigs and brambles snagging at her skin. Her exposed toes struck rocks and fallen branches with painful regularity, her lungs were aching from lack of oxygen, and the fierce wind pounded at her body.

Branches cracked and brush snapped as Beryl covered ground in front of her, audible even above the sounds of the storm, and before long Lily realized he was moving at a pace well below his capability. A couple of times she took a wrong turn into one of the maze's dead ends and heard him pause, waiting until she found her way back. He was luring her. Using Shala as bait. Clearly, Sebastian had learned of her affection for the girl. But how?

Soon she recognized a rock formation alongside the trail and noted that the temperature was falling. They were heading south and upward, closer to the canyon rim. The saguaro and chaparral were thinning, replaced by scrub oak and grasses. If they continued on this path, the oaks would grow taller and be joined by pines and ash.

Shala began singing in the Dawn People's language, still enchanted and unaware of the danger. Beryl made no attempt to hush her, confirming Lily's conclusion that she was walking into a trap.

A loud clap of thunder drowned out the song, and when the echoes subsided, and Lily again heard Shala's voice, the full horror of their situation crashed down on her. She'd been pushing it back while she raced after Beryl, but now she recognized the fiendish perfection of Sebastian's scheme.

He knew of her weakness for children. They'd quarreled about it once. He'd been hungrily eyeing a boy who couldn't have been more than two, and she'd stepped between him and the toddler. He joked that he wanted an appetizer, which had sickened Lily, and she sarcastically accused him of demeaning himself by preying on such defenseless ones.

He called her "unnatural," and they'd quarreled bitterly, but eventually he had just laughed and indulged her sensibilities.

Since that day, Lily had protected hundreds of children she hadn't even known, but the child in Beryl's arms meant more to her than any person on earth. Sebastian somehow knew that and was using it against her.

And he wasn't feeling indulgent anymore.

Tony regained awareness filled with the glowing aftermath of lovemaking. He rose and poured one last scoop of water on the smoldering Stone People, offered thanks for his vision, then left the sweat lodge. He headed down the hill, suffused with so much energy that by the time he reached the river there was a bounce in his step.

The rainless storm he'd expected had materialized, but he ignored the danger of the lightning and waded into the river, where he dipped his head and drank his fill. Then leaning back to float, he allowed the water to rinse the grime from his hair, combing the tangles free with his fingers. He felt cleansed, renewed, filled with oneness and having no need to analyze what he'd been told. The Great Spirit had answered his prayers; he could ruminate deeper meanings later.

He luxuriated in the cool water for some time, letting

it soothe his parched body. Finally he climbed out, shook out his wet hair, then went to his satchel and pulled out a slice of jerky. As he was about to take a healthy bite, he felt a sudden need to check on Shala. With an ease he took for granted, he sent the hawk form up into the windswept sky.

The impulse hadn't particularly alarmed him; he was accustomed to this periodic need to connect with his daughter. Ripping off a hunk of meat with his teeth, he chewed, savoring his first taste of food in over two days and letting his awareness idly follow the hawk's.

When the images came, he dropped the meat and shot to his feet. His beloved Shala was in the arms of a werewolf! A second werewolf plodded beside them. A tribesman he couldn't identify from that height lagged behind, struggling to keep pace. Undoubtedly the hapless man had tried to come to Shala's aid and had become a captive himself.

Farther back, he saw Lily, her breath heaving as she hurried to catch up. For a second Tony thought she was trying to rescue Shala. But that couldn't be. Werewolves could travel at dizzying speeds, and surely with their keen hearing they knew she was there.

He'd just held that woman in his arms. In a vision, true, but one so real he might as well have lived it. A cry of denial and rage erupted from Tony's throat, the emotions so overwhelming he lost his connection with the hawk.

He forced himself to concentrate on the bird's movements—the flutter of wings, the shallow dip of the neck with each stroke, the wind blowing through feathers. Soon he again saw what it saw. Lily.

With a small cry of pain, she stumbled and grabbed for her injured foot. The werewolves paused, looking back. She inspected the injury, then dropped her foot. Hesitating uncertainly, almost as if reconsidering, she reached in the pocket of her jacket. Then, taking some deep breaths, she started after the werewolves again.

Something about the gesture made Tony recall her earlier defense of Sebastian. His conclusion clicked into place, confirmed. Lily hadn't abandoned her king after all. She'd merely become his homing device to lead him to the Dawn People.

His renewed hatred combined with his fear for Shala and threatened to debilitate him, so he honed his resolve with action. Stripping off his loincloth, he ripped clothing from the satchel. Moments later he was in hemp breeches, clasping the belt of his hunting knife sheath around the waist.

Next he checked a small pocket on his belt for the supply of ammonia inhalant capsules he'd put there after he'd purchased them in Flagstaff—his only true defense against the werewolves. Reassured, he stepped into his moccasins.

Putting his hand firmly on the hilt of his knife, Tony loped toward the riverside trail.

He should have wondered why the spirits hadn't delivered him from hate as they'd promised. But he didn't. His heart was so full of it he could only imagine the pleasure he would take in killing Lily.

Chapter Fifteen

The desert terrain had disappeared miles back, and Beryl was leading Lily ever higher, deeper inside the forest, into parts of the canyon she knew like the back of her hand. Although the deliberately clumsy footfalls of the werewolves and Shala's high, sweet voice still reached her ears, she had no idea how far ahead they were.

On her right, Lily saw an earthen embankment from where she might get a better view. Trotting over to it, she grabbed a tree branch and hoisted herself onto a narrow ledge that formed a foothold in the dirt. Although the damp soil was somewhat slippery, the drought-hardened ground beneath was still firm and supported her easily. The rising wind made the branch she was holding insecure, so she reached for a larger one. Steadying herself, she peered through bobbing leaves, searching for the two enormous wolfish heads.

They were about a half mile ahead, moving slowly, making a lot of unnecessary noise. Behind them was the man she'd seen at the village. The sky suddenly crackled with lightning. Thunder rumbled. The werewolves' noises were momentarily lost, as was Shala's song.

Beryl undoubtedly didn't know her vision and hearing were nearly as acute as his. Lily also suspected he'd sent out his telepathic threat to her at the village instinctively, and had no idea she'd received it. His ignorance would work to her advantage.

Extending her psyche, she tentatively and quickly probed Beryl's mind. What a simple mind he had, lacking complex thought, merely following instructions, and she easily read his intentions.

An alarmed cry left her lips. Dear God! Beryl was leading her to the Clearing of the Black Hands.

For an instant she thought she might be sick. Images of fire and snow, a white flowing gown, a golden-eyed raptor, flashed before her eyes. Blood—Morgan's, Jorje's, her own—flowed thick and red. Finally the images came to rest on Jorje's lifeless body.

Her emotions whirled around a vortex of fear. Even for the love of Shala, could she face that fateful spot and all the memories it revived?

Just as abruptly as it had arisen, the thunder stopped, and in its wake rang the tones of Shala's sweet song.

With trembling hands, Lily grasped the tree branch firmly and swung off the ledge back to the ground.

The grotesque events of the night Dana Gibbs had invoked the Shadow of Venus in Morgan's behalf were coming back to haunt her. As a werewolf she'd had the courage born of invincibility. Did she possess even one ounce of that courage now that she was mortal?

For Shala's sake, she hoped she did.

"You fools," Sebastian growled. "Why didn't you keep her in your sights?"

"She was right behind us, Lord," Beryl whined. "I never thought she'd leave the trail."

"Bah! I told you how well she knows this country."

"She'll come." This reassurance was spoken in a human voice. "We have the girl."

"Don't underestimate Lily, mortal," Sebastian retorted. "It could be the end of you." Sebastian rapped his walking stick on the ground and shook his head in annoyance. "Very well," he finally said. "We will wait. Put the girl in the ring."

Lily pressed her body tightly against the stone wall behind the clearing and inched along until she could see everything. The effort of blocking her thoughts against Sebastian's continuous psychic scan was taking its toll, but her brief foray into Beyrl's mind had given her a wealth of information beyond the location he was bound for. She knew Shala was safe, for the time being at least, and the reason Sebastian had sent Beryl, his trusted prince, out on that particular night. And also why she hadn't sensed Sebastian's presence since she and White Hawk had climbed down into the canyon.

Sebastian had been biding his time until it was auspicious for the Song of Hades. Tonight the moon came close to Pluto, an aspect needed to perform the ceremony that created werewolves. While the perfect aspect for the Shadow of Venus occurred only once in seven years, the planet Pluto moved slowly, and if Sebastian failed tonight, he'd have several chances before the moon passed away. As usual, he could bide his time, although she suspected failure wasn't something he'd considered.

Lily didn't find it coincidental that he'd selected the Clearing of the Black Hands as a site for the ceremony. Large and relatively free of vegetation, it had the requisite fire pit. The black stone outcroppings, some of which jutted up several stories high, gave it a dramatic air that would appeal to him.

Obviously, they didn't doubt she'd come. The fire was already laid and burning steadily, waiting for more fuel. One of the eight werewolves, whom she recognized as the omega wolfling Philippe, was walking in a circle, cautiously sprinkling water on the dirt.

Sanctifying the ring. In preparation for me. Fingers of dread traveled up Lily's spine.

Inside the route that Philippe traveled, sobbed Shala, her blissful enchantment obviously gone. She climbed to her feet and started to leave the ring. Philippe growled. She scooted back to the center.

Including Sebastian, nine werewolves were in the clearing. Off to one side stood the mysterious man who'd accompanied them, his face again shadowed by the limb of a tree.

Lightning flashed, illuminating the man's familiar, arrogant expression, and though she was startled, Lily wasn't at all surprised. So Ravenheart had found someone to accept his unholy bargain. How she wished he'd failed. Not only would he be unaffected by the holy water, she wasn't willing to kill another member of the Dawn People, no matter how twisted he was.

She slipped one of the bottles out of her pocket, positioned the small knife so it would be easy to reach, then glanced up at the dark sky, hoping the ever-increasing streaks of lightning would offer a glimpse of soaring white. Where was that filthy fowl when she needed it? She couldn't remember ever needing help more. The creature had come to her aid once before. Why not now?

She heard Sebastian give Philippe another instruction and turned her attention back to him. He was wearing a maroon tuxedo and top hat—which he kept having to secure against the blowing wind—and looked as if he were about to attend an opera.

All signs of his encounter with the holy water were gone, although this was to be expected, since alchemizing to human form never failed to heal a werewolf's injuries. He did, however, stay well back as Philippe nervously spilled the dangerous water and chanted the litany that accompanied the drawing of the ring. During Sebastian's unusual bout with anxiety, his psychic probe ceased. Seeking a moment's rest and praying she wouldn't regret it, Lily dropped her mental block.

She didn't have time for regret.

With an incredible speed, Sebastian whirled. His hat flew off his head and he made a titanic leap, landing in front of Lily. He ripped the vial of holy water she'd been clutching so dearly in her hand and sent it soaring over the treetops.

"So you did come, dear one," he said. "I am pleased. I have such a treat in store."

Lily tried to fight but it was useless, and she quickly gave up, allowing Sebastian to pin her arms to her body and carry her to the edge of the ceremonial circle, where he deposited her.

"The Song of Hades is about to begin," he said, adjusting the tail of his maroon waistcoat. "The child will make a fetching werewolf, do you not agree?"

"Damn you, Sebastian, you can't do this. No one's ever initiated a child before. She could die."

"Relax, my dear. We rarely see such robustness in Europe. I doubt the rigors will prove too much for this healthy wild child. And—if you will pardon my pun—you shall have a ringside seat for my little experiment."

He was toying with her like an overfed cat might a mouse. To test her theory, Lily took a step toward the ring. A quick sly smile crossed his face. She returned his smile knowingly.

"Me for the girl, Sebastian. Let me take her to the village, then I'll submit to the ceremony."

"The child would make a unique addition to the pack." Sebastian brought his hand to his chin reflectively. "I must think on this."

Lily knew he was posturing. She waited quietly.

The silence grew longer. And longer. Still she didn't speak.

"You will submit willingly?" he finally asked.

"After the girl is safely in her village."

"No, Lily!" Shala cried from inside the ring. "You can't become a werewolf again! You promised!"

Lily forced herself to ignore Shala's plea, meeting Sebastian's eyes as only an alpha queen might do. After another span of silence, he laughed. "You must think I am still the fool for you, Lily. I know you will not return, so do not seek to deceive me."

"Deceive you, Lord? How could I? I'm not one of you anymore and have lost my skill at trickery. But even if I hadn't, I couldn't possibly be strong enough to deceive a great leader like yourself."

He laughed again. "Oh, Lily, I have missed your sugary praise almost as much as your peppery tongue. All right." He pivoted toward Ravenheart. "The child can go free. But I will ask the young warrior here to take her in your stead."

Ravenheart looked stunned. "But, I—"

"You *will* take her!"

"Yes, yes, of course I will," Ravenheart replied obsequiously. He started toward the ring.

"Wait!" Lily said. "I won't agree to this change unless you give me another promise. After the ceremony we'll leave Ebony Canyon and never come back."

Sebastian's gaze shifted between Lily, Shala, and the eagerly waiting Ravenheart. A werewolf's promise was bound by Law, and if Lily extracted one, Sebastian could not go back on his word. It was a hellish bargain, but if she saved Shala's life and protected the Dawn People it was a bargain well worth making.

"Agreed," Sebastian replied. "Get the child, Warrior."

Face unaccountably lit with triumph, Ravenheart entered the circle and grabbed Shala's arm.

"I won't go!" Shala screamed, pulling back with all her tiny might. "I won't leave Lily! I won't!"

"Shut up, girl!" Ravenheart growled. "You're too stupid to know what's good for you."

"Don't treat her that way," Lily ordered, crouching to Shala's level. "Come out now, Shala." She pulled the girl to the edge of the circle and embraced her. "I'll be all right, but I won't be coming back."

"No, Lily, p-plee-ease. I–I–I was just about to f-forgive you. Please don't s-stay here."

"It's the only way, sweetheart. Go with Ravenheart now. Tell Star Dancer I appreciated her kindness." Lily blinked hard and looked away for a second. "When . . . when your father returns . . . tell him justice was served."

Shala frowned.

"I know that doesn't make sense to you, but he'll understand."

"You take me, Lily. I don't want to go with Ravenheart." Shala shot the warrior a quick glance, then lowered her voice. "I don't like him."

"Nevertheless, he'll get you to safety. Go with him, sweetheart, if only because I ask you to."

New tears formed in Shala's eyes and she threw herself on Lily's shoulder, wrapped her small arms tightly around Lily's neck, and began sobbing. Lily stroked her tangled hair, fighting with the fierce wind to smooth it. Thunder and lightning punctuated Shala's sobs, causing them to pierce Lily's heart ever deeper.

"I love you, Shala," she whispered. Shala loosened her hold on Lily's neck and looked into her eyes.

"I l-love you too," she said. "And I d-do forgive you."

Lily inhaled sharply, struggling to hold back the ache in her chest. She held Shala until her tears subsided.

"I'll go," she whispered, rubbing her reddened eyes. "I'll get help."

"Yes," Lily said, standing up and taking one of Shala's hands. Slipping her other hand into the pocket of her jacket, she palmed a vial. Whether one would be of much use against nine werewolves, she didn't know.

With her hand still in her pocket, she reluctantly gave Shala over to Ravenheart. "Be good to her," she warned, "and keep your word. You won't want to pay the price if you don't."

She received a baleful glare in return, but was gratified to see him lead Shala gently from the clearing. When the pair reached the forest, Sebastian grabbed the collar of her jacket.

"Let me relieve you of that, dear one." With a smooth move, he pulled it down her arms, forcing her hand from the pocket.

But not before her fingers curled neatly around the vial.

Her jacket in hand, Sebastian gave her a werewolf nudge that sent her sprawling into the center of the ring. Beryl moved to the pit and stoked the fire. The other werewolves began shrinking to the smaller wolf form. When the last one alchemized, they lined up single file and marched around the ring until they'd surrounded it. Sinking to their haunches, they lifted their large heads in unison and emitted a synchronized howl.

"The Song of Hades begins," Sebastian announced, raising his hands to the sky.

Chapter Sixteen

"*Yeafanay cawfanay naylanay may,*" Sebastian recited in front of the wind-tossed flames, his long tail coat flapping around his legs as lightning flashed above. The tall black obelisks behind Sebastian darkly reflected the fire. "A she-wolf shall be born this day. *Yeafanay cawfanay naylanay may.*"

"Powers of darkness, heed our cry," Lily translated, cringing on the ground inside the circle. Steeling herself against dread, she rolled to a sitting position, fingering the slim plastic vial between her fingers. Already she felt twinges in her knees and elbows. Soon they'd spread into the long connecting bones. She must escape before the ceremony caused those agonizing changes in her body.

"Wait!" a panicked voice called. Ravenheart bolted

out of the woods, the kicking and squalling Shala tucked under his arm like a bundle of clothing.

"Let go!" Shala bellowed, beating on the warrior's back. "Let me go!"

He thumped her on the head, which did little to check her pugnacity. Sebastian turned toward Ravenheart with a sardonic smile, obviously amused by Shala's spirited battle, then waved his hand toward the circle. The wolves sitting in Ravenheart's path moved apart, and Sebastian turned back to Lily. "I did not promise my follower would necessarily obey my orders. Only that I would issue them."

"He offered me what you refused," Ravenheart said. "In exchange I agreed to deliver you and the shaman's child into his hands."

"Damn you both!" Lily leaped from the ring at Ravenheart. The wolf beside him pivoted and snapped his jaws near Shala's head. Lily halted. "All right. All right. Don't hurt her."

Backing up with her arms behind her, she gingerly uncorked the vial. It was a last desperate effort, but their only chance, and she was determined not to waste a single drop.

Spilling just the smallest amount on her fingers, she flicked it on the wolf who'd snapped at Shala. Although some of the water got lost in the wind, enough hit its target. The wolf yelped in agony and fell on its side, fluctuating rapidly between wolf and man-wolf form.

Shala screamed at the hideous sight. Ravenheart

gaped in horror, obviously not comprehending what was happening.

"I told you the bitch could not be trusted," Beryl bellowed from his place beside the fire.

Lily flicked a few more drops. The other wolves broke rank, scurrying back with fearful whimpers. Lily scattered more water. Sebastian roared in outrage, then leaped forward and tore Shala from Ravenheart's hold. She shrieked as Sebastian's hands closed around her neck.

"Enough, Lily!" he commanded, dangling Shala in front of him. Gasping for breath, the girl tore frantically at the werewolf's hands. "Toss that fluid into the fire or I will break this mortal young one's neck like the match stick that ignited the flames."

Lily paused, trying to gauge the extent of Sebastian's resolve. If he killed Shala he would lose his power over Lily, something he dearly wanted. But his fear of the sanctified water was great. Enough to make him follow through on his threat? She considered hurling the entire bottle at him, but he stood too far away. She might miss.

Shala let out a sickening gurgle.

"Put the girl down first, Sebastian," Lily said, holding the vial in front of her.

"No tricks, Lily, or you will sorely regret them."

Lily nodded, and Sebastian returned Shala to the ground. She dashed forward and wrapped her arms around Lily's waist. The wolf who'd been injured took on human shape. Immune to the water's effects now and glowering at Lily, he wiped the last remnant of water from his body, then quickly resumed wolf form and joined the other six.

Lowering their heads, the seven of them crept toward Lily and Shala, fangs bared, gleaming eyes reflecting the flames of the fire. Thunder shook the clearing. Renewed wind gusts battered their clothes and hair.

"Recork the vial," Sebastian commanded. "And throw it toward the fire."

With a show of insolence she didn't feel but knew was vital for their safety, Lily replaced the stopper, then tossed the bottle in the air. The wind carried it to the right of where she'd aimed, and it landed not far from Beryl's feet. He jumped back.

"Dispose of it," Sebastian said.

Beryl's eyes darted around the clearing, and he moved to collect two long sticks, which he then used as pinchers to gingerly lift the bottle. With a look of immense relief, he dropped it in the flames.

"The ceremony resumes," Sebastian intoned dramatically.

Ravenheart stepped eagerly into the ring. Sebastian gave Lily a commanding look, then glanced meaningfully at Shala. With the child still clinging to her, Lily backed over the line in the dirt.

"L-Lily." Shala hiccuped. "What's going to happen?"

Kneeling, she cupped Shala's dirty tear-streaked face, then looked up at Sebastian. "Please let her go. She's just a child."

"You've grown fond of these mortals, have you

not?" He looked vaguely puzzled that anyone who'd been so close to him could do such a thing. "I warned you such sensibilities would bring you to doom. Am I not proof of that? Look how I doted on you. Yet you, the daughter I once cherished, have caused me terrible pain. No, Lily, this girl will become what I always hoped you would be. So 'tis your choice. She stays in the ring and becomes one of us, or . . ." He licked his man-wolf muzzle as if anticipating a treat.

Lily's shoulders sagged. She pulled the trembling Shala close, feeling more miserable than she had the morning she'd keened over Jorje's lifeless body. She'd brought on this horror as surely as she'd taken Jorje's life. If not for her, Sebastian and his godless eight wouldn't even be here, Ravenheart wouldn't have been tempted to take a shortcut to shamanhood, and Shala wouldn't be trapped in this ring. White Hawk should have let her die.

"Sebastian, please . . ."

Giving no reply, Sebastian stretched his arms to the moon. The sky lit up with lightning, as if he'd commanded it. "*Yeafanay, cawfanay, naylanay, may. Yeafanay, cawfanay, naylanay, may.* Werewolves shall be born this day."

Defeated, Lily sank to the ground and settled Shala in her lap. The girl had grown eerily silent, her eyes huge pools of fear.

"Hang on to me, sweetheart," Lily said. "No matter what happens, hang on."

Sebastian began reciting words that Lily had often

used herself in the same unholy ritual and knew by heart in all their variations.

"Lady moon doth touch dark Pluto now.
Yet fickle lady waits for none
and soon moves on.
Oh, phantoms of the dark beneath rise up
to heed my cry."

A log crashed in the fire; the ensuing sparks swirled on the fierce wind.

"Bring fang and claw and strength beyond
what mortals know.
Bestow these gifts upon your servants now
that they may roam
the earth as wolf and man, as man and wolf
forever more."

The seven wolves emitted long, piercing howls. From somewhere above, a bird of prey gave out a shrill, foreboding cry. Shards of pain ripped at Lily's body as she fought back alchemization. Ravenheart wailed in torment beside her, clawing at his belly. Shala twisted feverishly in her arms, whimpering. Lily stroked the child's mud-smeared arms and dropped kisses on her teary face.

"It's all right," she whispered, though her body felt as if it were shattering into pieces. "It's all right."

"Rush, yeah, rush, Great Phantom," cried Sebastian, his voice growing ever more fervid. His eyes glinted red with angry intent. Fingers of flame reflected in the unclothed portions of his silvery coat. Lily closed her eyes in resignation. With a sob, Shala writhed out of her lap, but Lily was in too much pain to hold on.

"Race, Great Phantom, race, yeah, race.
The Lady rolls on, time grows short.
Heed us now. Heed us now.
Time grows short. Heed us now.
Yeafanay cawfanay nayla—"

Yealanay cawfanay nayfanay may. Lily didn't know where the unbidden refrain came from, but it raced through her mind in contradiction to Sebastian's words. "Spirits of light, hear our plea," she whispered weakly. *"Yealanay cawfanay nayfanay may."*

Her pain was now so intense she could barely lift her head, but at Sebastian's hesitation she forced it from the ground. He paused. A look of outrage crossed his face. Arms still raised in invocation, he eyed her suspiciously. At least she thought he did. Her vision was so blurred nothing was truly clear. And what was that, sitting on the stony rim of the fire pit, all white and golden-eyed?

"Cease that babble," he barked.

"Yealanay cawfanay nayfanay may," Lily choked out again, encouraged by his outburst. Her vision cleared a bit. Shala stirred beside her, moaning softly. Ravenheart grunted in discomfort. One of his feet extended beyond the edge of the circle and a wolf snapped at it. Sebastian snarled an order to desist, and it backed away.

With a shrill, ear-splitting shriek the white shape

rose from the wall enclosing the fire, swooped down and buried its talons into Beryl's head. Beryl yelped and clawed at it, but the bird deftly avoided his flailing hands, soaring to the fire pit again.

Suddenly it was gone. In its place stood White Hawk, a knife in one hand, a bright yellow scarf tied around his face. With a war cry, he rushed toward the circle, scattering small white objects in his wake. Wolves flew in all directions, howling and spraying dirt. Beryl doubled over, coughing. Sebastian dropped his arms and covered his muzzle with a kerchief pulled from his suit pocket. Wolfish noses began receding. A hairless arm appeared on one wolf, a leg on another. Coughs and gasps mingled with the whine of the wind.

Ravenheart made a strangled sound. Lily rolled into a ball as the acrid ammonia seared her lungs. Forcing herself not to resist, she inhaled another dose, feeling the familiar tingle of ebbing body changes. She glanced over at Shala, alarmed to see her lying limply on the earth, apparently not breathing. Scrambling to her knees, she tilted the girl's head back, inhaled another breath of ammonia, then pressed her mouth to Shala's and exhaled.

Coughing, Shala jerked upright. "Breathe," Lily rasped, almost too overcome to speak. The girl broke into sobs, trying to escape the ammonia but breathing nonetheless. Breathing . . . Oh thank God, she was breathing.

Springing to her feet, Lily swept Shala from the ground. Mayhem surrounded her. Sebastian bellowed as his height shrank and his fur began to fade. Already in human form, Beryl huddled on the rocky soil, retching from the fumes. The seven ceremonial wolves, having reverted to human shape, were ripping at their own bodies as fangs and paws dissolved. Ravenheart screamed inside the circle, pallid and in obvious agony. White Hawk whooped incessantly.

With Shala against her shoulder, Lily ran from the circle, dipping to reclaim her jacket from the ground as she raced toward White Hawk. When he saw her, he gave out another whoop, then crouched and swept his knife in front of him, waiting to see what move she would make.

The obvious motive behind his act stunned Lily. He thought she was part of this!

"Always the fool," she snarled, moving cautiously closer. "Take your daughter quickly. And run! Now! Before they recover."

A look of pure shock crossed his face. He tucked Shala against him, then reached for Lily's hand, spinning and pulling her toward the forest.

"No!" she cried, yanking free. "I have unfinished business here."

White Hawk hesitated, glancing first at her, then at the protection of the forest. Shala let out an ugly cough.

"Go!" Lily screamed.

He nodded, ripped the scarf from his face and handed it to Lily, then broke into a sprint and quickly vanished amid the thick pines.

Lily tied the yellow scarf around her face. The clearing still reeked of ammonia. White Hawk must have dropped every damned capsule he owned, and thank God for it too. She then shimmied into her jacket and reached for the knife. To her relief, it was still there. Small, but keenly edged and sufficient for her needs.

She carefully weaved through the yipping and whimpering werewolves, who were as a unit writhing on the ground. Sebastian had sunk to his knees beside the fire pit, still shifting between man-wolf and human shape. He fixed her with a stare as she approached.

"So," he groaned defiantly, eyeing the knife in her hand, "you hope to slay a king."

"I *will* slay a king."

He laughed harshly. "You do not have the stomach for it."

Holding the knife with both hands in front of her, Lily moved closer.

Sebastian sighed heavily and fell onto his side. "Much like Zeus dethroning Kronos, is it not, my dear?"

"If I recall correctly, Kronos swallowed his children," Lily replied, continuing to move forward. "Just as werewolves swallow mortals. I believe this is a fitting end to your infamy."

"You judge me quite harshly for one who shares in my crimes."

Lily was so close now she could see the irregular rise and fall of his soft underbelly, the werewolf's Achilles' heel. Although her knife was small, its deadly point could inflict a fatal blow. Even alchemizing to human form would not save him from such a wound.

She crouched, knife poised and aimed at his stomach, then hesitated. The ammonia stench was waning and, unlike the others, Sebastian wasn't completely immobilized. He'd tricked her once that evening with his slyly worded promise to free Shala, so it wouldn't surprise her if he possessed more strength than he was demonstrating.

Yet she'd never have a better chance. She coiled like a leopard and prepared to jump.

"Ah, the coup de grâce," Sebastian whispered satirically.

Thunder clapped, followed by a flash of lightning that illuminated the clearing. In that brief instant Lily took in Sebastian's disheveled appearance. His stylish tuxedo was covered in dust, one ragged lapel hanging limply on his chest. His top hat lay crushed on the ground beside him, and he clutched his natty pocket handkerchief. His face was etched with lines of pain.

Her gaze finally came to rest on his eyes, taking in the way the azure shade had dimmed to lackluster gray. She'd been his constant companion for years and knew him well. Knew his habits; the subtle variations of his moods. The pain she saw didn't come from the effects of the smelling salts. It was the signpost of a soul in agony.

An unwelcome wave of sympathy swept over her, stirring the deep love she'd once felt for him. She darted a panicky glance at the blade in her hand, saw firelight reflected in the shiny steel. A single downward sweep of her arm. That's all it would take to be free of him forever. Now! her soul screamed. Now!

Wild-eyed with inner conflict, Lily lunged, arching the knife toward her target. In that same second, Sebastian twisted. A hand closed around her ankle, sending her sprawling to the ground. In the space of his enraged bellow, she found herself soaring through the air, then landing inside the ceremonial ring on top of Ravenheart's prone body. Recoiling, she rolled off, rocked upright, and stared lividly at Sebastian.

Sebastian grinned mockingly, levering himself up until he leaned against the wall of the fire pit. He raised his arms.

"Yeafanay, cawfanay, naylanay, may," he cried thinly. *"Yeafanay, cawfanay, naylanay, may.* A she-wolf is born this day."

The last line of the Song of Hades! Sebastian had completed the ceremony! A reddish haze filled Lily's eyes, blinding her. Her joints creaked and groaned. No! No! She mustn't let this happen!

"Yealanay cawfanay nayfanay may," she murmured, barely able to speak. "The power of love . . . triumphs this . . . day." She'd once hated these words from the Shadow of Venus, but now . . . now she clung to them as her only . . .

. . . hope.

"The power of love . . . the power of love . . . triumphs this . . . day."

The pain ceased. Her vision cleared. She looked down, horrified to see a thick covering of fine white hairs on her arms. Sebastian had collapsed against the fire pit, his head lolling onto his stained white shirt-front, his hair dancing in the wind. His slitted eyes stared at her, almost blindly.

She scrambled to her feet, horrified by this change in her body, wanting to rip off the covering on her skin, hair by hair. But though he looked dazed beyond awareness, she knew Sebastian saw her, realized she'd been given another chance to kill him.

Looking frantically around for her fallen knife, she moaned when she saw it lying many yards from the circle. The bodies of the other werewolves were slumped together in clusters, most appearing unconscious from the effects of her litany, but they would stir soon, as would Sebastian.

No she wouldn't kill him. Not this time, she realized with deep regret. Not this time.

She bolted for the path leading through the pines, but as she reached the trees she looked back over her shoulder. Sebastian's ice blue eyes were open now, taking her in. A sly smile covered his ravaged face.

Lily stopped and addressed him in a deadly cold voice. "Don't ever touch that girl again, Sebastian. If you do, I *will* kill you. I swear it."

Then she whirled to run through the forest, knowing her words hadn't scared him off, knowing her smooth human skin was covered with wolfish fur, knowing she'd become an outcast, unloved, belonging nowhere.

Across the needle-covered carpet of the forest floor, over the rugged desert, onto the path along the river, heedless of the needles, twigs, and rocks slicing her exposed toes, of the windswept branches scratching her face and snagging her hair, she ran. From Sebastian. From herself. From the hellish fate that had brought her to this point.

She didn't stop until she ran straight into White Hawk's arms.

Chapter Seventeen

Chest heaving, Lily let out a gasp and backed out of Tony's arms. The wind tore at her hair, and her wide dark eyes darted in all directions. Clearly she was terrified.

"Lily," Tony said gently. "It's okay. It's only me."

Looking down at her hands, she brought them up and stared as if she'd never seen them before. Then she ran her fingers quickly over her arms as if checking for something. Finally, she met his eyes. "Sebastian . . . I thought—" Her voice choked. "But I'm all right, aren't I?"

"Yes, Lily. You're all right. Just fine in fact."

"What are you doing here?" she asked in panic. "You shouldn't have left Shala. The ceremony almost killed her."

"She's with Riva, Lily, and she's recovered. But she

wouldn't settle down until I agreed to come after you."

Not that he needed his daughter's urgent pleas. He'd only left Lily behind for Shala's sake, and because he'd seen how intent she was on carrying out her purpose. Nothing he could have done would have persuaded her to leave.

"Sebastian?"

"He's still alive." She looked defeated. "I should have—" She shook her head sadly. "I'm sorry."

"Sorry?" Tony put his hands on her shoulders and forced her to look at him. "Lily, you saved Shala's life. What do you have to be sorry for?"

"Are you being kind to me?" she asked suspiciously.

Tony laughed.

"Was that funny?"

"Not funny, but—Lily, I'm so filled with gratitude . . . You can't imagine."

Swaying trees admitted streaks of moonlight that shone on Lily's face. Gone was her usual haughty expression. In its place was a vulnerability Tony had never seen there before. She looked away uneasily, and he reached out to touch her cheek.

"You're hurt."

"It's only a scratch." She brought her own hand up; it trembled as it brushed against his.

Involuntarily, Tony closed his hand around hers. She clutched at him for a moment like a frightened child, then let go and dropped her arm. Strangely unnerved, Tony stepped back. Twigs and leaves were tangled in her windswept hair and in the shifting moonlight they almost resembled a halo. Her eyes possessed an unusually brilliant sheen.

Tony cleared his throat. "Let's get out of here before the werewolves show up again."

Lily shook her head. "They won't recover until morning. How many of those capsules did you throw anyway? I've never seen such violent reactions."

Tony grinned. "Several dozen."

"Then you still have plenty left. Good, we'll need them."

He shook his head. "Star Dancer issued a warning for no one to leave the village."

"It won't help. Ravenheart led Beryl through the maze. I think he died from the ceremony, but it doesn't matter. They now know how to find us."

Us. Although Tony understood the importance of her information, that word *us* stuck in his mind. Lily didn't think of herself as a werewolf now.

"Did you hear me, White Hawk?"

"I heard. I was just taking it in." He inclined his head toward the village, then started walking. Lily moved slowly forward, and he reduced his pace, thinking she was still winded. "I don't understand why Ravenheart betrayed us," he said after she caught up.

Lily gave him a sideways glance. "Jealousy. He wants to outdo you." She paused, obviously considering her next words. "He asked me to initiate him as a werewolf."

"What?" Tony looked at her sharply. "Why didn't you tell someone?"

Lily laughed bitterly.

"You thought no one would listen."

She nodded, then immediately let out a soft moan and stumbled.

"Good Lord, Lily. You're only wearing sandals."

"I didn't have time to pull on boots, White Hawk," she said testily, lifting a foot and rubbing it cautiously.

Tony stared down. A deep gash on the side of her big toe oozed blood. A sliver of a pine needle protruded from a spot just above the small toe. He bent and touched her instep, which was bruised and beginning to swell. Righting himself, he untied his yellow scarf from her neck, which must have long ago slipped off her face.

"Here, let me." He bent again, lifted her foot, and tied the scarf around the worst of the cuts.

"I'm all right," she said curtly, planting her foot sharply on the ground the minute he let go. Stifling a gasp at the abrupt movement, she started forward, stumbling after just a few steps. Her independence drew Tony's admiration, but he knew much of it stemmed from lack of trust. Could he blame her? He'd essentially kidnapped her, then brought her to the village where she'd been shunned and left to contemplate the outcome of her inquisition by the Tribunal.

"I'll carry you."

"I can—"

"I'll carry you," he repeated. Moving forward, he swung her into his arms.

He expected a struggle, but the minute he settled her against his bare chest, she shuddered. He felt her fatigue as acutely as if it were his own and knew that, relieved of its own weight, her body had finally succumbed to it.

Tony broke into an easy lope. Lily was feather light in his arms, and no burden at all. After a short while, she sighed and let her head fall on his shoulder.

"Thank you," she murmured. "My feet hurt so much."

"It's my honor."

How could he say otherwise? Although Lily had killed Tajaya, her courageous acts had saved Shala's life. But as he jogged along the river toward the village, he wondered just how much of the tenderness filling his heart was caused by gratitude.

Star Dancer and White Hawk had bathed Lily's battered feet, their faces mildly troubled. Now Shala held her hand, as the High Shaman gently probed the area around an imbedded pine needle.

"It's very deep," she said. "Get me the mineral mud, Shala, if you will."

Shala let go of Lily's hand, went to a low bench along one wall of White Hawk's wickiup, and picked up a wooden bowl. She brought it to Star Dancer, who dipped her fingers inside for a handful, then handed the bowl to White Hawk. Singing softly in the Dawn People's language, Star Dancer slathered mud over Lily's foot. White Hawk did the same with the other foot.

She was the center of their attention and efforts. She hadn't been touched with so much tenderness since her nanny Gwen's traumatic departure heralded the arrival of the militant Mrs. Preston. A lump formed in her throat and her chest began to ache.

"This might hurt," Star Dancer warned, then gave a quick tug on the pine needle.

The pain was brief and minuscule compared to the merciless ache in Lily's heart, but it sent her over the edge. She jerked into a sitting position and doubled over.

"Lily," Shala cried, falling to her knees beside the sleeping platform and putting a hand on Lily's back.

White Hawk moved to stand behind Shala and put one hand on Lily's forehead, the other at the base of the skull. "Be at peace," he said. Star Dancer gently took her injured feet, murmuring identical words.

Lily's eyes drifted shut as a sweet wave of calming peace flowed from their hands into her tense and battered body. Her turbulent mind slowed down. White Hawk began singing in the tribal language, his rich baritone filling the room. Soon he was joined by Star Dancer's lovely contralto and the sweet high notes of Shala's soprano. The unbearable ache in Lily's chest subsided. She felt light, in body and in soul. She felt joyous, she felt peaceful, she felt . . .

Loved. She felt loved.

Laughter bubbled in her throat and she opened her eyes to see Shala, Star Dancer, and White Hawk smiling at her. His hands were still on her head and she turned, nestling into his soothing touch. Then she glanced at Star Dancer's serene face and remembered the Tribunal. She'd given no thought to what would happen during the inquisition because she hadn't intended on staying around that long. Now she wanted to stay.

Remembering that Star Dancer had said she *doubted* Lily would survive, implying there was a chance she would, Lily knew she wanted to take that chance.

She looked imploringly into the woman's eyes. "Please," she said, "tell me when the Tribunal will be held."

Star Dancer's smile faded. She let go of Lily's feet and straightened up. "I'm still waiting for the sign."

"What *is* the sign?"

"Your advocate must come forward."

Lily frowned. "My advocate?"

"I can say no more." She lowered to sit on the edge of the platform. "But let me impart a parable."

Lily watched uneasily as Star Dancer's eyes began to glaze. It reminded her uncomfortably of her meal with Tony on the train, and she was unwilling to listen to a similar indictment from this woman she'd come to admire so much.

"After White Wolf Woman returned to the Deer People as Sienna Doe," Star Dancer began in a voice considerably deeper than her normal tone, "she was greeted with fear and contempt."

Even her own children avoided her, and none spoke except to give curt orders. At first she thought their cruelty would ease with time. But days passed, then weeks, then finally months, and ever they treated her thusly. One afternoon, after being chased away from her grazing by a pair of young bucks, she wandered into the wild forest, sobbing from the pain of her loneliness.

"Oh, Great One," she cried through her tears, "lift this censure from me and make me one of my people again."

Quetzalcoatl suddenly stood in front of her.

"Daughter," he said, "again I find you full of sadness. Do you wish to return to the way of the wolf?"

"No, no. My heart desires acceptance from the Deer People as I once had."

Before he spoke, Quetzalcoatl adjusted his crown, which had fallen askew in his haste to aid Sienna Doe. "You have lived as Wolf and Deer, Sienna Doe, which gives you a deep comprehension of my universe. As Wolf you understood the nature of Deer. Now as Deer you understand the nature of Wolf. Would you have me take that away?"

"Yes, if I would gain acceptance from my relations."

"Alas, I cannot grant that." He gave her a look of deep chagrin. "Some wishes are beyond my power. What has been learned cannot be unlearned."

"But I shall die of loneliness, Great One."

"Endure, my learned daughter, endure. For if you do, you shall become a bridge between predator and prey. And in the end, all shall revere you."

Then Quetzalcoatl vanished in the blink of Sienna Doe's eyes. She didn't understand why, but she felt better, and she returned to the grassy clearing with her head held high and began to feed.

This time none disturbed her grazing.

Star Dancer sat very still, her eyes still closed. White Hawk looked at the floor reflectively, and Shala had curled up by Lily's side. The story obviously had meaning to the three of them, but it had none for her.

She waited until Star Dancer opened her eyes. "I

don't understand. What does the story have to do with my advocate?"

"Absolutely nothing, Lily," she said, standing and turning to White Hawk. "Finish tending the woman, if you will."

White Hawk returned the High Shaman's gaze, an enigmatic expression on his face. Actually, Lily thought, he looked as confused as she felt, a word she would never before have applied to him. Finally, he simply nodded, and Star Dancer left the wickiup.

When she'd gone, White Hawk said to Shala, who was now snuggled under Lily's arm. "You'll have time with Lily in the morning, but you both need rest now."

"Can't I sleep here?"

White Hawk smiled. "Don't forget Lily's scratched and bruised. You would disturb her with your tossing and turning."

"Oh." Clearly reluctant, Shala disentangled herself and got up and went behind one of the several reed screens that divided the larger room. A moment later she reemerged, carrying a circular object crisscrossed with webbing and decorated with colorful stones and feathers.

"A dream catcher," she said, presenting it to Lily with a proud grin. "I made it for you after you told me you had nightmares. Before—"

She knew what Shala had been about to say. No matter how lovingly they treated her, the matter of Tajaya's death would always hang between them. But Lily forced herself to smile in spite of this sobering realization and took Shala's gift, running her fingers over the carefully wrapped leather webbing and admiring the unique striations of the turquoise.

Her throat clutched again—it had been such an emotional night. "Thank you, sweetheart."

"I'll hang it above her pallet," White Hawk said. "Now will you go to bed, Shala?"

With a pleased grin, the girl disappeared behind the screen.

Still clutching the dream catcher, Lily listened to sounds of clothing being shed, blankets rustling, the faint creak of slats as Shala settled down. She knew she was grinning like a fool, and White Hawk's cryptic stare made her uneasy.

"It was sweet of her," she said, feeling a sudden need to explain her smile.

"Shala has a loving nature—Here, let me wrap your feet." He sat on the pallet and applied soaked leaves. "Do not abuse it."

"My foot?" Lily asked, confused.

Without answering, White Hawk picked up a roll of gauze, let a length fall free, and sliced it with his knife. He resheathed the blade, then picked up her foot and began deftly wrapping it.

"Don't abuse her loving nature."

"I'd never hurt her, White Hawk."

He finished with her foot and secured the loose end, taking obvious care not to cause her further pain, then started on the other foot. When he finished, he took the supplies back to the table, then returned with a comb.

"I'm going to try to get the burrs out of your hair. Sit up, if you will."

Lily had frequently heard the Dawn People add that phrase to their requests and had assumed it was their version of "please," but White Hawk had never shown her that respect before.

He was grateful, she thought, only grateful. And in his gratitude he was probably trying to make up for his earlier treatment. So, as he pulled the comb through her tangled hair, mindful not to tug too hard and occasionally tossing a burr or twig in a basket, she simply allowed him to make this small amends.

He paused suddenly. "I don't know why," he said brusquely, "but I believe you."

Lily's breath caught. "About Shala?"

"Yes, about Shala."

He returned to tending her hair. When he finished, he told her she'd do well to rest, then covered her with a blanket and went behind another screen. As Lily snuggled deeper into the soft mattress, she thought of how she'd accompanied White Hawk to the canyon only because she had no place else to go and Sebastian was on her heels. Now, in one roller-coaster night, everything had changed. A woman she admired had shown her both respect and kindness. A child she loved, loved her in return.

And a man who once scorned her like a worthless beast was treating her like a woman.

Chapter Eighteen

Lily woke up the next morning with a smile on her face. She'd dreamed of cool meadows, laughing children, a strong and steady man standing by her side looking at her with love. She opened her eyes and the first thing she saw was sunlight reflecting off the crystals in the dream catcher above her bed. White Hawk's last act before retiring had been to hang it.

Still smiling, she stretched, luxuriating in the relaxing aftermath of her night of sleep. She arched her back, wiggled her fingers, wiggled her toes. It felt good to be alive.

Even her feet felt good, although they should be throbbing, especially after the workout she'd just put her toes through.

But they *should* be throbbing.

She sprang upright, not quite so happy anymore.

Bending over, she began unwinding the bandage on one foot. The gauze fell away, taking most of the poultice with it. Flakes of the mud pack appeared on the bedclothes, and she brushed them away fretfully, not wanting to look. Finally, the last speck of mud disposed of, she gave a tentative glance at the unbandaged foot.

Her skin was pink and healthy. The punctures left by the pine needle had vanished. Not a scratch or bruise remained. Lily touched her face, searching for signs of the many scratches made by tree branches the previous night. The skin was smooth, unbroken.

A sound rose from her belly as she ripped the gauze from the other foot, already knowing what she'd find.

It too was fully healed.

Dear God, she must have alchemized in her sleep! When she'd found Tony in the forest and realized hair no longer covered her skin, she'd wanted to believe that Sebastian's jerky, interrupted ceremony had failed. But the only explanation for her instant healing was that it had succeeded. Clutching the bloodstained gauze to her chest, she started rocking on the bed.

This can't be happening. Please, God, she begged, this can't be happening. Not now. Now when—

"Are you okay, Lily?"

Startled, Lily dropped the bandages and spun her head to see Shala frowning with worry in the open doorway. When Lily didn't answer right away, the girl ran to her side. "What's wrong?" she asked fretfully. Involuntarily, Lily's eyes moved to her bare feet.

"Oh, Lily!" Shala exclaimed. "Look. The healing's

worked already!" A proud smile lit up her face. "I'm not supposed to brag, but Papa and Star Dancer are very powerful shamans."

"Of course! The healing!"

Shala wrinkled her nose. "What else did you think it was, silly?"

Lily broke—in peals of unbroken laughter. Finally Shala asked her what was so funny.

Lily shook her head. "I don't know, sweetheart," she replied through ebbing bursts of chuckles. "My . . . my mind's still foggy . . . from sleeping so long." She looked out the open door. "What time is it?"

"The sun is in the middle sky, long past the morning meal. Are you well enough to get up?"

"Yes. I'm very well." Another small chuckle erupted. "You don't know how well. Although I would dearly love a trip to the woman's pool."

"After we eat, if you will. We're having roasted buffalo, and there's still some left at Kessa's fire. She's the best cook in the village, so we must hurry before it's all gone."

"Buffalo?" Lily queried as she climbed off the pallet. "I don't remember buffalo in the canyon."

"It came from—" Shala's eyes widened. "I'm not supposed to tell."

"Tell what?" She suspected the information had something to do with the bustling activity surrounding the canyon by the pueblos.

"Papa will be angry." Shala bit her lower lip. "But not anymore, I think." Taking a resolute breath, she blurted out, "The warriors brought it back from Quakahla."

"Does this mean I'm finally going to learn what Quakahla is?" Lily smiled as she asked, not really caring. She'd just awoken from a living nightmare, and all other mysteries seemed mundane in comparison.

Shala paused uncertainly, then squared her small shoulders. "You're one of us now, and you should know. Quakahla is the true home of the Dawn People. When the dark moon rises we will all return—" She whirled around, obviously frustrated.

"What is it, sweetheart?"

Troubled blue eyes stared up at Lily. "I don't want to go! I want to see the mechanical world, the moving pictures, and the Disney lands. The great fish at the world by the sea. Maybe go to a mall, except I don't even know what that is." She gave out a little hiccup. "Won't you take me?"

"And leave your father?"

"Papa." Shala plopped down on the pallet. "No, I can't leave Papa." Then, forlornly, "I guess I never will see the mechanical world."

"You're not missing much, truly you aren't," Lily assured her as she slipped on her sandals. She nodded at a pile on a nearby chair. "How did my clothes get here?"

"I fetched them for you."

"You're so good to me."

Shala bounced off the pallet and gave Lily a fierce hug. "I love you."

"Not as much as I love you." Lily could barely keep the tremor of emotion from her voice.

"Oh yes I do, even more."

"Impossible." Lily gave the girl a kiss on the forehead. "Now, about that buffalo. You think there will be any left?"

"We'd better hurry."

Lily agreed and slipped behind a screen to change, then took Shala's hand and walked with her toward the village center. As they approached Kessa's hearth, she noticed a crowd gathering. Probably a council to discuss the werewolf threat, Lily thought, having no expectations that their attitude toward her would change as much as White Hawk and Shala's had.

But as they got nearer she saw everyone was staring at her. She lifted her chin a notch higher, only half aware that her grip on Shala's hand had tightened.

Suddenly a cheer filled the village. Arms upraised, fists pumping, they began chanting, "Lily! Lily! Lily!"

Kessa was there, smiling and holding little Joey, surrounded by her entire family. And the gossipy women from the bathing pool, the boy Ravenheart had yelled at, Gerard, and his brave grandson. Even old Frieda leaned on her cane, revealing her dark teeth with a wide smile. The whole village had shown up, it seemed.

Lily stared in astonishment, still not quite comprehending that they were cheering for her. At her side, Shala grinned so wide the remainder of her face almost disappeared.

"Did you know about this?" Lily asked, her eyes brimming with tears.

Shala bobbed her head. "That's why I told you to hurry."

"B-but . . . why?"

"A tribute," Shala replied. "For fighting the werewolves."

White Hawk stepped from the crowd, looking almost as bemused as Lily felt, and took Shala's hand, then draped an arm around Lily's shoulder. She sensed hesitation in him, but his touch felt reassuring nonetheless.

Then Star Dancer came forward, carrying an object. As she got closer, Lily saw an exquisitely braided thong from which hung a perfectly faceted spear of quartz crystal.

"In honor of your bravery, Lily." Star Dancer dropped the necklace over her head.

Lily thanked her, then whispered, "Does this mean I don't have to face the Tribunal?"

"That is beyond our power to change. It is already done."

"I see." Lily's hand drifted to the crystal and rested there. Star Dancer's eyes followed the movement.

"The gem may help you endure," she said, then turned toward the crowd, cutting off the possibility of any further questions.

The villagers cheered again, repeating Lily's name, calling her the werewolf slayer, which wasn't true, of course. Then White Hawk took her elbow, guided her to Kessa's fire, and sat beside her. Shala took a seat on her other side. Someone brought food.

Her thoughts and emotions were a jumble when she took the offered plate. She looked at White Hawk. "I don't understand . . ." She made a circular gesture, taking in the entire scene.

"This is to celebrate your help in returning Shala. We value every one of our members, and to save even one life is considered a noble act."

"How do they know?"

"I told them." His tone suggested he'd done it from duty, but Lily sensed qualities she'd felt from him with increasing frequency—tenderness, protectiveness—and many more she was afraid to hope for.

Then people milled around, patting her shoulders, saying appreciative words. More food was offered. Thanks were given to Grandfather Sky for sending Lily to them.

What a crazy world, she thought, biting into the buffalo steak, which tasted more delicious than anything she'd ever eaten. This was the best and worst day of her entire life. She'd finally earned what she'd always dreamed of—acceptance from a loving people.

Yet they were still going to execute her.

Later, Kessa brought Lily a piece of fresh fry bread dusted with powdered sugar. "I know it's your favorite," she said.

Then she joined the others. As if on cue, people began drifting toward the longhouse. White Hawk excused himself, taking Shala's hand and walking toward the crowd. The celebratory mood popped as quickly as if someone had pricked a balloon.

Star Dancer stood at the threshold of the building, and White Hawk took a place beside her. Soon a low murmur ran through the crowd. A prayer, Lily realized, spoken in a mixture of English and their native language. She heard invocations to Grandfather Sky and Mother Earth. Arlan Ravenheart's name was mentioned several times.

So White Hawk had also relayed the young warrior's fate. Lily felt a moment's sadness. Ravenheart's ambition had either ended his days or cursed him for the length of several lifetimes. But she found herself unable to condemn him. She knew too well the lure of the werewolf powers.

The group began to disperse. Some headed toward the fields, some to the pastures. Still others bustled toward the cleft in the canyon wall. Remembering what Shala had told her, Lily assumed they were preparing for Quakahla.

The event would happen on the dark moon rising. She'd been so overcome by relief when Shala first mentioned it she'd given little thought to the importance of the girl's words. Now she remembered why she'd felt this year's fall equinox held unusual significance: It would be accompanied by a total eclipse of the moon.

Eclipses held great import in astrology. This one obviously heralded the end of an era for the Dawn People. And that day wasn't far away. By her markings outside her quarters, the date was September twentieth. The equinox would occur on the twenty-third.

Where was Quakahla? she wondered. In another deeper, better hidden region of Ebony Canyon, or someplace quite distant? She couldn't blame the People for retreating. She'd heard the sounds of encroachment herself, although she'd been in the village but a short time. Hikers and campers were becoming ever more frequent in the once remote Ebony Canyon.

Would the Tribunal convene before their migration? The thought made her uneasy, and soon she felt immensely sad. These people had feted and fed her, yet even this would not stop her from being judged—and probably executed. She didn't deserve this. Sebastian had made her a werewolf, and she'd been true to her nature. The People's stories about White Wolf Woman showed they understood that this was so.

Why didn't they adhere to their own beliefs? Why did they seek revenge for acts she'd committed while she was something other than what she now was?

These charming people were hypocrites! They spoke from both sides of their mouths! Hadn't they slain the buffalo she'd just eaten with the same indifferences with which she'd once slain mortals? Although she vaguely recalled their custom of honoring the spirit of their fallen prey, she brushed the memory away. This was unfair! Unjust! Who did they think they were, sitting in judgment of her?

A bolt of pure outrage shot through her, and she wanted to howl it to the sky. She arched her neck, throwing back her head, tempted to let the sound emerge.

The first twinge in her knee went unnoticed. Then she felt another. And a third. A familiar stretching sensation radiated through her fingers and toes.

Lily leaped up.

"Is something wrong?" asked Kessa, who had returned to her hearth.

"No, no, nothing." Lily forced herself to walk calmly forward with the plate in her hand. She gave it to Kessa, whose brow was still wrinkled with concern. "I'm—I'm just desperately wanting a bath."

Kessa smiled, took the plate, and turned back to her fire. Lily headed for her pueblo, climbing as rapidly as she could without slipping, then ran to her quarters and pulled the curtain shut behind her.

Her heart raced, but she walked calmly toward her pallet and sat down. Shala had assured her the rapid healing came from White Hawk and Star Dancer's medicine, and Lily had wanted an explanation so badly, she'd clung to it without examination. But she still had scars from the wounds White Hawk had treated on the train, while not a mark remained from last night's injuries.

Just will it, she told herself. *Will it, then you'll know.*

She brought her hands to her lips and rubbed them absently, only vaguely aware her breath was coming in ragged heaves. Some time passed before she found her courage. Staring at the backs of her suntanned hands, she breathed the word: *Alchemize.*

Instantly, a layer of silver hair covered her arms and hands. The swiftness of the transformation stunned her. She'd always alchemized more easily than most werewolves—Sebastian had said it was because she hadn't fought her new nature—but never this quickly. Even the Lupine King did not alchemize with such speed.

In bewildered agony, she stared down. Where was the wiry coat of the werewolf? This hair looked like the down of a newborn pup. She ran her tongue along her teeth and discovered she also lacked fangs. She had no claws, nor did she have the werewolf's prodigious height.

She recalled the fate of a man who'd fled from the ceremonial ring into the thick woods before the ritual was finished. The pack never found him, but whispered stories returned of a creature half human, half monster, unable to shape-shift and doomed to eke out his existence with the other beasts of the wilderness.

She killed the scream before it left her throat. Panicked, she willed herself into human form. Again the transformation came instantly.

Pulse still racing, she tried to logically assess her fate. Was the botched ceremony effecting its changes slowly? Would new attributes appear each day until . . .

. . . until she was again filled with bloodlust?

Poor Morgan, she thought unexpectedly. All those years of fighting his werewolf urges. What horrors the struggle had driven him to—crawling through snow and bogs, seeking lesser forms of life to fulfill his dark needs. But Morgan was safe now, redeemed forever, while she could only contemplate living as he once had.

She let out a whimper. Where was God, or the Great Spirit the Dawn People so revered? She'd been deserted.

But this wasn't a curse from the deities, it was Sebastian's handiwork!

And she'd been moved with sympathy for him! Like a father to her? No! He'd needed a devoted follower to keep his pack in line. See how quickly he'd replaced her with the jealous Beryl!

Her joints creaked again; a sharper pain streaked through one knee, jolting her. Swiftly she calmed down and willed the changes to cease. They stopped immediately.

But now she knew this wasn't a fluke. Her werewolf nature had returned. What was she to do? She'd already brought danger to the Dawn People by leading Sebastian to them. Now she herself was the danger.

She saw only one solution. And she would have to carry it out that night.

Chapter Nineteen

"Why didn't you tell me?" Tony demanded without preamble, not bothering to hide his anger from Riva.

She looked up from her work at the loom, the corners of her mouth lifting. "Tony, it's always a pleasure to see you."

"Cut the crap, Riva! I want to know why you kept this from me."

"My, I see your time in the mechanical world has renewed your colorful vocabulary." She cocked her head to the right. "Let's sit on the dais. We have much to discuss. I want to hear of your vision quest."

"Not until you tell me about Lily's part in the journey to Quakahla." But he moved to the platform anyway, knowing Riva would reveal only what she wanted and only in her own time.

After they settled on the sheepskin, he turned to her, his eyes still blazing. "Lily may not have understood your parable last night, but I understood it fully, and deserved to have been given this information before I went after her."

"Would it have changed your feelings toward her—this woman who killed Tajaya?"

Tony shifted his weight and readjusted his legs. "No, but I would have better understood the purpose of bringing her back alive."

"Yet you did bring her safely back even without that knowledge." Riva rose and went to the table, lit incense in a pot, then brought it back to the sheepskin. "I observed you with Lily last evening, Tony. Your feelings for her are changing."

Breathing in the sweet scent, he slowly shook his head. "I am in her debt for saving Shala, that is all."

Riva's sharp glance told him she knew he was hedging. But if he revealed his turmoil—if he said out loud what he feared was happening between him and Lily . . . He couldn't speak of it. Even thinking the words dishonored Tajaya.

"I don't understand, Riva. Tajaya was your daughter, yet you still respect her killer. How are you able to do it?"

"Sometimes . . ." She glanced away for an instant. "The absence Tajaya's death left in my heart cannot ever be filled. Sometimes I do hate the wolf woman. But then Quetzalcoatl comes to remind me the world is as he made it. You must also remember that."

He took another whiff of incense.

"Speak to me of your vision quest, Tony."

"White Bear came to me . . ."

"A powerful animal guide. You were greatly honored."

"Yes, but that is of little consequence. His words were—they were harsh, yet heavy with truth."

Tony paused. After leaving Lily's side the night before, he'd lain awake thinking of Riva's parable. As a latecomer, he hadn't grown up listening to tales of White Wolf Woman like the trueborns had, and in his skepticism about the existence of Quakahla, he'd paid them little attention. Not until the previous night had he connected Lily with the legends. If they were true, then Lily was the bridge between the two worlds and they couldn't pass successfully without her.

The urgency of the council's request should have triggered the memory, but it hadn't. Bear's message implied Tony's reasons for hiding the truth from himself went far deeper than revenge. Revealing this to Riva made him feel vulnerable and unworthy of his shaman's title.

But she'd been his teacher for years and had never condemned him when he faltered. He had no reason to believe she'd do so now.

"Bear told me my hatred for Lily comes not from my love of Tajaya," he said, feeling his spirit lighten even as the difficult words left his mouth, "but from my own self-deception."

"What do you think?" Riva probed. "What true reason lies behind your hate?"

"I'm questioning whether I want to remain with The

People," he replied, heart aching at the thought of leaving, yet feeling the call of the outside world. "Since . . . since Tajaya died, something has been missing from my life. I can't put my finger on it, but . . .

"Shala begs to visit the mechanical world and tells me she doesn't want to go to Quakahla . . . When I explain how wonderful our new home will be, I feel the falseness in my assurances . . . I miss computers, Riva. I miss the feel of the wind from the back of a horse, automobiles, and . . ." He smiled wanly. "I miss Snickers candy bars."

"But you've decided to come with us anyway?"

"My home's with the Dawn People now. And so is Shala's. She is, after all, your granddaughter and destined to become a great shaman herself."

"So for her sake, and for mine, you'll go, even though your spirit calls you elsewhere?"

"Yes."

"It is your choice, Tony. I won't stand in your way if you choose otherwise."

"I know that, Riva." He hesitated, reluctant to tell her the rest, yet knowing he must. "There's more."

He told her then of the vision—no, it was more than a vision, it had been realer than many of his conscious encounters—of caressing Lily, joining with her, whispering loving words.

"And I awoke filled with love. Lily seemed like a piece of me then." He glanced away in self-reproach. "So quickly I turned back to hate. When I saw her following the werewolves and Shala, I immediately assumed she was going back to her pack."

He forced himself to meet Riva's eyes, although the horror of the barely averted outcome of his misjudgment almost overwhelmed him, and said in a hushed tone, "If Lily hadn't been there, Shala would have joined her mother."

"As usual, you judge yourself too harshly. You've received the gift of greater self-knowledge. Give thanks for it."

"This is one time where ignorance feels like bliss. I don't feel thankful at all. Another sign I've failed in the shaman's way."

"You don't mean that, Tony, and you know it." Riva straightened her back abruptly, indicating she was about to change the subject. "Will you be Lily's advocate before the Tribunal?"

Once again Riva had guessed what was truly on his mind.

"I don't yet know."

"Time is slipping away."

"Do you have another if I refuse?"

"Only myself."

Tony nodded, then climbed to his feet. "I'll let you know by morning."

As he turned toward the door, Riva said, "You had a second shape-shifting experience last night, didn't you?"

Long ago he'd stopped asking Riva how she knew such things, and now he only looked back and nodded. "It happened the same way it did in New York. When I saw what peril Shala was in, I suddenly became the hawk. I still have no control."

"Control will come."

"But not until I resolve my conflict?"

Rising, Riva smiled in agreement, then said, "I'll wait for your decision. Walk in beauty."

She accompanied him down the length of the longhouse, stopping beside her loom. As Tony was about to move on, she touched his shoulder.

"All that was foretold is not already done, Tony. The fate of the Dawn People hangs in the balance."

"Yes," he replied somewhat impatiently. "Just as the legends foretell."

Riva ignored his tone. "You have not heard it all. The final story hasn't yet been fully written. It concerns Lily, and to amend for not telling you of her part in our migration, I will tell you how the story stands now. If, as you say, your feelings for her run no deeper than gratitude, my words will be of little importance."

Tony nodded, waiting with more apprehension than he dared admit. When the words came, he almost staggered under their weight. Of little importance? He only wished they were.

Lily grabbed at a quivering tree branch, seeking leverage to navigate a particularly steep section of the trail. She'd scraped her hand on the scrub oak during her leap from the catwalk wall, and the rough bark made the cuts hurt all the more. When she finally reached a flatter area, she paused to blow on the abrasion.

Anticipating the colder weather at the top of the ridge, she'd put on her blue jeans and the linen jacket, which were now damp with sweat. Now she wiped her dripping forehead with the hem of the jacket, then looked up at the dark sky. Another monsoon gale was brewing. Pulsing heat lightning brushed the churning thunderheads with silver, and the round moon glowed through streaks of dark clouds. Wind battered the trees clinging to the steep wall of the canyon. Thunder periodically rumbled in the distance.

A fitting night to die.

She resumed her climb, stopping now and again to brush her flapping hair from her eyes. Tiring, she briefly considered alchemizing to speed her journey and heal her cuts. Although the idea tempted her, she resisted and continued on, using the weaving branches for support whenever she could catch one.

Finally, after an interminable climb, she arrived at the top. The moon poured its cold light on the rain-starved grass in the meadow and illuminated the remains of Morgan's charred and crumbling cabin. She shivered, not only from the onslaught of the brisk, cold wind, but from the memories it stirred.

She'd once traveled to this place through the worst snowstorm in recent Arizona history, protected by her thick werewolf coat and impervious to the cold of this higher altitude. She'd been filled with the hunger then, and also fearful of Sebastian's censure. Her acts had been heartless. And she was doomed to repeat them if she didn't end it now.

She shivered again, this time from apprehension. Would she have the courage to follow through on her decision?

She didn't know. Ducking her head to ward off the chill of the wind, she tightened her lightweight jacket around her body and hurried south toward the Clearing of the Black Hands.

Thunder clapped and the sky lit up with jagged streaks that ripped through the angry clouds, converging as they met the earth.

Lily stopped and stared upward, wondering if the stormy weather was a sign the gods were judging her. How odd that she'd so badly wanted to escape the Tribunal and was now headed to carry out the sentence they would have undoubtedly passed.

Her options had narrowed. She couldn't live as one of *them* again, and *they* were only here because she'd lured them. When she was gone, they would leave. The Dawn People would know peace again. Her deepest regret was that she'd never be able to show Shala the wonders of the mechanical world.

Tony couldn't sleep. After spending the day with a team of men rerouting the path through the maze, he should have dropped off immediately. But his pallet felt as hard and unyielding as his desire to punish Lily for Tajaya's murder. Listening to the thunder and the wail of the mounting wind, he tossed and turned, thinking about Riva's request.

Be Lily's advocate? What defense would he use? Shouldn't her life be sacrificed to atone for Tajaya's? Or had saving Shala's been atonement enough?

Tony rolled in his bed again, yanking irritably at his blanket, which had gotten tangled around his legs. By all that was sacred, he didn't want to be part of a legend. And though he'd devoted his entire adult life to the shaman's way, at this moment he wasn't sure he wanted that either.

Surrendering to his restlessness, he got up and fetched his hemp trousers, not sure why he was dressing or what he'd do once he had. Bear's message came back to him, and as he left the wickiup, walking to an unknown destination, he mulled it over. Since Tajaya died, dissatisfaction with the People's life *had* troubled him.

He'd told himself he missed his wife and his disquiet sprang from grief. But as he placed a hand on the rung of the ladder leading up to the pueblos, barely troubled by the high wind that dogged his every step, he asked himself if his purpose for being in Ebony Canyon had died with his wife.

She'd been his teacher as much as Riva, and though his affection for the High Shaman ran deep, she didn't fill the void Tajaya had left. Was Bear right? Was he truly nourishing his hatred for Lily to hide these doubts from himself?

Yes! That's exactly what he'd been doing. In violation of everything he'd learned from his beloved wife and her equally beloved mother, he'd ignored the teaching, rejected the compassion that was the way of The People, and focused all his self-deception on Lily.

The wind cooled the waves of shame that heated White Hawk's body, and when the waves finally passed, he felt a weight lift. He climbed faster, taking the rungs two at a time, nearing the top where Lily's quarters were, no longer hiding his destination from himself. His answer had come. He would defend her before the Tribunal.

A glowing smile spread over his face, and he practically flew up the remaining rungs of the ladder.

Chapter Twenty

Tony held Lily's note in his hand, fighting a reflexive desire to crumple it in his fist. In his other hand he clutched the crystal necklace and one of the small plastic bottles. She'd dumped them all on the washing table, atop her hastily scrawled explanation that the gemstone belonged to the tribe and the liquid in the bottles was deadly to werewolves. He was so stunned by her absence—and the message within her message—that his feet felt glued to the floor.

Breaking his paralysis, he spun around and marched out to the walkway. He had no idea where she'd gone. Was she even now surrendering herself to Sebastian in exchange for the Dawn People's safety? Or—

Or what? He refused to think of it.

Staring up at the churning sky, ignoring the wind that threatened to rip his hair from its restraining thong, he struggled to find his center, the place from which his thought-form sprang. Finally he felt energy gather. A few minutes later the white winged shape soared into the air, screeching a warning.

Its vision joined with Tony's and delivered images of Lily clinging to a fragile handhold on the side of the canyon wall. Tony sped toward the catwalk, knowing it was the only path she could have taken.

Although he'd scaled these walls many times, his pace was brutal and by the time the cold blast at the top hit his bare chest, he was both scratched and dripping with sweat. Ignoring his chill, he bent into the fierce wind and broke into a sprint.

The hawk's cries had grown louder and more repetitive, and his keen eyes brought images of Lily racing along the rim. More than a mile behind her, Tony forced his legs to move faster, pumping them almost beyond endurance.

Soon he saw she'd reached the path to the Clearing of the Black Hands. Instead of going down it, she stood at the edge of the cliff, her hair billowing around her face and shoulders. He saw her shudder, saw her lips mouthing words the hawk could not hear. The bird dipped low, passing right before her face. Her eyes widened in alarm, and she moved closer to the precipice.

The earth rumbled from the assault of thunder. Flashes of blinding light filled the sky with jagged streaks that backlit her like a statue of an ancient dryad arising from the trees. She crept ever nearer to the edge, now hesitating, now moving again.

Suddenly Tony understood what she meant to do. No! He wouldn't let death rob him a second time! Forcing yet more speed from his aching legs, he raced against the clock.

The hawk cried out once more, and suddenly Tony was soaring with it, battling the turbulent up-and-down drafts, dropping to the ground just as Lily prepared to take her final step. With a roar of denial, Tony resumed his human form and snatched her from the edge.

"White Hawk!" She wrestled to free herself from his restraining hold. "Stop it . . . stop . . . You don't understand."

He grabbed her pummeling hands and shook her fiercely. "What the hell do you think you're doing?" he demanded, then pressed her close to his chest.

She continued to struggle, writhing against his chilled skin, warming it with her heat. Her hips brushed the thin fabric of his trousers, heating his lower regions.

"Let me go, you fool," she ordered, her voice thin and breathless. "This is for your own good . . . it's for Shala. For all your people."

"Killing yourself won't help anyone, Lily." This time he spoke softly, burying his face in her whipping hair. It grazed his face, the bare skin of his shoulders, and smelled of herbs and spices and pine. She was so tiny, barely reaching his shoulder, so fragile. Why hadn't he realized earlier that this woman needed his protection, not his censure? He inhaled, his breath catching, and trembled at the knowledge of how close he'd come to losing her.

"I don't understand. Even now you save my life although the Tribunal soon plans to take it. Why?"

"We need you." His words came out with a ragged exhale.

"N-n-need me?" She tilted back her head, shaking it slowly. "No one needs me, White Hawk. None of you are safe while I'm alive. Please, please let me go. Turn around and forget you ever saw this."

"I can't." He pulled her head back to his shoulder. She didn't struggle this time, and he whispered in her ear, "When I—When I found your note and realized you were gone . . . I went to your quarters to tell you I'll be your advocate."

"Why? You still believe I killed your wife." She was trembling now. They both were. And though the cold wind bit at their bodies he knew that wasn't the cause.

"For many reasons. But the true reason is I—I . . . I care about you. I'll defend you well, Lily, to my death if that's what it takes. Trust me, if you will."

She chuckled bleakly and lifted her head, fixing her dark gaze on him. "What makes you think you can trust *me*?"

"You saved my daughter's life." His golden eyes met hers levelly. "That's enough proof."

"You don't know . . ." Lily looked away. White Hawk's gaze held so much tenderness she could hardly bear it. "Sebastian . . . the ceremony . . ." Would he kill her when she showed him what she'd again become. With his own hands? The ones that had combed her tangled hair the night before and even now held her tenderly against his chest. Would he kill her when he knew?

What did it matter how she died?

"Let me go. I need to show you something."

His eyes took on a suspicious cast, but he dropped his arms. "No tricks," he said warily, clearly prepared to stop her if she bolted toward the canyon.

She glanced toward the drop-off, then smiled weakly, steeling herself against the disgust she knew would arise on his face. Will it. She only had to will it.

Alchemize.

Again the change came instantly. One moment she was shivering in the freezing wind, the next moment she noticed it not at all.

She'd expected a startled cry, a quick jerk of revulsion. Instead he uttered a soft, "How?" She heard no loathing in his voice.

"After you left, Sebastian forced me back into the circle and completed the Song of Hades. That's what he was doing when you arrived. He almost succeeded in transforming Shala too."

He flinched at that but said nothing.

"I thought the ritual was unsuccessful—you'd interrupted it and—" She gave a short ironic laugh. "It was . . . well, untraditional. It shouldn't have worked, but it did. You see now why I can't live."

She couldn't read his expression nor discern his thoughts, and felt only an overwhelming sense of amazement from him.

"Aren't you going to say something?" she snapped.

"You look like no werewolf I've ever seen."

"What are you talking about?"

"Look at your hands, Lily."

She dropped her gaze and again saw the pale down covering her hands. Only this time the hair seemed incandescent. She still didn't have claws, though the ragged edges of the fingernails she'd torn on her climb were now smooth and perfectly rounded. She lifted her hands to her face and touched the flat, even features of a human, not the short muzzle of a werewolf.

"I know it doesn't make sense. But the ceremony was disrupted." Then, almost in a whisper, she added, "Over time, I'm sure it will get worse."

"Do you know that?"

She shook her head.

"Do you feel an urge to dine on my bones, Lily?"

"What a stupid question," she replied sharply. "I'm not hungry."

"If you were, how would you do it? Where is your werewolf height? Your fangs, your claws?"

"I don't know! But I can't risk it!" She swung her arms in agitation. Why the hell couldn't he understand? "You, Shala, Star Dancer, you're all in danger. And I'm the only reason Sebastian brought his pack to Ebony Canyon. When I'm gone, they'll leave! Can't you see—"

Tony turned abruptly toward the nearby trees. His expression grew distant and unfocused, and he lifted his arms to the cloud-covered moon. "And White Wolf Woman shall leave the deer and the wolf people, and come to live among the Two-Leggeds," he intoned in an altered voice. "Although they shall first revile her for what she had once been and blame her for the howling and gnashing of the beast of the forest, White Wolf Woman shall hold high her head and remain. Her mastery of the hungering natures of the meat-feeders, the plant-feeders, the feeders on both, will bestow her with strength beyond any known to this world. She shall join with the bear and fend off the monsters.

"Thus aided, the people shall gather their belongings and under the dark moon rising pass unto their true land."

A whirlwind suddenly enclosed them both, spiraling leaves, twigs, and small rocks. But they stood untouched inside its calm eye. As quickly as it arose, the tempest vanished, leaving Lily staring at the shaman before her. Slowly White Hawk's eyes cleared and he looked at her.

"What was that about?" Lily asked, vaguely noticing that her hands were trembling and sending out tiny sparks of light.

"An omen. I don't know its portent, only that you have a place in it." He reached out and took her hands. "Return to human shape and come back to the village with me. Come back, if you will."

Lily heard the plea in his voice, felt it draw her to obey. Oh sweet heaven, she wanted to. This man who asked it of her was extraordinary in every way. A loving child waited down below, and a giving people seemed ready to accept her. Oh yes, she wanted to obey.

With one lingering look at White Hawk, she spun and leaped toward the abyss. One jump took her to the canyon's edge, where she alchemized to fragile mortal form and prepared to take the final plunge.

Then Tony was upon her, calling her name, cursing her, holding her, pulling her back. She tried to fight him off and they tumbled. Arms and legs entwined, they hit the earth with a force that knocked Lily's breath away. His weight pressed her against the uneven ground. Rocks and twigs poked her skin, but she ignored their bite and pounded on White Hawk's back, demanding that he let her up.

Thunder clapped so loudly it drowned out her words. Lightning flashed in dizzying strobes that nearly blinded her. But still she fought. She twisted, drove an elbow into White Hawk's stomach. He grunted, then captured both her wrists and forced her arms to the earth.

"You won't die, Lily. I won't let you."

The words, so reminiscent of those he spoke that night in her bedroom, held an entirely different meaning this time, and gave her such a jolt she stopped fighting. Still panting from exertion, Lily looked directly in his face. There was a shimmer of unshed tears in his golden eyes, an emotion she couldn't quite identify. She felt it in her heart. His nostrils flared slightly, his mouth softened.

Slowly he lowered his head.

When his lips met hers Lily thought she truly might die from the sheer bliss of it. An unexpressed sigh filled her heart. She felt a sweet rush as White Hawk moaned against her mouth and parted her lips, returning his kiss with a hunger she'd never known.

Tony had felt as parched as the canyon, and Lily's kiss was like life-giving rain. He should be horrified at wanting her this way at this horrendous time, but horror eluded him. He felt fulfilled, as though he'd been designed by the Great Spirit only to kiss this woman, hold her in his arms. And the passion with which she returned his kiss made his heart swell.

Their kiss was hidden from the world by a swirl of silver hair, and he held her hands against the earth, arching his back ever so slightly to gentle his claim on her mouth. He ran his tongue across her lower lip, then inside her mouth, feeling the smooth moist surface, slipping slowly between her teeth. She met his tongue passionately, made mewing sounds in her throat. Her body began to tremble.

"Lily," he groaned, releasing her lips and rolling to bring her on top of him. Her legs parted and slid on either side of him. She swayed almost imperceptibly against the swelling beneath his pants.

Rocks pricked at his bare back, making his muscles quiver, but he felt no pain. Every inch of his body was alive with need for her. The thunder roared again. Their kiss broke, and his eyelids fluttered open. He saw her above him, hair flying in the wind, dark almond-shaped eyes clouded with desire.

"You shouldn't have stopped me," she said. "Why did you do it, you who have wanted me dead for so long?"

He touched the hollow of her throat. Her pulse throbbed visibly, rapidly. Such a tender spot, one he'd often dreamed of slicing with his hunting knife. But now? Now?

"Duty," he replied, dropping his hand. He saw a faint widening of her eyes, knew he had hurt her. "That night when I saved you from Sebastian, I acted out of duty. But tonight?" He reached up and took the lapels of her jacket and began slowly slipping it down her arms. "I don't know, Lily. I couldn't bear to see you die. My heart's on fire from wanting you. It's torture not to touch you . . ."

Torture. Yes, torture. He jerked the jacket down her arms, revealing the clinging cotton camisole she wore. Shimmying out of the sleeves, she took his hands and brought them to cover her small, firm breasts. He held them for an instant like precious jewels, then slowly rubbed his thumbs across the nipples. They hardened for him, small aching nubs that begged for his caress.

Lily let out a muffled cry. Exquisite sensations raced through her body, tingling up and down her spine, moving through her limbs to her fingers and toes. White Hawk lifted his hands and she felt the bite of freezing wind against her skin as he pushed up her camisole. She moaned in protest, but when his mouth closed over her throbbing nipple her protest died and she thought she might scream from ecstasy instead.

She arched her neck, and through her closed eyelids saw the pure white field of flashing lightning. Thunder roared, shaking the earth beneath her knees. Wind whipped her hair relentlessly against her chilled and naked arms. But the rest of her was hot. Blazing hot. And wild like the storm.

Beneath her White Hawk trembled like a stallion primed to mount his mare. She'd known what was in his mind before, had felt his hate, his desire to slit her throat with that deadly knife of his and take her life. But now he would take from her what she'd never before been able to give. She loved him, this man who'd once prayed for her death. Which felt like a little death itself, she realized, the pain of it piercing her heart.

She shuddered again as his tongue moved toward the under curve of her breast, and then he was kissing her belly, quickly, hungrily as though he wanted to devour every inch of her body. Tightening her thighs against his hips, she began to rotate her own. He was hard and full of wanting, a wanting she needed him to spill into her.

If there was life after death, she'd remember this moment forever, remember the unrelenting hardness of his muscled chest, remember the poignant tenderness of his mouth . . .

For despite his belief that she wasn't a werewolf, Lily knew she couldn't risk finding out she was. The zenith of the full moon was but three nights away, bringing the werewolves' blood frenzy to its peak, and if White Hawk was wrong, his people would suffer for his mistake.

But she would seize this night in White Hawk's arms. Tonight was theirs. Tonight.

Tony had started to unbutton Lily's jeans when she exploded above him. Like the beast she once had been, she clawed at his trousers, bucking her hips, yanking them down. He kicked his feet, sending the pants flying somewhere into the meadow, and she began tearing at her own clothes. The camisole soared, the jeans were discarded, and she hovered over him, shoulders heaving from the force of her need.

Her hands, her fingers were everywhere. Stroking and massaging his taut biceps, exploring the rise of his chest, moving down the rippled muscles of his abdomen, and finally closing over the center of his need. He was hot and engorged—her hand was chilled from the wind—and his body turned rigid from the electric pleasure her touch evoked. He let out a cry. She whimpered in response, elevated her hips, and guided him into her.

Her movements were uncontrolled. She swayed and bucked like a wild thing, crying out uninhibitedly, touching him here, touching him there. He brought her mouth to his, taking it in a brutal kiss that matched her passion.

The cold wind gusted, blowing dry leaves and grass around them, whipping her hair like a nine-tailed whip, and still he held her mouth. She sheathed him fully, tightening around him. He swelled inside her, growing larger, growing hotter, feeling her, wanting her, needing her . . . loving her.

She let out a throaty cry and shuddered from head to toe. Tearing her mouth from his, she collapsed onto his chest, gasping and moaning. A second later, Tony felt his own release approaching. He tried to hold back, but she rotated her hips, tugging at him, holding him.

When his explosion came, he felt one with the

thunder and lightning, one with the raging wind, one with Lily.

She whimpered again, and Tony took the sound, merged it with the waves of pleasure exquisitely tearing his body apart, and pulled Lily tight against his heart, never to let her go.

Chapter Twenty-one

White Hawk pulled Lily closer to his chest. "You're cold. You need your clothing."

"No . . . yes." Lily settled against him for just a little longer. The ground was hard, rock-filled and unforgiving, and the wind felt like a freezer blast, but she didn't want to end this last moment between them. Not yet.

White Hawk stirred and gently moved her to a sitting position. Then he stood up, searching the rim for their clothes.

"Your trousers are over there." Lily pointed to a pale mass atop the dying grass of the meadow.

As he went to retrieve them, she saw her chance. Her jacket was at her feet. She put it on, then started for the rim where her jeans and camisole had landed.

He wouldn't guess her intent, not yet. By the time he did, it would be too late.

She picked up her jeans, then glanced at the meadow. White Hawk was stepping into his trousers. As he began tying the drawstring at the waist, Lily made her move.

Dropping the jeans, she sprinted toward the canyon, breath catching, hesitation in her every footfall. But she must do it! Now! Before she changed her mind.

Suddenly a bird screeched. She saw that hated flash of white. Before she knew it, Tony again clutched her against his chest, whispering questions, murmuring crazy reassurances.

She didn't fight. Instead she trembled, clung to him with equal ferocity, knowing she'd hoped he'd do this all along. Tears filled her eyes as she contemplated the result of her selfishness.

But she wanted to live! Especially now, with this strong and steady man she'd dreamed of holding her in his arms and begging her not to do it.

"You're one and the same, aren't you?" she asked, when she regained her voice. "You and the hawk."

He nodded, and she wondered why she hadn't made the connection earlier, but didn't really care. He was here now and she was still alive.

She tried to pull away, but Tony tightened his hold on her. "It's over, Lily. You'll have to find the courage to live."

"I won't try again." She shook her head sadly. "But we both may come to regret it."

"Then you'll come back with me?"

"White Hawk . . . I—I—"

"Tony," he said gruffly.

She stared at him blankly.

He drew a finger softly along the curve of her jaw. "When a woman makes love with a man it gives her the right to use his first name."

She continued to stare, feeling dazed.

"You're important to me, Lily." He looked away, but not before she saw the vulnerability in his eyes. "I care for you."

Now it was her turn to look away. Why had she hoped for something deeper, more impassioned?

"I don't deserve your caring. You of all people should know that."

"But you've got it regardless. Don't ask me to explain, or to vow that a part of my soul doesn't still rail against it, but my feelings are what they are." He tilted her chin up, forcing her to meet his eyes. "Will you come back with me?"

Lily sighed heavily. "Yes, White Hawk, and may God help us both."

Moonlight glinted off his straight white teeth as he let out a laugh of pure joy. "Call me Tony, darling. Call me Tony."

"Tony," she echoed, then she tilted back her head to receive his kiss, trying to convince herself she hadn't hoped he'd say he loved her.

Lily sat on the pallet in her quarters and clutched the crystal she'd replaced around her neck, still shaken by the events of the previous evening. When they'd returned to the village, she'd gone with Tony to Star Dancer's hogan, where he'd informed the High Shaman he would defend Lily.

"Excellent," Star Dancer had replied. "You leave in the morning."

So soon? Lily now thought, as the creeping light of dawn appeared in her window. She dreaded the events the next few days would bring. What frightened her most was knowing Tony would be alone with her while these changes were taking place in her body. He'd assured her more than once that she wasn't becoming a werewolf, but . . .

She reached for a vial of holy water.

Tony had kept his sights on her ever since they returned, and she wouldn't be surprised to find him sleeping at the base of the ladder to prevent her from escaping. She must protect him by learning the truth. Rolling the bottle between her fingers, she eyed the stamp of sanctification as if she'd never seen one before. If Tony was right, this simple test would tell. But if he was wrong . . .

She'd never personally experienced the agonizing effect of holy water, but she'd seen the tortured expressions of those who had.

She alchemized.

The same soft fur blanketed her skin, and the glow she'd seen the night before seemed even brighter. So odd, these changes, unlike anything she'd ever seen, but they didn't mean she wasn't a werewolf.

Bracing herself for the pain, she pulled the stopper

from the vial, shuddering as she spilled a drop on her palm.

Nothing happened.

She felt fine, okay. More than okay. A peaceful feeling flowed from her palm into her fingertips, up her arm. Soon her whole body sang with well-being. Her heart skipped a beat. This couldn't be true, yet her unscathed palm proved it was.

But if she wasn't a werewolf, what was she?

Failing to find an answer, she recorked the bottle, averse to risking another precious drop. They'd need the water soon enough. Although the tribespeople had rerouted the maze, if Ravenheart was still alive he'd undoubtedly find a way through. It was only a matter of time.

Returning to human form, she put the bottle back into the pocket of her jacket, then got up. Suddenly her legs gave out. She fell back on the pallet, trembling and shivering, wanting to cry, wanting to laugh. Instinctively, her hand moved to the gemstone between her breasts.

Tears of relief and joy streamed down her face. She wasn't a werewolf! She was alive and mortal, with so much to live for!

And with every reason to survive the Tribunal. She looked up at the ceiling and wondered if she was searching for guidance. Maybe she was. Clearly something or someone was guiding her destiny. What else could explain the bizarre life she'd led?

She got up to get dressed. It was time to meet the Tribunal, and she was as ready as she'd ever be.

* * *

"By Hades," Beryl grumbled to Sebastian, "this wolfling will not live a fortnight. He cannot even alchemize without tearing the ceiling out with his screams."

Arlan Ravenheart shivered on the floor of the filthy cave and tried to get warm by wrapping himself up in a thin, patterned rug that looked so old it must be worthless. Mice droppings and spiderwebs clung to the faded fabric. He brushed them off with a shudder of revulsion and tried to glare at Sebastian's critical follower.

But he had no strength to glare. The transformation—what the others called alchemization—had drained his vitality to alarmingly low levels. Never had he experienced such pain, not even as a child when old Frieda had yanked out his aching molar.

Sebastian paced the floor in human form, chewing on a gold-plated piece of metal that held a smoldering cigarette. He took it from his mouth, blew out a circle of smoke, and went to a portrait of a man with a red feather in his cap that hung on the sloping stone wall.

"Lily has let this place go to ruin," he complained as he straightened the painting's tarnished frame. Then he glanced at Ravenheart. "The wolfling is young yet. He has not had his first kill. We will introduce him to that pleasure when the sun goes down."

"And how will we do that?" Beryl questioned. "Those people have altered the path. Philippe and I traveled through their maze last night and got hopelessly lost. We almost failed to find our way out." He whirled toward Ravenheart. "Destroy this puny wolf-ling, Lord. His presence will only hinder us."

Sebastian gave out a low growl. "The Law *forbids* it!"

Ravenheart's tensing body relaxed at Sebastian's answer. Although the others were now in human form, he didn't have enough strength in this unfamiliar Lupine body to defend himself if they chose to kill him. He didn't understand his misery. Had the Great Wolf deceived him? Had it truly been Coyote, full of his usual trickery? But all true shamans were tested before they attained full power. Clearly this was his test.

Sebastian walked over, stooped, and brushed back Ravenheart's disheveled hair, reminding Ravenheart that he'd lost his own red feather sometime during the limb-wrenching ritual. The rabbit's foot too had long since fallen out.

"This one can lead us through the maze," Sebastian said to Beryl, although his eyes remained on Ravenheart. "Can you not?"

"Yes," Ravenheart croaked, although he wasn't actually sure he could.

"Yes?" Sebastian repeated tartly.

Ravenheart lowered his eyes, hating the need to assume a servile tone. "Yes, Lord."

"Better." Sebastian again regarded Beryl. "See? This young one learns quickly. He, I am certain, would never suggest ignoring the Law."

Taking another leisurely drag of his cigarette, he straightened. "We have three nights yet to perform the Song of Hades. I erred in trying to do it when the astrological aspect was not yet ripe. But the ritual will not fail the next time. We'll reclaim Lily yet. The new wolfling knows the way and will be of great use to us."

Of use to them. No, Ravenheart thought, they would be of use to him. He would take them to the village, lead them to the former she-wolf, to Star Dancer and to Shala. And most of all to White Hawk. He'd let them feed in their beastly manner, then when they'd had their fill he'd let them take the she-wolf wherever they willed.

But he would stay. The Dawn People would turn to him as their rightful leader, respectful, worshipful, as he led them through the gates. Then with the Great Wolf at his side, he would rule the realm of Quakahla forever.

Forever.

It was already done.

With that gratifying thought, he curled back into a ball and stifled another moan.

"How're your feet?" Tony asked, mindful of the blisters Lily's boots had caused during their original hike to the village.

"So far so good."

She dropped a rock into the blazing pit, then scurried back to avoid sparks. Glancing quickly at the glaring sun, she asked, "When are the others arriving?"

She wore tight shorts and one of those skimpy cotton tops he'd so hastily pulled from her drawers back in New York. An inverted V of perspiration stained the spot between her breasts, revealing the crisp edges of the crystal that rested underneath it. The damp cotton clung to the shallow indentations between her ribs. Her hair was held back by a thong, and a band of bright cotton was wrapped around her forehead to keep sweat from her eyes.

Her appearance reminded him of the comic-book heroines he'd pined over as a boy. Cosmic Woman or some such name. Like them, she hadn't complained about the arduous tasks they were performing.

Without taking food or water, they'd collected the firewood, log by log, twig by twig. Then they started gathering the rocks. As they worked, Tony explained the ritual. When the sun set, they'd transfer the blazing Stone People into a pit inside the sweat lodge and would stay there until Lily had a vision. Apparently, Tony now thought, he'd left out a very important detail.

"You're expecting people?"

Her expression turned quizzical. "Of course, people. What else?"

"Your inquisition is too important to be left to Two-Leggeds." He straightened to readjust his loincloth. "The Tribunal consists of spirits and guides who have greater understanding of the Universe's harmony."

"Ghosts?" Her voice rose, partly teasing, partly incredulous. "I'm going to be judged by ghosts?"

"Not ghosts, Lily. Higher beings."

She smiled wanly. "When I was small, I believed I had a guardian angel. I'd like to believe that again. Do you think she might show up?"

He pulled her against his naked chest and stroked her damp hair, surprised as always by the slightness of her body. "Call on her and she will come. You must have faith."

"I don't want to die, Tony." Her dark eyes looked up at him longingly. "I have so much to live for now."

Taking her face between his palms, he kissed her, then whispered, "I'll do everything in my power to protect you."

She sighed. "But you can't promise, can you?"

"No. This isn't already done."

"I see." She put her hand over the gemstone. "Then it's up to me. Tell me what to expect while we finish our work."

Tony explained what was to come as they carried rocks to the fire, pausing now and then to catch his breath. He would see her visions as clearly as she would, he told her, and could speak in her behalf, but couldn't advise her how to respond to her accusers. If she appeased their spirits, the vision would end.

"My accusers? You mean the Tribunal."

"No. Your victims."

Goose bumps appeared on her arms. She blinked several times. "And if I don't appease them?"

Hesitant to answer, Tony adjusted his slipping sweat-band. When her impatient stare told him he could delay no longer, he continued. "You'll either go completely insane or perish from the heat inside the lodge."

"What will you do with me if I die?" she asked unexpectedly. The slight upward curve of her lips made him think she believed she'd succeed. He returned the smile.

"What would you like me to do?"

"Bury me under a tree by the river, where I'll be cool and can hear the water flowing."

"Lily," he said, broadening his smile as though he thought the subject was silly and irrelevant. "You'll be dead. You won't know."

"Maybe." Her smile faded and she touched his cheek. "But do it anyway, okay?"

"Okay."

Without another word, she bent down and picked up some kindling. They collected wood until the pile overflowed, then gathered more rocks. Lily sometimes nearly staggered from their weight, but she still didn't complain. Finally Tony told her they'd done enough. The sun was heading west, still pouring searing heat on the mesa.

"We'll rest until Mother Earth swallows the sun."

"You don't really think that, do you?"

"Think what?" He picked up a long branch and prodded the fire, driving the stones deeper into the fire.

"That Mother Earth swallows the sun."

He grinned. "Of course not. I'm a college grad."

"Then why do you say it?"

He shrugged, watching a burning log split, its pieces falling between the boulders. The heat used to make him recoil, especially during midsummer, but of late he found he enjoyed it.

"It's poetic. Isn't that reason enough?"

"I bet there's more behind it than that."

He moved to her side, and they began the climb down the steep sides of the mesa toward the river-bank. "Metaphors touch people's feeling place. It's a shaman's job to open that place in others so they can access their own inner guidance."

"But I thought shamans healed."

"It seems that way, but it's the patient who does the healing by drawing on their own resources. The shaman merely helps them do it."

She looked down thoughtfully as she made her way over a particularly treacherous spot. "Do you think I'll survive? Be honest, Tony."

He put a hand on her shoulder. "Only you can know what's inside you, which is what will decide your fate. I believe your strong spirit will carry you through. But you have to believe it too."

They'd reached the river, and Lily moved away without comment, settling on the blanket Tony had spread beneath a cottonwood when they'd arrived. Her gaze went to the parched desert beyond the river oasis, to the water-starved scrub oak, the withering chollas, saguaros, jumping cactus, then on to the low, rounded structure of the sweat lodge.

After some time, she leaned over and began unlacing her boots. Tony watched her, amazed that he enjoyed observing her perform these simple tasks. As if she felt his attention, she looked up, smiled, and patted the spot beside her.

"Tell me about your life before you came to Ebony Canyon." She lifted her eyebrows teasingly. "Are you really a college graduate?"

"Absolutely." He lowered himself onto the blanket, reclining beside her with an elbow on the ground and his head supported by his hand, still watching her.

"I'm a computer engineer. I was the first member of my family to graduate. I even worked at Microsoft for a couple of years."

"Why did you leave it all behind?"

Tony hesitated, reached out to pluck a blade of grass and started nibbling on it. "Tajaya . . . I used to hike on the rim when I was a teenager, and I met her there one day. At first I thought she came from one of the surrounding reservations too. We met for several years before she told me the truth."

He was surprised and a bit dismayed to realize talking about Tajaya hadn't stirred his anger toward Lily. He looked over at her, saw the slender curve of her bare leg. A twig clung to her calf and he leaned to flick it off, expecting the touch to ignite his rage. It didn't, but he wasn't sure he wanted to test it any further.

"Eventually Tajaya introduced me to Star Dancer. We married . . ."

Tony felt a need to stop talking, which Lily must have sensed, because she abruptly said, "Tell me one of your legends instead. I'd like to hear more of White Wolf Woman and Sienna Doe."

"How many have you heard besides the one Star Dancer told?"

"Shala told me a few. The last one was about White Wolf Woman becoming Sienna Doe again."

Glad she'd changed the subject, he sat up, crossed his legs in tailor fashion, then closed his eyes and waited for the spirits to deliver the story. Soon the words came, and he began to talk.

Chapter Twenty-two

Although White Wolf Woman again lived as Sienna Doe, hatred was in the hearts of the Deer People. When they spoke to her, which was seldom, they vented their rage at the loved ones she had taken. She lived among them, yet not one of them, and as the days passed, her loneliness grew until it was a dense stone inside her heart.

Winter came. A hard winter, with many snows, killing the sweet sprigs that usually sprouted on warmer days. The herd grew painfully leaner—some died of hunger—and as their prey dwindled the wolves became bolder.

A snowstorm sent the deer into the dangerous shelter of a one-way canyon, and had now passed, but when the herd prepared to leave they heard wolves yapping and howling near the canyon mouth.

"Sienna Doe," cried Jeshra, a stag who had lost a mate to

her ravenous appetite. "Speak to your brethren the wolves, and ask for safe passage. By this you shall be redeemed."

Of all the Deer People, this stag bore the greatest malice toward her, but Sienna Doe so desired acceptance she bowed her head and backed toward the canyon mouth.

A high alpha wolf waited for her, fangs exposed, flanks tightened to attack. As she approached the wolf, she heard the deer whisper among themselves. "Surely, she shall die, and while the wolves feast on her dead flesh, we shall escape."

Even knowing she'd been sent as sacrifice, White Wolf Woman did not hesitate. Better death at the hands of those who were once her kin, than a life amid those who hated her. Lifting her head proudly, she walked steely-eyed toward the alpha wolf.

She'd returned from her wolf life bigger and stronger than ever before, but she'd never had an opportunity to test her full powers. Now, as the alpha wolf threw himself at her throat, she lifted a foreleg and kicked him, sending him soaring into a tree. Stunned, he gathered himself and flew at her again. Another wolf leaped at her flanks. She kicked both predators into a snowbank. The second wolf collapsed and died with a whimper, but the alpha wolf climbed to his feet and sprang at her again.

He sank his teeth into her shoulder, tearing flesh. Bleeding badly, she reared her hind legs and struck the wolf's head with her sharp hooves. With a half yelp he somersaulted through the air, then collapsed onto the snow-covered ground. This time, he didn't get up.

Leaderless, the other wolves stared at their fallen relations. One let out a mournful howl, then whirled and fled. The others immediately followed.

Tony stopped and opened his eyes. Why had the spirits sent this tale? As much as Lily tried to hide it, he knew she was frightened and thought the Tribunal was an execution squad. It was a misinterpretation he'd fostered, one all his present assurances hadn't changed.

"Go on," she urged, fluttering her hands to draw the words from him.

"It might be better if I didn't."

"So it doesn't come out well?"

"No," he replied flatly.

"Finish it anyway. We've got nothing better to do until sunset."

Although doubting the wisdom of it, Tony lowered his eyelids and went on.

Jeshra ran to Sienna Doe. "You've saved us from certain death," he declared, nudging her with his great rack of antlers as a sign of tribute. "We honor you."

Her heart soared. Finally her brothers and sisters had found forgiveness. She was about to tell him how happy she was to be back, then Jeshra spoke again.

"We now ask that you go into the forest and slay the rest."

Tony fell silent and opened his eyes again. Lily looked at him, her expression growing impatient.

"Is that it?" she asked sharply. "They send her out to certain death?"

"I'm sorry." Tony touched her arm. "The spirits deliver the tales. When I began, I didn't think of how it would . . ."

She tossed her head, jogging loose a strand of hair.

It fell over her eyes, and she brushed it away crossly, then flopped back on the blanket and stared up at the swaying trees. "It's just a story."

"That's right, just a story." Tony lay down beside her, tucked the flyaway strand beneath her damp headband, then took her in his arms. "I'll ask for a happier one."

She wrapped her arms around his neck, put a light kiss on his lips. "Not now."

She kissed him again, lingering this time. Tony nipped at her lower lip. With a sharp intake of breath she deepened the kiss. Tony felt her almost imperceptible tremble and returned her kiss with equal hunger.

"Make love to me, Tony," she breathed against his mouth. "Whisper some colorful poetry into my ears, and let me forget for a short time why we're here."

Tony groaned, involuntarily tightening his hold on her. "We can't, Lily. Such intimacy is expressly forbidden before a Tribunal."

"Forbidden . . ." She rolled out of his arms. "How unfair."

She stared up at the trees again. Behind them the river babbled pleasantly. Birds called out overhead, and occasionally a frog was heard. Then she sat up abruptly, as if she'd made an important decision.

"Please, Tony," she said, unfastening the waistband of her shorts. "I'll take my chances. Please make love to me." She jerked down the zipper and slipped off the shorts in one fluid movement, then fell back against the blanket and looked up at him with hungry eyes. "If I'm to die, at least I'll have that."

Had any others ever joined together beforehand and survived? Would violating the ban cost Lily her life? Lily rolled on her side, slipped her hand beneath the flimsy covering provided by his loincloth. When her fingers touched him there, he immediately came to life, hot with wanting her.

"We shouldn't," he murmured hoarsely. "We mustn't."

She nibbled on his lower lip and flicked her tongue against the sensitive skin inside. "Shh," she whispered against his mouth. "Shh."

Still kissing her, Tony groaned and rolled on top of her, sliding his hands underneath her body and taking her small buttocks in his hands.

Her hand still enclosed him, moving rhythmically up and down. With a smooth twist of her wrist, she dislodged his loincloth, exposing him fully.

She could die during the inquisition, he realized. They both could die, whether they defied the ban or not. A moment like this one might never come again.

He entered her, swiftly, possessively, finding her hot and moist and ready. This time she took him without the urgency of the night before, rotating her hips so sensually he burned with need for her. As she wrapped her legs around his thrusting hips, she suddenly broke their kiss, opened her eyes, and stared pensively into his.

"Tony," she asked in a ragged voice, "did White Wolf Woman survive?"

"Yes, Lily. Yes, she did."

She sighed, tightened her legs around him, then claimed his mouth again.

* * *

Night fell with a blaze of crimson and orange. With obvious reluctance, Tony withdrew his arm from around Lily and stood up. He had put the backpack he'd carried with him from the village not far from the blanket, and now he crossed to it and pulled down the zipper.

Lily sat up, feeling a little light-headed. As custom required, they'd taken neither food nor water since reaching the sweat-lodge site, but she wasn't sure whether her dizziness came from that or was an aftermath of their lovemaking.

She watched Tony's purposeful movements. The drapes of his loincloth had split, displaying the flexing muscles of his thighs, and she licked her parched lips, remembering how they'd felt between her own parted legs. Her skin tingled even now, and she felt another wave of desire.

But his grim expression told her she wouldn't tempt him a second time. With a muffled groan she reached for her discarded shorts.

"You won't need those," Tony said, rising with a buff-colored garment in his hand.

He walked over and handed it to her. "Our women wear these during mixed gender sweats," he said.

She smiled up provocatively. "And what do you wear when you're alone?"

"Nothing," he said curtly, then returned to the backpack.

He came back with his satchel, which he put on the ground. Solemnly, he began taking out items. Lily smelled the aroma of tobacco seeping through the leather wrapping of a small packet, saw a sage stick tightly bound with vines. Then he opened a larger bundle, from which he took the wing of a big bird and a round drum. Next came a clay pot, and he filled this to the brim with water.

"You look like a traveling medicine show," she joked, trying to ease her unrest.

"Talk no more unless it is of these matters," he said with a sharp look.

"Sorry. I didn't realize there was a protocol."

"Lily!"

She jerked her head in assent. Suddenly a bundle of nerves, she climbed to her feet, becoming aware of the soft feel of the garment in her hand. Holding one edge, she let it fall.

It was a shiftlike dress, constructed in the meticulous manner of the tribespeople. Deerskin, she thought, wondering if this was another metaphor. The Dawn People were full of them. She glanced up and saw Tony looking at her.

"It absorbs the heat from your body and makes the fires of the lodge easier to withstand," he said.

She raised her eyebrows in question.

"Yes, it is deerskin, but has nothing to do with the legends. Put it on now. The sun will soon set."

He turned back to the satchel, dumping its remaining contents on the blanket. Then he put the items he'd taken out back inside, except for the clay pot. By the time he finished, Lily had gotten into the dress, which ended at the middle of her thighs and was as soft and supple as her own skin.

When Tony looked up, his eyes widened. "Free your hair, if you will."

Lily untied the thong, and her hair fell around her shoulders. Barefoot, clad only in the dress and the bright scarf around her forehead, she felt suddenly self-conscious beneath Tony's riveted gaze.

"If beauty were any defense, the Tribunal would surely acquit you." His words were so soft they sounded like sighs. "Here," he said, louder and more gruffly, shoving Lily's sandals toward her. "Although shoes aren't allowed inside the lodge, you'll need these for the climb."

She thanked him and slipped the sandals onto her feet. At that he got up, swung the satchel over his shoulder, then bent for the bowl. Cradling it against his chest, he turned to her. "We must go now."

Lily walked behind him, noticing that though he wore only moccasins himself he kicked away the larger rocks to protect her feet, making her ascent relatively easy. When they reached the top, Lily waited beside the blazing fire pit; the colors in its depths matched the sky. Tony hurried toward the lodge, lifted the leather curtain, and put the satchel inside. He came back with an enormous, scorched scoop that appeared to have been carved from a type of gourd.

He scooped out the fiery rocks one by one onto a rusty sheet of metal that had once been the fender of a car. When he'd gathered about a dozen, he looked at Lily. "Help me drag the Stone People to the lodge."

She took one corner of the metal. Horrific heat emanated from the glowing rocks, and perspiration beaded her forehead as they lugged the metal sheet to the sweat lodge.

Although it was dark in the lodge, Lily's keen eyes still saw the smooth dirt floor and the large hole that marked one corner. The eastern corner, she noticed, remembering there was some significance in that location. She asked Tony about it.

"East is the spirits' door to our world."

"Oh, the spirits," she said numbly, looking up at the sky. The colors were fading, and like the nights before, the wind was rising. Surprisingly, she felt no fear, even though she was facing the greatest unknown of her life. Although it was foolish, Tony's affirmation that White Wolf Woman survived her ordeal had given Lily a hope she hadn't possessed earlier.

After kicking off his moccasins, Tony positioned himself in the middle of the sheet of metal, then asked Lily to take hold of the opposite end, adding, "Be careful not to burn your hands."

He pulled and she pushed. When the metal sheet was halfway inside the lodge, Tony raised his hand. He knelt in front of the corner pit and transferred the rocks by means of the gourd. Soon Lily felt as if she were standing in front of a sauna. Only the blowing wind kept her from becoming faint from the intense heat.

When the last rock was in place, Tony pushed the metal aside, then stood and said, "Wait here."

He walked barefoot to a nearby chaparral. Taking

his knife from its sheath at his waist, he cut off a branch and brought it back to the lodge.

"Remove your shoes and enter," he instructed, waiting beside the door.

Lily stooped to clear the low entrance, then fell to her knees and crawled on the leather floor as far as possible from the heated rocks. Tony scooted in behind her and sat in front of the pit. Using the edge of his knife like a razor blade, he sliced leaves off the chaparral branch, dropping them in the clay bowl. This he carefully placed on top of the glowing stones. After that he unwrapped the tobacco packet and put it at the center of the lodge.

Then he shoved the sage stick against the blazing stones. When it began to smolder, he pivoted at the waist to reach toward the door.

The heavy leather curtain fell. Total darkness descended on the small space, and even with the light coming from the pit, Lily could barely see. A trill of panic ran up her spine. The Tribunal was about to convene.

Chapter Twenty-three

Lily's eyes quickly adjusted to the darkness. Although she didn't know how he could stand the heat, Tony remained next to the pit, the glow silhouetting him in the darkness. Now he placed the drum between his legs. His lips moved wordlessly and he began tattooing out a rhythmic beat.

"South," he cried, tilting back his head. "Home of Earth Mother, who was present when life began. We honor you."

The drumming stopped. Lily smelled the scent of sage and saw red flashes as he waved the burning stick in the air.

He made a quarter turn and the drumming resumed. "West. Grandfather Sky, the seed of thought and consciousness. We honor you."

Another waft of sage, another turn, another beating

of the drum. He spoke to the east, honoring the Four-Leggeds for providing guidance and nourishment. As he uttered each prayer, the timbre of his voice grew more impassioned. When he turned to the north his voice rang like a bell.

"North. Home of the Great Spirit, creator of all that the Two-Leggeds know. Send your lords and demi-lords, your spirit guides, your animal guides!"

Thunder shook the sky, rumbling in deafening waves from the north. Although she'd never feared the weather, Lily cringed.

Tony resumed his drumming, raising the crescendo until it filled the lodge with a mighty song rivaling the thunder outside. As the beat slowed, growing quieter, gentler, Tony said, "The Storm Gods have heard our call. It's a good omen."

"Good?" Lily repeated shakily.

"Yes, very good. Now rise on your knees."

She did as he asked, and he fluttered the bird wing above her skin, starting at the ground and moving gradually up her body. It created a heavenly breeze and Lily let her head drop back. Her eyes closed.

"Your daughter is here, Great Spirit. Her heart is open to your guidance. Steer her well as she meets her accusers."

Lily's eyes snapped open. For an inane moment, she thought of how her mother would respond to Tony's prayer. Ridiculous! Superstitious! But Lily's experiences of what lay beyond sight and sense did not allow her to share those sentiments. She knew these things existed. Her firsthand knowledge was of dark powers, though, and she had no faith the powers of light would appear—at least for her.

"How can the Great Spirit steer me, Tony? I don't see or hear him. I don't even sense him."

"You will, when the need arises. In the meantime, I'm your advocate in these proceedings. I'll share your visions and know what you experience. But you have to ask for my help. No matter what happens, don't forget I'm by your side. When all seems lost, turn to me." He leaned forward then and rested his hand lightly on her hip. "I fear for you, Lily. We shouldn't have made love."

She took his hand in hers. Although her own skin was already growing clammy, his was dry. "It was worth it."

Then she smiled, sank to the ground, and gave herself over to what was coming.

Arlan Ravenheart shivered as he led Sebastian and his pack through the darkening maze. The King had been impatient to find his lost Queen, and had rushed them from the cave before the sun had fully set.

He tried to concentrate on finding small signs that the maze had been disturbed. He'd assisted in reroutings himself many times and knew what to look for—a broken branch, a freshly cut twig, grass trampled by many feet, then raked back to conceal the damage. But the wind had picked up, bringing the scent of impending rain, and the stiff breeze made him shiver even in the sultry night. His limbs still ached from the rigors of alchemizing.

His companions appeared untroubled by the changing weather and moved stealthily over the pine carpet of the forest even as he struggled to keep from clumsily snapping twigs, a difficulty he'd never had in human form.

"This way," he said to Beryl, who'd remained close to his side, but was now veering off into a dead end. Beryl growled, moving uncomfortably close to Ravenheart's shoulder.

Nor was he as tall as they, he realized. Beryl topped him by half a foot or more. This new state hadn't delivered the power he'd expected. And when the others had dragged in the elk and expected him to dine on the ripped, raw meat, he'd almost gagged. Was this common for an omega? None of them would explain and had soon grown cross with his ceaseless questions, laughing and nipping at him like the runt of the litter.

"This is the correct path," he assured Beryl, who was looking at him suspiciously. The wolf Prince didn't like him, although he didn't know why. Perhaps Sebastian's protection had raised his ire.

Ravenheart stopped and looked back at the King, who was strolling in a lordly manner behind Ravenheart and Beryl, followed by the remaining seven. "Swear again, you will spare my people, and only take Lily and the shaman's kin from the village."

"A werewolf always keeps a promise," Sebastian barked. "And I promised to hurt no one unless they attack first."

"Yes, Lord," Ravenheart replied quickly. "Of course."

Sebastian's sly smile made him uneasy. Something wasn't right. But at least he could shape-shift, something White Hawk couldn't do. Surely, he would harness these new powers in due time. This wasn't a mistake, he assured himself.

No, he'd made no mistake. None.

Ravenheart stopped, raising his hand. Through the trees he saw people milling around the fires. Sentries were posted beside the entrance, standing with their hands on their knives. Old Frieda leaned on her cane, taking her slow nightly stroll around the perimeter of the village.

Beryl grunted something in the werewolves' language that Ravenheart vaguely knew meant that those behind them should also stop. He was already learning their tongue, although how he could do this in one day was beyond his comprehension.

Sebastian cocked his enormous head and pricked his ears. He frowned unpleasantly, then sniffed the air.

"Lily and the shaman are not here!" he roared.

Ravenheart cringed. The people by the fires pivoted their heads toward the maze. The two warriors at the entrance drew their knives, then reached into the pockets of their sheath belts. Whoops rose from the edges of the forest.

Dozens of warriors rushed toward the maze, arms raised and holding spears. Frieda, who was only feet away, shrank against her walking stick.

The werewolves bristled and howled in unison. "Change," Sebastian ordered, melting into full wolf form. His eight minions fell in line, their forms melting until they stood on all fours. Ravenheart tried to obey, but the agony was so intense that by the time he'd alchemized, the others were barreling toward the approaching warriors.

Suddenly the air was filled with noxious fumes. The wolves at the forefront gasped. One let out a pitiful cry and fell to the ground.

"Fall back," Sebastian choked out. His wolf body now had a human head. One paw had turned into a hand. Lumbering awkwardly, he retreated into the maze. Beryl and the other wolves turned and began slithering for shelter. Ravenheart fell on his haunches, horrified.

Then he gasped like the others. His body began to spontaneously alchemize, but not as painfully as before. The other werewolves slunk past, giving him little heed. Ravenheart stared down at his fingers, then turned to look at the fleeing werewolves, remembering Sebastian's last words before the chaos began: Lily wasn't in the village.

He moved his gaze to Frieda. The warriors were swarming around her, rushing toward the entrance of the maze. Ravenheart could smell her fear, hear the boom of her pulse straining to race through her calcified arteries. He felt a hunger unlike anything he'd ever known, not even in his darkest moments of hating White Hawk.

Pretending not to hear Sebastian's orders to follow him, Ravenheart ducked into the shelter of some bushes and waited until the warriors passed him. Then he stepped out of the maze.

"Arlan!" Frieda exclaimed. "You are alive."

He rushed forward, taking her in his arms as an expression of reunion. "Yes," he breathed hastily. "The werewolves captured me and were planning to trade me for Lily. But I escaped."

"Praise the spirits," she replied. "If the man-wolves had learned Lily is not here they surely would have slain you."

"Not here?" He inhaled deeply. Even in human form he could smell the salty scent of her skin, could almost smell her blood.

"No." Frieda leaned heavily on her cane and looked up at him. "She has gone with White Hawk to meet the Tribunal."

Ravenheart let go of Frieda and stepped back. She'd given him what he needed. Her usefulness had ended. At least while she was alive. He looked toward the fires. Everyone had scattered. He and Frieda were standing in the shadows out of view and he was sure no one had seen them.

"Follow me," he said. "I have something to show you in the forest."

Frieda had no reason to doubt him. She'd always liked him, regarded him as a powerful warrior who was destined to be a shaman. He moved into the dark shelter of a tree and waited as she cautiously made her way, eyes downcast to check for obstacles.

Already the changes were coming, and he bit his lips to keep from crying out. When Frieda reached the tree, she looked up trustingly, then gasped. Ravenheart felt a brief regret as his fangs closed around her stringy neck. He felt her scream, although it never left her lips. She collapsed against him, limp and lifeless. Sweeping her into his arms, he broke into a lope, his only aim to get far enough from the warriors and werewolves to feed alone on his bony kill.

Tony ladled water on the stones. Steam filled the lodge so densely Lily couldn't see. She felt weak and nauseous and unable to sit. Moaning softly, she fell to her side. Compared to the heat above, the leather felt cool against her cheek, and she pressed closer to it, seeking relief.

The voices came.

"I had three children who grew up without me," a young woman cried.

"My wife and sons were forced to live on the streets," a man accused.

"Because I was not there to heal them, half of my village died from a plague."

Lily looked up. The woman was barely past her teenaged years. The man was tall and strong. The middle-aged woman wore a peasant's shift; a medallion signifying she was a white witch hung around her neck.

"No, no," Lily moaned, clutching the crystal at her breasts and curling into a ball. "Go away. None of you are real."

Suddenly she was in a field, running on the four legs of a wolf. The man ahead of her glanced back in terror, his feet trampling the crops in his attempt to elude her. She narrowed the space between them and his face contorted in fear. She lunged. . . . The scene changed. A woman wearing black hugged two small boys who wept over an open grave. Two children clung to the legs of a grief-stricken man; he held a wailing baby in his arms. A mass of quaintly clothed people mourned their recent dead.

The steam swirled, then Morgan stood before her. "You ripped my life away," he said, "and cursed me with a living hell."

"You would have squashed me like a beetle," Dana Gibbs cried.

Lily's head spun, and another vision arose. Jorje at her side, racing through the pines toward the enticing scent of live human flesh. Dusk was falling. They were in wolf shape, and she savored the feel of the ground beneath her paws, the wind ruffling her silver coat.

"There," Jorje said in Lupinese, skidding to a stop. A meadow lay just beyond the edge of the trees. He crept forward. Lily followed, eagerly anticipating their first mortal kill in more than a week. A woman knelt on the ground, humming as she plucked various plants and tossed them in a basket.

One of those elusive Dawn People, she thought. What satisfaction this kill would bring. Jorje inched closer, licking his muzzle.

"I'll take the little one," he said.

Little one? Lily's head moved beyond the woman. Not far away, a small child, barely old enough to walk, toddled after a butterfly.

"No!" she said.

But Jorje sprang from the cover of the trees and darted into the meadow. The woman raised her head.

Her startled blue eyes, streaked with shades of lapis, widened in terror and she leaped up to run toward the baby.

"Noooo!" Lily screamed the order this time, tearing after Jorje. He was almost on the child now. She continued shouting, but so intent was he on capturing his morsel, he didn't hear.

Lily alchemized to man-wolf shape, and vaulted over the space separating them. She landed in front of the child just as Jorje prepared to lunge. The mother was speeding toward them now, her battle cries filling the air. She had a gleaming knife in her hand, the rage of a mother bear upon her face.

"Take the mother," Lily commanded. "She is yours."

She bent down and swept the baby from the ground. A girl, she realized, noticing the feminine beading on her short hemp smock. A defenseless, fragile little girl. The child was crying now, distressed by her mother's whoops, frightened by the hairy creature that held her.

Lily cradled the girl against her chest and whirled toward the forest. As she entered, she heard the woman's final whoop abruptly end. Careening through the forest, burning up the ground, she ran down, down, deeper into the desert terrain she so despised.

The child calmed down, curled her hands into Lily's coat, hanging on. Soon they reached the brush and trees of the river. The unnavigable maze was not far ahead. She heard movement inside, still a distance away, but approaching. The warriors had heard the woman's screams. She waited by the entrance, rocking the baby in her arms, unwilling to leave her undefended.

A small hand brushed her cheek. Lily looked down and saw the girl staring at her with eyes identical to her mother's. The child explored Lily's face, touched her eyes, her short muzzle, then reached for her pointed ears. She gurgled and her face broke into a smile.

Lily felt a wave of tenderness she'd never known before. She smiled back. At the sight of fangs, the girl's face twisted and she broke into a keening wail.

The sound must have reached the warriors' ears. Lily heard their voices, loud and close and alarmed for the child. Sadly, she put the crying baby down and turned away.

Returning to wolf form she sped toward the meadow. She wouldn't punish Jorje. She'd initiated him just recently so she'd have company on the solitary journey to Ebony Canyon at Sebastian's command. The wolfling was being true to his new nature. He was slow too, slower than most; it might take years before he attained even beta status. He'd undoubtedly forgotten her instructions that they always spared the children.

It wasn't his fault.

She found Jorje among the dandelions and sunflowers, basking in the sun and licking blood off his muzzle.

It wasn't *his* fault.

Chapter Twenty-four

Lily shivered; chills ran through her body. Vaguely she realized no one shivered in the heat. Where was she?

Her eyelids fluttered up, but she lacked the strength to keep them open, and they closed again. She rolled into a ball, trying to get warm. Her skin felt hot and dry, and as cold as she was she also felt feverish.

Something wet touched her head. Water trickled into her hair, streamed down her face, and onto her neck. It should have made her colder, but it didn't, and she rolled onto her back, welcoming it.

Rain? Again she wondered where she was.

The water was all over now. On the leather dress, running down her legs, her arms, moistening her hands and feet. Someone lifted her shoulders and then she was sliding across the leather floor.

Light struck her closed eyes. Heat beat down on her bare arms and legs. Through her misery she realized they'd been in the lodge all night. Then a glorious wind caressed her, taking the fever, taking the chills. Strong arms lifted her from the ground, cradling her against smooth, damp skin.

She lifted her eyelids, squinted at Tony's face, and saw his worried gaze. She smiled weakly.

"I survived?" Her voice was less than a whisper.

"You survived." He was smiling too, hugging her fiercely against his bare chest, his breathing ragged. Lily wanted to cry, but couldn't, so she just inhaled his glorious scent. He straightened up, moved his legs, and she surmised he was slipping into his moccasins.

A moment later he carried her down the steep side of the mesa. Then they were at the river, and he waded in. Wordlessly, he splashed cooling water over her, then let her float, supporting her with one hand as she turned and dipped, at times submerging herself completely.

Soon she could stand on her own, but she was too tired to walk. Tony scooped her up again and took her to the blanket under the trees. After draping a second blanket over her soaked body, he lay down beside her and took her in his arms.

"Sleep," he said. "We'll rest during sunlight and start again come dusk."

"It isn't over?"

Flinching at the alarm in her voice, he shook his head. "You did fine," he said. "Don't think about it now. Just rest."

She snuggled into the crook of his arms, needing him near, feeling peaceful despite the horrors she'd just faced.

Just as she was about to drop off, Tony spoke. "Why didn't you tell me?"

She didn't ask what he meant. "You wouldn't have believed me."

He brought her close to his heart, then whispered, "I do now."

As she fell into slumber, she thought he said he loved her and sadly feared she'd heard him wrong.

Sebastian was waiting for Arlan Ravenheart when he returned to the cave just before dawn, the sly smile again on his face, although he was now in human form.

"So you had your first taste of mortal flesh, wolf-ling," he said. "Incomparable, is it not?"

Ravenheart licked his muzzle. The taste still lingered, tantalizing and fulfilling. "Yes, Lord." Then fearing the King's anger might emerge, he offered, "I've learned where Lily is."

Sebastian rubbed his hands together in satisfaction. "Excellent. Where do we find her?"

"She has gone with White Hawk to a sweat lodge in the desert."

"Nearby?"

"Near enough for us. We can be there in an hour."

"And the shaman is with her," Sebastian asked with great interest, stroking his chin. "Good. I have a score to settle with him."

He strode past the mass of sleeping followers, all

huddled together in wolf form on the filthy rug, and crossed to Beryl, who slept as a human on a mat several feet from the others. He nudged Beryl with his toe. "Wake up."

Beryl groggily lifted his head and peered up with sleepy eyes. "W-what is it?"

Sebastian moved back and draped a proud arm over Ravenheart's shoulder. "This young one has informed me that Lily is with the shaman at a sweat lodge not far from here. He is a wondrous wolfling, is he not?"

Ravenheart preened under the werewolf's praise. At last the recognition he so sorely deserved. Beryl rolled off the mat and climbed to his feet. He kicked the others and as a group they sprang awake.

"News from our Lord," Beryl said, his voice heavy with hostility.

The seven omegas sat up, giving Sebastian their full and respectful attention.

"Alchemize to man-shape," Sebastian ordered. Although some of them whimpered, all obeyed.

"Arlan has brought news of Lily's whereabouts. We leave at dusk to bring her back into our fold. The shaman is fair game and belongs to the one who reaches him first."

"Will this earn us favor in your eyes, Lord?" Philippe asked.

Sebastian smiled so broadly his teeth gleamed even in the dim light inside the cave. "Indeed it shall," he said. "Indeed it shall."

Still enclosed in Sebastian's approving embrace,

Ravenheart couldn't keep a smirk off his face. The King didn't notice, but Beryl did. As he returned the envious alpha werewolf's glare, Ravenheart thought not only of the reward killing White Hawk would earn, but of the pleasure he'd take in feasting on the shaman's flesh.

Lily's mind surged with every beat of Tony's drum and ebbed with every chant he uttered. Night had come so soon, too soon, and thunder rumbled above the roof of the lodge once more. She drifted . . .

Adults of all shapes and ages glowered at her. "My son. . . ." An old woman wept. "The light of my life."

"You took my husband," cried another.

"My brother was my best friend. You didn't leave enough of him to bury."

"I couldn't help myself," Lily cried out in defense.

They faded. Children appeared. Hundreds of them, from infancy to adolescence.

"You took my parents," accused a blond boy. He looked about Shala's age, young and vulnerable. "My grandparents don't like me. All I did was get mud on the kitchen floor, and they sent me to my room for days."

A baby wailed, its thoughts filled with images of lying abandoned in a crib. A dark-eyed toddler screamed, unable to comprehend why her parents hadn't returned.

One after another they spilled their tales. Their cries increased, hammering at Lily's ears. She curled up, pressing her hands to her head, trying to block out their accusations.

An Hispanic teenager swaggered forth, his eyes dark with loathing. He wore a battered leather jacket. A gold earring glinted dully from one ear. "My parents had hopes for me," he spat. "I was an athlete, an honor student. The first of our family to be accepted to college." He bent forward until his nose almost touched hers. "Without them, I was lost. Strangers fed me, but gave me no love. Then I found friends. They showed me another way."

He turned. The name Crips, emblazoned on the back of his jacket, was ripped clean through by a gaping, oozing hole. "I was shot during a war with a rival gang. At fifteen, my life wiped out. Our dreams are gone . . .

"Gone . . . gone."

She hadn't realized . . . hadn't even thought . . . The agony she'd caused went far beyond the ones she'd slain. How could she ever atone for this? No spirit, no angel, no god, would ever forgive her. She buried her head in her hands, filled with the remorse she'd scorned for so long. "I didn't think . . ." She gasped. "I didn't know. I—I—I didn't . . ."

"Lily, the crystal," she heard someone say from far away. She was forgetting something—something important that the same voice had told her so long ago. She was supposed to turn . . . turn . . . turn to . . .

Then someone started screaming. One of her victims? One of those small orphaned ones? Who?

When Lily realized they were her screams, she scrambled to her hands and knees and crawled rapidly toward the door. She couldn't bear this anymore! She would go mad or die from the weight of her regret!

"No, Lily, don't," cried the disembodied voice.

She gave it no heed and slithered beneath the leather curtain. Wind yanked at her hair. Fat drops of rain fell on her head, cooling her burning body. She sprang to her feet, racing down the steep mesa. Rocks and brambles nicked her feet, but she barely noticed. She was fleeing from all she had been. Fleeing from the fear it was all she'd ever be.

The sky exploded, dumping bucketfuls of water on the earth. The wind blew fiercely as if the spirits were trying to hold her back. She thought she heard someone call her name, but the words got lost in the gale.

"Lily! Lily!" There, the words came again.

She looked back and saw Tony barreling down the slope. Lightning flashed, and his brown body glistened with raindrops. Already, water cascaded over the edges of the mesa, forming streams that churned the clay soil.

Tony slipped in the mud and windmilled his arms for balance. Regaining his footing, he called her name again.

Lily kept on running.

Then she heard him cry out. She spun on the desert floor and saw him tumbling down the slope. He crashed into a boulder at the bottom, then fell heavily at its base.

He didn't move. Lily waited, but he remained very still. Water gushed around him. Suddenly Lily's own torment meant nothing. She loved this man, but even if he'd been a stranger, she now vowed no one would ever again suffer from her actions, no matter how indirectly.

She sped to him, nearly falling herself as her feet lost purchase on the rain-slick ground. When she reached his side, she dropped to her knees.

"Tony . . ." Her heart hammered as she looked down on his motionless form, then eased when she saw the regular rise and fall of his chest. Bending over, she ran frantic hands along his limbs, checking for blood, misshapen bone, calling his name again and again.

His lids fluttered. Lily straightened abruptly and he opened his eyes. Falling on his stirring form, she dropped kisses everywhere. On his forehead, his cheeks, his naked shoulders, his mud-splattered chest.

"Whoa . . ." he said weakly, turning his head to catch her final kiss on his lips.

"Can you get up?" she asked, wanting to make absolutely certain he was all right.

"I, uh . . . I'm not sure . . ." He sat up and gingerly stretched his limbs, grunting from the effort. Touching a spot on his ribs, he winced. "Hurts. But nothing seems broken. Must've just had the breath knocked out of me."

He gave his body a double-check, then looked at her. "You came back . . . For me?"

"Yes."

Using the boulder as support, Tony levered himself to his feet. He took his time getting his balance before letting go and standing straight.

"We must go back," he said gravely.

Lily's eyes darted involuntarily to the lodge. Sitting high on the mesa, it seemed under assault by the intensity of the storm. It wasn't too late. She could still run. But Tony was staring at her imploringly, waiting for her answer. When she'd looked down at his motionless body she'd thought he was gone, lost to her forever. It had been more than she could bear.

"Yes," she repeated softly.

He took her arm and they started the treacherous climb back to the lodge, one or the other of them losing balance several times. As Lily righted herself once again, the fine hairs on her body bristled. She paused, turning to look at the riverbank.

"What is it?" Tony asked.

A howl rose above the cacophony of the storm. Another followed. Soon the sounds joined with the thunder and lightning in unholy discord.

"Sebastian's here!"

Tony turned from the howls and mentally measured the distance to the lodge. "We've left sacred ground," he told Lily. "We have no protection."

He was more familiar with the treachery of a desert storm, so he took her arm, supporting her, forcing her to practically leap up the slick mud slope. Soon his ribs throbbed. He almost lost her, and when he twisted to keep her from falling, he grunted and doubled over. Lily bent and ran her hands along his ribs and asked him if he could go on.

Then the wolves were at the base of the mesa, hunkering on all fours. Forcing himself beyond his pain,

Tony took Lily's hand and began the last leg of their slippery climb.

Suddenly Sebastian was ahead of them in man-wolf form. He ripped Lily away from Tony, scooping her into his arms, then whirled and sped down the slope. Lily kicked and screamed in his arms, but couldn't break free. Not wasting a single breath on words, Tony projected the hawk into the air to follow Lily, then turned to pursue.

From the base of the mesa, eight pairs of hungry eyes glinted red in the lightning flashes. Crouching, they slunk forward. Tony wrenched his knife from its sheath and began cautiously backing up the slope. The lodge was only feet away, but judging by the swiftness with which Sebastian took the hill, the four-legged ones would be on him in an instant.

Taking a chance, Tony pivoted and took the remaining distance in long, rib-splitting strides. When he was within feet of the door, he fell to the ground and rolled beneath the curtain. His side screamed in agony, and he held it as he crouched by the fire. His breath came in excruciating heaves.

The wolves let out an angry howl. One came crashing through the curtain. It yelped, somersaulted, rolled out the way it had come. Another tried and left just as quickly, *ki-yi-yi-ing* with pain.

None of the others attempted to enter. Except for the roar of the rainstorm, all was silent on the other side of the curtain. Then Tony heard feet approaching. Not the even beat of four paws on the ground, but the sound of a creature walking upright.

"Another time, Shaman," someone snarled through the curtain.

"Arlan?" Tony asked, sure he recognized the voice. "We thought you were dead."

"Yes, I'm alive. More alive than I have ever been. I am one of the Lupine now, and I shape-shift with ease. Soon you, Riva, and that mewling offspring of yours shall serve as our dinner. None shall mourn your names."

Tony's heart filled with pity. "It might not be too late," he said. "Lily has ways . . . She could restore you."

"Bah! I do not wish to be restored. I am destined for greater things. When the People pass into Quakahla I shall rule them in the ways of old."

"Arlan . . ."

But he was gone. Tony knew it by the way the Stone People flared again, filling the lodge with light.

Although he hated to lose sight of Lily, who was still pounding her fists on Sebastian's back, he called back the hawk. Its eyes soon told him the wolves had truly gone, and a few minutes later he saw them scurrying after their king.

He had no smelling salts, nor had he advised Lily to bring the sanctified water. They were to stay in the sacred lodge by night, and werewolves seldom ventured out by day except in human form.

His ribs still throbbing, he moved through the curtain, the knife in his hand. The raptor was again rising and falling with the currents above Sebastian's head. Lily had stopped struggling. From what she'd told him, he knew Sebastian's plan had been to return her to his pack. But what now? Had she angered him so much his plans had changed?

Tony started down the perilous side of the mesa, taking minimal care, his only goal to reach Lily while she was still alive. What he would do when he got there, with only his knife and the hawk to aid him, he didn't know.

Chapter Twenty-five

Tony raced along the river trail. The hawk's eyes told him Lily was as yet unharmed, but had no way of escaping. The pack was miles ahead of him. He compelled his legs to move faster. They gave him their best, which wasn't enough, and he considered sending the hawk in to attack. But even the agile raptor couldn't take on nine werewolves. Should it be injured, Tony would feel the pain as acutely as if he'd received the blows himself.

He'd never catch up this way. His only hope was to meld with his thought-form, glide down from the sky, and shape-shift to human form when he landed near the werewolves. He'd done it before. Surely the gift would come again.

Delving deep into his psyche, he willed himself to join with the hawk. He waited for the merging to occur as it had in New York and again at the Clearing of the Black Hands, but instead of feeling talons drawn against a feathered underbelly, he felt human feet pounding the riverbank. He tried a second time, again without success.

When his third attempt also failed, Tony's frustration mounted. As he fought off despair, he heard a small voice inside him speak: *Call on me in your hour of need.*

"Brother, I need you," he cried, more from hopelessness than faith that Bear would appear.

Suddenly, instead of looking down from the air, as his thought form had been doing, he saw leaves and pine needles. He moved with an awkward gait that still managed to deliver considerable speed. As the thought-form turned its head, he saw a round brown nose and got a glimpse of white shaggy fur.

Bear had heeded his call.

Rain fell in sheets off the leaves of the towering trees, soaking Lily to her bones. She bounced miserably in Sebastian's arms as he ate up the trail with his long strides. She'd almost forgotten how monstrously tall werewolves were. If he let go, she'd drop more than five feet.

Tony's safety concerned her the most. Her heart had fairly stopped when the hawk disappeared a short while before. But now it glided above them again, giving out an occasional shrill cry.

The rest of the pack had joined them, most retaining their wolf form. Beryl and Ravenheart, however, had returned to the man-wolf shape, and the latter wore an arrogant expression as he jogged behind Sebastian. With relief, Lily noticed that none of them showed signs of recent feeding, giving her additional hope for Tony's safety.

"Let me go, Sebastian!" she demanded again, although her earlier cries had fallen on deaf ears.

Sebastian lowered his muzzle until it touched her ear. "Give me no orders, bitch. You forfeited your queenly status the night you slayed the wolfling."

The old defenses sprang to Lily's lips: Sebastian had insisted she go after Morgan; Jorje had been about to kill him; she never would have—

Those excuses didn't work anymore.

"Yes, I killed Jorje," she replied sadly. "I'll live with that for the rest of my days. Take me back if you like, but you'll only be stuck with a sniveling mortal. I'll never go into the ceremonial ring."

Sebastian hesitated, the idea obviously troubling him. "You have no powers now, Lily. Do not pretend you do."

But she did. Although she had no idea what they were. If she alchemized now, how would she fare? Without fangs or claws, could she defend herself? She was five feet tall. They were nearly eight. Still, the element of surprise might cause enough confusion to let her escape.

She willed her alchemization.

Nothing happened. She tried again. Still nothing. Dismayed, she absently brought her hand to the crystal, thinking about Tony, where he was, whether he was hurt. She must find him. The crystal grew warm against her fingers.

Sebastian groaned suddenly, his pace turning choppy. Lily was so lost in thought she gave him little notice. The gem in her hand was hot now, warming the chill in her body.

As soon as she found Tony and knew he was safe, she'd return to the sweat lodge. The Tribunal was incomplete. Although its outcome remained nebulous, she suddenly knew she'd never find peace unless she finished the inquisition.

Escape, she must. But how?

Sebastian's groan accelerated to a whimper, tearing Lily from her thoughts. She looked at his face and saw his muzzle wrinkling with pain. He stumbled. His grip on her relaxed.

Lily seized the moment. Twisting, she jumped from his arms, landing bent-legged on the soggy ground. He didn't try to recapture her. Instead his hands flew to the sides of his head. His whimper turned into an agonized howl. Staring at him in puzzlement, Lily wondered if his agony had something to do with the crystal in her hand. It practically thrummed now, pulsing with so much heat it was slightly uncomfortable to hold.

Beryl and Ravenheart moved beside their king. "What is it, Lord?" Beryl asked.

"Stop . . . stop Lily," Sebastian croaked, grinding his hands into his head.

Just as the pair converged on her, the forest came

alive with noise. Hands still pressing on his head, Sebastian turned stiffly. His companions whirled.

A huge bear was charging at them, rain skittering off a shaggy coat, mud splattering beneath the force of gargantuan feet. Lily took it in with wide-eyed shock. What was this massive creature who barreled down on them so determinedly?

Enemy? she asked herself. Or friend?

From the riverbank, Tony saw the werewolves and felt the bear's massive head lower. The wolves had turned, prepared for battle, but Bear surprised the closest one with a swipe of his paw before it fully registered his presence. The wolf rolled with a yelp, then crouched to defend itself. Raising on hind legs, the bear lumbered forward and dropped on the wolf's back. When he reared again, the wolf didn't get up.

Now the pack was howling and caterwauling. Several shifted to the larger man-wolf shape. Up ahead, Sebastian held his head as if it were splitting apart. Lily stood before him, hand on the gemstone, appearing paralyzed by the sight of the rampaging bear. Ravenheart and another taller werewolf stayed close to their king, disregarding his orders to move in on Lily.

Still speeding beside the river in his human body, Tony's head suddenly swirled. He lost consciousness for the space of a breath. Then he was looking through the bear's eyes, feeling a rocking motion as his enormous body swayed above the approaching pack.

He had become the bear.

A wolf was in midair, aiming at his throat, and he

fell back on all fours, tossed his head, and caught the wolf's forelegs in his teeth. Shaking it brutally, he pitched it into the muddy runoff at the edge of the path. Another wolf flew forward, met Tony's swinging paw, and soared into the trees. Then a man-wolf approached, eyes blazing, fangs bared.

Tony rose on two legs again, wrapped his front ones around the charging beast. Sharp fangs punctured his shoulder, but still he held on. Two wolves hammered at his back, nipping and tearing. The man-wolf fought fiercely, driving a hind leg into Tony's stomach, its sharp claws tearing fur and flesh. Barely noticing his wounds, Tony upped the pressure of his hold to bone-crushing intensity.

He heard the spine snap even before the werewolf felt it. Its livid eyes widened in surprise, glazed. Then it grew limp. Tony let it slide to the ground as he whirled to deal with the two animals savaging his back.

One of the wolves fell off, landing on its fallen companion, its muzzle sinking into the muddy runoff. The other jumped down, hunkering on the ground, lips drawn back and revealing dripping fangs. Another man-wolf stood behind it. Still keeping an eye on them, Tony lifted his head to seek out Lily.

She was backing away from Sebastian, holding the crystal spear in front of her like a weapon. The minions stood protectively at their leader's side.

"Get her," Sebastian barked.

Beryl instantly lunged forward, but Ravenheart merely looked at his master. "The gem, Lord. It is enchanted. We cannot—"

"Get her!"

Reluctantly, Ravenheart moved to join Beryl, who even now was closing a hand on Lily's shoulder. A *ki-yi-yi* abruptly left Beryl's mouth. He fell to his knees. Ravenheart stopped in midstep.

Lily bolted for the forest. Although Sebastian bellowed orders, neither Ravenheart nor the fallen werewolf moved to obey. Whirling, he bayed, "Philippe!"

The man-wolf in front of Tony turned at the shout, heard the second order—"Catch, Lily!"—and dashed into the forest. The four-legged wolf backed up, whirled and joined his packmate.

Tony let his head drop. His body throbbed from the aftermath of the battle, but he didn't care. Lily was safely in the woods. He hoped the driving rain and wind would soon conceal her from her pursuers, but failing that, he hoped the crystal would protect her.

A few yards down the trail Sebastian and the others seemed like apparitions in the heavy downpour. They had their eyes on him, he knew, gauging him, assessing their chances, but eventually they departed in the opposite direction.

Tony sank to the ground. Bear's wounds were deep, and he shared every one of them. He needed to shapeshift soon, before it was too late.

He wasn't sure he could.

Her journey had taken eons, it seemed. Sebastian, of course, had sent others after her. Lily knew their keen ears could catch her slightest move, but she was running downwind, so they couldn't smell her. A few times she was sure they'd lost her trail, but then she heard them again. They got dangerously close at one point, and she hid in the bushes, doing her best not to fidget as branches scratched her face and water spilled fat, cold drops on her head.

She heard Philippe grumbling to another in Lupinese, saying Sebastian should forget about her. The second one told him not to blaspheme, but Philippe was obviously too disgruntled about creeping through the forest to stop complaining.

Lily almost smiled. Philippe had always been a city lover, preferring sidewalk cafés over these more primitive haunts. She'd shared his preference . . . but that had been another life.

Soon the pair drifted off, and when Lily was sure they weren't coming back, she crept from her hiding place and edged back to the riverside trail. Years of flooding had covered it with a fine silt that sopped up the rain and cushioned her footfalls, which was easier on her battered bare feet.

As she sped along, she finally gave thought to the bear. Where had it come from? Arizona did have them—black ones, an occasional brown, all small-bodied berry eaters. But a giant grizzly, pure white in color? Such creatures didn't exist in this part of the world.

Lightning flashed, silhouetting the dome of the sweat lodge, and Lily pulled one last burst of speed from her legs until she reached the base of the mesa.

Digging her bare toes into its slick sides, she climbed toward the lodge. Her body was a mass of scratches and bruises from the careless claws of werewolves, the battering from the wind-tossed branches. The perilous climb was made more so by the ferocity of the storm. But she would have *crawled* through the mud if that's what it took. Tony was inside, well and safe. She knew he was and wouldn't let herself think otherwise.

She just wished the hawk hadn't vanished when the bear arrived. Refusing to dwell on that, she told herself there was an explanation. Soon her faith would be rewarded. Very soon. She was almost at the top.

Then her feet hit firmer soil and she dashed for the lodge.

"Tony! Tony!" She ripped the curtain open. A distressed cry immediately left her lips.

Heartsick, Lily fell to her knees on the threshold and buried her face in her hands. Rain beat on her back. The curtain flopped against the outside wall, making a sick noise reminiscent of a death knell.

Could she go on without him? Not just with the inquisition, but with the remainder of her life? She'd never known tenderness before, and now that she had, could she live without it?

A wind gust blew the heavy curtain through the door, which struck her shoulders and sent her tumbling to the floor. Hot tears stung her eyes, and she angrily rocked to a sitting position and yanked the curtain closed. It throbbed like a bellows from the force of the wind, but stayed in place. Having tamed the wind, she looked around. The drum, the tobacco, the wand of sage were all in place. The Stone People glowed at her from their home in the east corner.

For once, she welcomed their warmth. Alone and staring at a fiery doorway that called forth the spirits, a sob stirred in Lily's chest. She choked it back, determined not to cry. Tony was out there somewhere, alive.

But with Sebastian's pack on the prowl he was in deadly danger. And she was to blame. Her impulsive, cowardly flight from the inquisition had put him at risk.

Shala had already lost a mother because of her. Had she now cost the girl her father too? Could Shala even endure this second loss or would that bubbly enthusiasm leave her big blue eyes for good?

This stirred memories of the children who'd come in her vision—the motherless and fatherless ones, the orphans. She gazed into the coals, realizing it was time to face the Tribunal again. The belligerent boy who'd lost his life to crime had not finished his accusation.

Leaning forward, she scooped water from the clay bowl and dropped it on the stones. Steam rose. She dipped out another ladleful, then another.

Soon the lodge filled with mist. She felt light-headed once more. . . .

CRIPS—large block letters, dripping with blood against a field of black. Slowly the field revolved. A dark angry gaze came into view.

Could she survive this without Tony's help?

With a fearful sigh she stretched out beside the pit, knowing she was about to find out.

Chapter Twenty-six

"What do you say to me, monster?"

Lily gazed into the boy's agonized eyes and took in the small scar beneath his shaved-off hair, the colorful scarf around his neck. What could she say? She'd taken everything from this child without a second thought.

"I'm sorry . . ." Weak, pitiful, no excuse, but it was all she had to offer.

The boy smiled, his teeth bright and even. His jacket dissolved, replaced by an oversized polo shirt. His hair turned thick and black. Then he was gone.

Lily drifted in a fog until a voice brought her back.

"You created me!" it accused.

"Jorje?" Lifting her head, Lily met the wolfling's recriminating stare.

"He whom you made, you destroyed? How could you, Lily?"

You were about to kill Morgan . . . . But she didn't say it. She knew better now. Had she not been so overwrought over the success of Dana's ceremony, had she not feared Sebastian's wrath, she could have saved Morgan without slaying her dear companion.

"You served me well, dear one, and I repaid you poorly."

"Poorly? You killed me!" Jorje stood up, an act rendered impossible by the low ceiling, Lily dimly realized, but he did so nonetheless. Then she gave it no further thought. Jorje had bared his fangs, raised his clawed hands, and was poised to strike.

How dare he, that puny wolfling?

"Yes. Yes, yes. I did it," she snarled. "Killing was natural to me!" Her voice gained volume, bringing back the feeling of the power she'd once known. She was filled with it, relished it. "I loved it. Loved the blood, the smell of fear. Even as your neck broke in my hand I was filled with glory. Should I atone for *that*?"

Jorje dropped his arms and backed away. Instantly, Lily's perspective changed. She lowered her face to her hands. "But I'm not that creature anymore . . . and I wish, oh how I wish I'd never done it." She looked back at him, knew her eyes were dark with pleading. "I loved you like a child. Can you forgive me?"

"In time," he said. Then, like the boy in the black leather jacket he was gone.

Suddenly remorseful tears she'd never before allowed to flow rushed to Lily's eyes. They stung like acid, spilled over and streaked down her face. Her shoulders heaved with the force of her sobs, which came in gulping waves she couldn't fight. After a while she stopped trying. The mist enclosed her again, filled with her torment and guilt, weighing her heart down until she knew it would split in two.

She could never atone for her acts. If she spent the rest of her life serving mankind, it could not make up for them. Jorje was right in wanting to kill her. He should have done it . . . should have done it. . . .

He should have . . .

"Arise, child of the Universe."

The words sounded like beautiful music, and Lily rolled to her side, wondering where they had come from. Her sobs were now just intermittent hiccups, but the pressure on her heart remained.

No one was there. The mist had cleared. She sat up leadenly and dropped another scoop of water on the rocks. Steam rose, spiraling toward the ceiling.

Then the lodge was filled with intense light. On the edges of the field she saw white feathers—on a wingspan ten times that of the hawk's. Then a being emerged. Long golden hair, eyes the color of the bluest sky, a robe so white it shimmered like polished silver. Man or woman she could not say.

"Wipe away your tears, Lily Angelica DeLaVega," the being said. "We have much to talk about."

* * *

He was lying in a pool of blood red water, battered by rain and wind. Mud clung to his ragged coat. The sound of thunder was growing distant. He barely noticed the lightning anymore.

The runoff was nearly to his nose. Tony weakly lifted his head and managed to move to higher ground before his thick neck gave out. His surroundings began to fade.

He wasn't going to make it, he realized. Bear would die of his wounds here in the rain-soaked forest, and he would perish with him. His lids fell shut over his round dark eyes. Filled with regret, he resigned himself to his fate. It would be easier, he thought, if he knew Lily was safe, that Shala would grow up all right without him. It would be so much easier.

Soon he'd lose consciousness, and knowing this, he tried one last time to change form. He thought again of Lily—how much he loved her . . . needed her. How much she needed him. Suddenly a shift occurred within his body. His eyes snapped open. He lifted his weary head. Something rose, taking the numbing pain away.

"Call on me again, Brother," he heard Bear say.

Then he was above the earth, white wings straining against the fierce air current. He let out a shrill cry of exaltation, caught an updraft that lifted him high above the leafy canopy. Another time he would have celebrated this success, but now he dipped earthward again, searching for Lily. Although she'd sworn Sebastian wouldn't hurt her, he didn't share her certainty, and each time he saw a shape on the forest floor his heart clutched in terror.

But when he descended to investigate, he found

only fallen trees or cringing animals caught in the fierce storm and seeking shelter as they could. Finally, convinced she wasn't there, he headed for the lodge.

Except for the wails of the rainstorm and the flap of the billowing curtain hanging over the door, all was quiet as he approached. He dropped to the ground several feet from the lodge, bereft over not finding Lily, and resumed human form. Where could he go from here? Nowhere, at least not in the driving rain.

He would crawl into the lodge for warmth and rest and search again come sunrise. As he neared the opening he heard voices. Flattening himself against the curved rail wall of the lodge, he cautiously lifted a corner of the curtain.

Lily sat cross-legged beside the pit, facing the center of the lodge. The ceiling appeared to have disappeared, and the sky above was a balmy blue, dotted with pure white cotton puffs. Beings of all types lined the walls—a fox and a bear, a small white wolf, a dark raven with intelligent eyes, even Coyote the Trickster. Quetzalcoatl was there, coiled in his feathered serpent form. Buffalo Woman, Grandfather Sky, representatives of the Stone and Standing People.

In front of the Native American deities was a chorus of angels dressed in pure white, their wings folded against their backs, forming a semicircle behind a taller angel.

The Tribunal.

All wore expressions of intense interest as they listened to Lily.

"I am guilty," she said without equivocation. The Tribunal nodded their heads. "Hundreds I killed, affecting thousands I never met like ripples in a pond. I loved no one and was loved by none. But my greatest sin was I didn't care. I reveled in my werewolf ways, relished the wildness, the invincibility, the fear I caused . . . the blood I spilled."

Again, the listeners nodded.

"Only now do I see the harm I've done. The children . . . the families—" Lily lifted her chin, dark eyes gleaming with tears of remorse. "I confess my crimes to you. Nothing I do or say can make amends. Do with me as you will. I am yours."

A murmur filled the lodge.

Tony scooted through the door. None gave him any attention except Lily, who looked at him with a tremulous smile. *Ask for my help,* Tony mentally cried. *Ask.*

But she turned back to the Tribunal. "What is my punishment?"

The beings broke their formation to talk among themselves.

"Loved no one, loved by none," several murmured.

"Thousands suffered from her acts," several more intoned.

"Banishment to the Himalayas," said Raven.

"Return her to the One Mind," said a small angel. "She is a danger while she walks this earth."

"Seven lifetimes of abject service," cried the wolf.

Ask me! Tony wanted to scream. But he didn't. Lily must turn to him of her own free will.

As though she'd heard his mental cry, Lily glanced

his way, eyes filled with despair. "Tony . . ." She spoke his name as though she hadn't seen him before. Her attention returned to the discussion, then back to him, looking like she was trying very hard to remember something. Then a light of recollection replaced the despair in her eyes.

"Help me, Tony. Please help me."

He got up and walked over and stood beside her. "Tribunal," he said. "I wish to be heard."

The discussion ended and all eyes turned to him. Tony hesitated, unsure what to say. His own words would be inadequate. Only the Great Spirit could move these beings. Putting a hand on Lily's shoulder, he tilted back his head and allowed his eyelids to drift closed.

"Honored beings," he said, still not knowing what his next words would be. But they flowed regardless. "Your child belonged to the wild, running free, following the nature the Universe gave her. She believes she loved no one, but she judges herself cruelly. I saw her keening over her slain companion's form, nearly mad with remorse. Is that not love? She risked her own life to save my daughter's. Is that not also love?"

The animal guides and nature spirits moved away, again lining the walls. The chorus of angels reassumed their semicircle. Quetzalcoatl slithered forward, coiling up next to the tallest angel and ruffling his feathers.

"Remember the children she spared," Tony continued. "Not all of them suffered from poverty and neglect."

On those words, a young man materialized. "Hear me," he implored. "I entered medical school last year. They tell me I'll be a great surgeon."

"Yes," the tall angel said, "and many lives you'll save."

The boy became a teenaged girl. "I will enter politics," she told them. "Change is in the wind."

"She'll bring a new era of compassion," said Bear.

"There are more of us," the girl continued. "We live to enrich the world." Then she disappeared.

"Listen to these children, Tribunal," Tony cried. Lily shuddered beneath his palm. He looked down, saw she was crying, and his voice became impassioned. "They show this woman's worth. She says she's loved by none, but Shala loves her like the mother she lost. Show this woman mercy. She is your child as much as I, as much as those she's slain! She deserves your mercy!"

Quetzalcoatl's long forked tongue flickered. Instantly he was a man, the great ruler of the Aztecs, his bronze skin gleaming in the brilliant light. He straightened his golden crown and met the tallest angel's eyes. The angel subtly inclined his head, and Quetzalcoatl turned his gaze to Tony.

"Well spoken, Shaman," he said. "This woman means much to you?"

"I love her," he said softly. "She is part of my heart."

Lily looked up at him, a dazed expression on her tear-streaked face.

A hushed discussion began anew. Tony couldn't make out the words, but he wasn't drawn to listen.

Lily was still staring at him, adoration shining on her face, and he could concentrate on nothing else.

"If my life ends now," she said softly, "I'll die fulfilled. I love you too, Tony White Hawk. More than words can tell."

Bending, he chastely kissed her lips, breathing in the smell of her.

"Stand, wolf woman," Quetzalcoatl commanded.

Tony straightened. Taking Lily's hands, he helped her to her feet. She looked at him so trustingly his heart almost shattered. Had his words been enough? Would the Tribunal heed the messages of the exceptional children who had spoken?

Taking a place beside Lily, he kept one of her hands, waiting with her. He expected the Aztec ruler to speak, but instead it was the angel.

"You have done well, Daughter, yet there is more for you to know."

Eyes now dry, Lily faced the angel's light without flinching.

"The judgments you heard us reflect on, Lily, were only echoes of your own self-condemnation. Your crime was not in adhering to your werewolf nature. You lived that life in accordance with its Laws, yet retained some spark of your humanity, as the testimony of the children attest. But your fear of your leader's censure sapped your integrity. When you killed the wolfling, you parted from yourself, and became lost and unanchored, searching for meaning." The angel fluttered its wings. "By coming back to face the Tribunal alone, unaided by your advocate, you surrendered your defenses. And in your defenselessness you found salvation."

"But there is one more task ahead," interrupted Quetzalcoatl, "before you are redeemed."

"What?" Lily asked.

"It will be revealed in its own time."

"I will fulfill it as well as I can."

The Aztec ruler bowed. "This is all we ask of you. Remember, wolf woman, stay true to yourself. In doing so, you cannot fail."

He moved his eyes toward Tony. "And you, Shaman, have stared into your doubts courageously, but have still failed to make a choice. You can't delay much longer."

"I understand."

Instantly, the light inside the lodge grew in brilliance, although the moment before Tony would have thought it impossible. A sense of peace unlike any he'd ever known embraced him. Lily's hand was still enclosed in his. As the light increased, he felt a subtle change in the feel of it, and he looked at Lily, then blinked in astonishment.

Again, a fine silver down covered her skin. But now it seemed like filaments of light instead of hair. Her body was brighter than the field that enclosed them, and her face radiated serenity.

She returned Quetzalcoatl's bow. With a smile the god resumed his serpent form and vanished. The angels, animal guides, and nature spirits lingered an instant longer, then they too evaporated in the mist.

Soon the rough branch and mud ceiling of the lodge

came back, and only the radiance left in the spirits' wake confirmed the beings had even been there.

Lily released Tony's hand and sank slowly to the floor. Stretching out on her side, she folded her hands and put them beneath her head. Still radiating light, she gave a sigh of complete fulfillment, then fell fast asleep.

Tony settled beside her to wait until she awoke. The Stone People stared at him, giving him the full import of what had occurred, and he took it in, knowing he was meant to share it with Lily when the time came. It pained him that her ordeal wasn't over, but even before he'd taken her to the lodge he'd known it wasn't. He'd felt the injustice of it then, but now it nearly tore him apart.

But she was alive, she'd survived both the werewolves and the Tribunal. He'd be at her side for her next and final challenge, and for the moment he was determined to just appreciate having her here. He swung away from the pit, let his eyes drink her in. The shimmering cover had left her body. She reclined quietly on the floor, very human, very tired.

Then he noticed how still she was. Her chest wasn't moving. Rising to his knees, he bent over and put his ear to her face. Was she breathing? Oh gods above, he didn't think so. And she was so pale.

Berating himself for making love to her in defiance of tradition, he put his fingers on her throat and found a pulse.

So why the hell didn't she breathe?

He rolled her onto her back, placed his mouth over

hers, and blew air into her lungs. After several exhales, she still didn't move.

Breathe, Lily, he willed, *breathe*. He shouldn't have done it, shouldn't have touched her, despite her pleas—she hadn't fully understood the consequences. But he had understood and still allowed his desire for her to put her in this danger.

Suddenly she coughed. Never had Tony heard a sweeter sound, and he rocked back on his knees, flushed with relief. Her chest rose and fell rhythmically again. Her face looked more serene than he had ever seen it. Now the only thing that stood between them was Quakahla and the passing of his people. Exhausted himself, Tony reclined beside Lily. Knowing he was now free to love her with all his heart, he took her in his arms and fell asleep.

Later, when he felt Lily stir in his arms, he came fully awake. The Stone People had ebbed to small sparks of red. The lodge was cooler now, and dressed only in his loincloth, he shivered and moved closer. Lily slowly opened her eyes and smiled at him luminously.

"Oh, Tony," she said, "I had the most wonderful dream."

Chapter Twenty-seven

Lily had expected sunshine and singing birds to greet her that morning, but the raindrops drizzling on the top of the lodge told her differently. She and Tony crawled out of the sweat lodge into a gray day. She wasn't even sure it was morning because the sun was nowhere to be found.

She'd wanted to tell Tony about her dream, but he'd insisted they leave for the village immediately. Now, after making their way down the muddy slope of the mesa, they stood beneath the dripping tree where they'd left their provisions and Tony was rummaging through the backpack.

His urgency should be making her uneasy, but it wasn't. Tony had escaped Sebastian unharmed. She'd survived the Tribunal, and it had ended so blissfully she almost wished it weren't over.

The experience had irrevocably changed her. Not anything she could quite put her finger on, but she wasn't angry anymore, or bitter or sad, regretful or guilty. Everything was okay now. The future was full of promise.

The Tribunal had taken her to a world of white upon white, a place so filled with joyful possibilities she'd wept from sheer happiness. She'd floated on clouds and felt herself rocked by loving hands as if in a cradle. Voices had crooned words of forgiveness, words of encouragement. Never had she known such peace.

"Don't you want to hear about my dream, Tony?"

"Later, while we walk to the village." He handed her some water with terse instructions not to drink too much, then reapplied himself to his search for the backpack.

Although Lily had neither eaten nor drank since the morning they'd walked to the lodge, she wasn't hungry or thirsty. She felt marvelous, better than she ever had. Her bruises and scratches were gone, and despite the rain, the radical drop in temperature, and her wet and muddy feet, the deerskin dress was keeping her comfortable. Her only uneasiness came from the suspicion she was fooling herself.

A dream? Truly, the experience had been as crazy and blissful as any dream she'd ever had, but the content . . .

Well, even though werewolves were considered imaginary by mortals, they were still bound by natural law. They couldn't appear, disappear, and reappear the way her nocturnal visitors had. And she'd been visited by dead ones, angels, *gods,* for heaven's sake, creatures that didn't just drop in on mortals every day.

No, it was easier just to call it a dream—a wonderful, cleansing, heart-lifting dream—and leave it at that.

"Why are we in such a hurry?" she asked, taking a small sip of water. "It's a beautiful day."

"Put that on," he said, lobbing a small packet her way and glancing dubiously at the dripping sky. "It'll make the beautiful day a bit easier to endure."

The packet contained a thin plastic rain cape, which crackled as Lily let it unfurl. After slipping it on, she pulled up the hood, realizing she'd been cold after all.

Then, still all business, Tony shoved her boots and socks in her hand. She kicked her sandals off. After she'd laced up her second boot, she looked down. The wrinkled cape was a putrid shade of green, hung well below her knees, and was the ugliest thing she'd ever seen. The boots, already battered from two long hikes they were never meant to undertake, ended a short distance above her ankles and revealed a span of mud-covered leg.

Lily almost laughed. In all her life the only thing she'd adored almost as much as the smell of fear and blood was clothing. What had become of her?

She looked over at Tony, who crouched on the blanket pulling on his own boots. Still in his loincloth, he was half naked, rain-soaked, and covered with mud, but to her he seemed the most magnificent man who ever lived.

The other Lily, the one who'd lusted for blood and clothes, had died last night. And this new Lily wasn't consumed with how she looked. She found pleasure in simply being alive and with the man she loved, in anticipating reuniting with the child she adored, and getting to know the Dawn People better. She'd finally found a place where she belonged and she would hold on to it the rest of her days.

"How are you doing, Tony?" she asked. "I'm ready to go home now."

Home. She'd never used those words before. My house, the house, my den, my hotel room, yes. But home? None of those places had felt like a home.

Tony had already donned the rain cape and was lacing up his boots. "Get the water bag, will you?" he asked, standing to fold up the blanket.

"Sure." His melancholy perplexed her. She'd survived the Tribunal. They were together. What more could he want?

He remained pensive during their walk to the village. At first Lily tried to tell him about her dream, wanting to share and get his feedback on what it might mean. But he responded so halfheartedly she finally gave up.

Even though the river trail was more protected than the higher ground, the desert's riparian washes channeled water across it in several places. On one occasion, Tony carried her. She laughed and called him gallant, but he only smiled weakly as he put her down.

What was wrong with him? For some reason, the question brought to mind the man with the golden crown who'd told her she had one more task before she was redeemed.

She glanced at Tony, who looked very morose as he resettled the pack on his back.

"What's bothering you, Tony?"

"Nothing." He wiped the troubled expression off his face before looking at her. Although he'd kept his thoughts guarded up until then, she got a sudden quick flash of what was on his mind and all her self-deception vanished.

"It *wasn't* a dream, was it?"

"No, Lily, it wasn't."

She caught a second thought from him, which reminded her of what day it was. Suddenly, she understood his urgency.

"Tonight's the eclipse of the moon," she said. "Does my final task have something to do with that?"

His face remained impassive, but his mournful eyes told her he knew what lay ahead even before he nodded. "But it isn't time to tell you about it." He sighed, no longer bothering to hide his distress. "The Stone People advised me to withhold that information until we meet with Star Dancer."

"But—"

"You'll have to wait." His voice rose with urgency. "When . . . when we made love, although I was your advocate, I defied a taboo. You almost died in there, Lily. By all that's sacred, you stopped breathing!" He stepped close, took her shoulders, and stared into her eyes. "I won't take that chance again."

His thoughts were no longer shielded. She heard words of love running beneath his spoken ones, felt his relief, his guilt. But there was something else, something he refused to bring to the surface and would not share with her.

But she could ease some of his guilt.

"No," she said. "I wasn't dying. I was simply visiting heaven."

"It looked like death to me!" His grip on her shoulder tightened almost painfully. "I've already lost one woman I loved! I will not lose another!"

She'd caused him so much pain by permitting his wife to die, and now she felt the full weight of it. She might as well have killed Tajaya herself.

One last task to redeem herself. If that was the case, she'd complete it, no matter if it took her life, which Tony's agonized face told her it might.

"But you have to risk losing me anyway, don't you, Tony?"

He nodded sadly. "And I refuse to do anything else to increase that risk."

"We must go tonight, Lord," Arlan Ravenheart said fervently. "The dark moon rises."

"Bah!" Sebastian sat on a wooden spindle chair, drumming his fingers against its splitting back. "The dark moon is of no concern to me. But my pack is." He waved his hand at four wolves, who licked their wounds atop the rotting rug. "We lost two of our number to that hideous bear, and some enchantment keeps the others from alchemizing. We must give them time to heal."

"But—"

"No! I will listen to no more of this drivel. Can you not see the others need time?"

Sebastian's roar made the four wolves cringe. Beryl and Philippe moved a greater distance away. The show of temper also gave Ravenheart pause, but he alone knew time was critical. He pressed his case. "We cannot wait, Lord. After tonight, it will be too late. The people will be gone, taking Lily with them."

"What?" Sebastian leaped from the chair. "Gone? Where?"

"To Quakahla."

"Then we shall follow them."

"None can enter Quakahla after the dark moon passes."

The werewolf king stroked his muzzle and strode around the cave. He glanced once or twice at his wounded followers, his nose wrinkling in distaste.

"Something's happened to my pack," he mumbled, almost to himself. "Too seldom do they change into human form these days. Nay, not even into man-wolf. They become more beastlike with each passing hour."

He circled the room several times, growing more beastlike himself with every turn. He growled, he snarled, he whipped his tail in agitation. Finally he looked at Ravenheart.

"Very well. If the others have not mended before sunset, you, Beryl, Philippe, and I shall go to the village. I will not suffer Lily to escape. If I need to travel to the earth's ends to find her, I vow to do so. She will know my wrath and beg for death before I finish with her!"

One of the wolves on the rug whimpered. Beryl and Philippe exchanged worried glances.

Ravenheart saw only a failing king and toyed briefly with the idea of taking his place. But Quakahla beckoned, promising glories far above that of commanding a pack of sniveling cur, so he simply smiled at Sebastian and said, "Wise as always, Lord."

"Ah, Arlan, you remind me so of—" He stepped to Ravenheart's side and put a fatherly arm around his shoulder. "I weary of toadies." This was accompanied by a quick glance at Beryl and Philippe, a lowering of the voice. "When Lily is recovered, the shaman shall be yours to slay."

Ravenheart smiled with satisfaction and ignored Beryl's threatening glare. The dark moon was upon them. The destiny promised by Walking Wolf would soon be his.

King of Quakahla. He could not wait.

"Papa! Lily!" Shala cried, throwing herself into Tony's waiting arms. "Terrible things have happened. Werewolves attacked last night. The warriors fought them off but now we're almost out of the smelling salts, and . . . and, oh, poor Frieda."

"Frieda," Lily asked in alarm.

"They found"—Shala's voice choked—"they found her walking stick inside the maze! Warriors are out searching for her re-re-remains! I was afraid they got you too!"

While Tony comforted Shala, Lily stared at the chaos surrounding them. Although the sky was still thick with clouds, it provided a glimpse of the sun that told her night was rapidly approaching. The rain had stopped for the time being, giving the people respite as they herded pigs, goat, and sheep into a hastily constructed pen beside the canyon that led to the cave. Gerard passed, shooing along several goats. When he saw Tony, he said that Star Dancer wanted to see him.

"Can you stay with Lily?" he asked his daughter.

"Yes," Shala replied weepily. "But don't be long, okay?"

"Okay." Then Tony took off for the longhouse.

Kessa sobbed by her fire, surrounded by other women, some of whom were also crying. Holding Shala's hand, Lily went to Kessa's side.

"I'm sorry," she said.

Kessa stared up, tears streaking down her face. "What if no one ever finds her body? All Grandmother ever wanted was to f-finish her years in Quakahla and have her ashes scattered there. N-Now she n-never will."

Lily sat down beside her, only half aware the other women had deferentially stepped aside for her. She embraced Kessa until her tears subsided.

Then Gerard approached, an urgent expression on his face. "Star Dancer needs to see you, Lily. It's very important."

Again telling Kessa she was sorry, and leaving Shala with her, Lily followed Gerard. He was hurrying toward the longhouse at a pace that belied his age, and she didn't catch up until he'd reached the longhouse door. He opened it for her, but after she went through the door, it started to close. She stopped, peering out. "Aren't you coming in?"

Gerard shook his head. "This is between you, Tony, and Riva."

Both the urgency and the secrecy alarmed Lily. She let the door fall shut and turned apprehensively to the center of the room. Tony and Star Dancer were sitting on the dais, obviously waiting for her. Lily's alarm turned to annoyance.

"Frieda is probably dead," she scolded as she approached. "Half the village is looking for her and the other half is in mourning. Why are you two just sitting here?"

Star Dancer laughed.

"It's not funny. These are perilous times. Obviously the werewolves found their way through the maze despite your efforts. Something must be done."

The High Shaman patted a spot on the sheepskin that faced both she and Tony. "Sit," she said. Still smiling, she turned to Tony. "Already she feels the urgency of her new role."

"What are you talking about?" Lily lowered herself gracefully to the floor, landing in a cross-legged position.

Star Dancer's amusement faded. "More serious matters, Lily. Tony was guided to keep this from you, but we have talked long about it and have come to an agreement. You should be told."

Told what? Lily wondered, but kept her peace.

"For a thousand years," Star Dancer began, "the

Dawn People have passed down the legends of Quakahla. After many generations some no longer believed they were actually prophesies." At Tony's sharp glance, she looked over. "No, you weren't the only one. Many of the council privately shared your views."

Star Dancer paused to light some incense, then returned her gaze to Lily. "Skepticism vanished on the last full moon when the gates opened inside the cave. You have seen the cave, haven't you?"

Lily nodded.

"The gate is a doorway into a different reality, another dimension if you will, where buffalo still roam and corn grows high and wild in the meadows. No Europeans have ever seen that land. The confirmation of this legend tells us that the other legends are also true. You've been told of White Wolf Woman?"

Lily knew Star Dancer was aware she had, but nodded anyway.

"And these changes in your body? The ones that made you fear you were again a werewolf. What of them?"

Now Lily was on uncertain ground. Clearly Tony had told his teacher what he'd seen on the rim above the Clearing of the Black Hands. But what did it have to do with their legends?

"I, uh, I know I'm not a werewolf. After . . . well, I poured holy water on my hands and felt no pain, so I'm sure— What am I?"

Star Dancer and Tony simultaneously said, "White Wolf Woman."

"What? No." Lily shook her head vehemently. "I'm not. I can't be."

Two pairs of golden eyes regarded her calmly. The silence grew, and in it Lily scanned the stories she'd been told, the most recent one from Tony beside the river. Her confusion and denial changed to dismay.

"You're sending me out to fight the werewolves." It wasn't a question.

"Not exactly, Lily." Star Dancer leaned and touched Lily's clenched hands. "That's what Tony and I have been discussing. He rather heatedly argued that we aren't Four-Leggeds and should be expected to show more compassion than they. Regardless of the counsel he received from the Stone People, he believes you should be given a choice."

"About what?"

"The legends say that on the night of the dark moon rising, the beasts will try to stop us from passing through the gate. White Wolf Woman shall rise up, filled with glorious light, and hold them back. Thus the Dawn People will return to their true home." Star Dancer paused. "But it is not already done, Lily. The beasts have arrived, but the outcome of our passing remains a mystery."

Lily looked down at her hands, which were still covered by Star Dancer's. "Unless I play my role?"

"Even then. There are no guarantees you'll be successful. That's why we've decided to inform you of what is to come. You don't have to participate."

"It's your choice," Tony added. She sensed his mixed emotions. Fear for her, fear for his people, uncertainty about her response and his knowledge that he'd stay behind and fight even if she chose not to.

"You can leave by the escape route you so cleverly found," Star Dancer added. "We'll give you food, water, warm clothing. You'll be gone before the beasts arrive."

Gone? Where would she go? She had no other home. And the very idea of leaving Tony and Shala was abhorrent. As she was about to say she really didn't have a choice, Star Dancer asked, "You want to come to Quakahla with us?"

"Everyone I love will be there," Lily replied, nodding her head. "There's nothing for me in this world."

"Then you must know this." A sheen formed on Star Dancer's eyes, alarming Lily, and she leaned closer, wanting to know, but terribly afraid.

"The legends say that The People honored White Wolf Woman for a thousand years. But nothing tells us whether she lived in Quakahla . . . or even if she survived the battle with the wolves."

Chapter Twenty-eight

Lily left the longhouse with Tony, armed with advice to mull over their discussion before making a decision. They circled the village several times, with Tony continuously urging her to leave. Eventually Lily threw up her hands and demanded that he stop.

Saying she needed time to think and would meet him in an hour, she went back to her quarters to wash off the grime, change into dry clothes, and get rid of the chafing boots. Although her feet were cold, at least the leather of her sandals didn't bind.

She hung the deerskin dress on a rail attached to the washing table, smoothing it out lovingly and wondering if she'd ever see it again. Then she faced the fear that troubled her most. She'd been unable to shapeshift when Sebastian captured her. Had she lost the power?

Trembling slightly, she willed herself to change. It came instantly. Heaving a relieved sigh, she again stared in awe at the filamentlike hair that covered her body. A human body, though, with its rounded fingernails and teeth. What possible threat could such a mortal form pose to Sebastian?

"Lily."

At the sound of Tony's voice, she willed herself back to normal, put on her rain cape and walked toward the closed curtain.

"Your hour's up." Tony looked impatient. He'd washed also, she noticed, but his face looked gray and grim.

"Let's walk by the river," he suggested, taking hold of her arm in a way that made her think he wouldn't let her refuse. He wanted to talk privately, she supposed.

But what was there to talk about? Everything she valued was going to a new dimension that night—Tony, Shala, Star Dancer, and all the other people who had finally come to accept her. When they vanished, nothing remained for her except the prospect of running from Sebastian the rest of her life.

After descending the ladder, Lily let Tony guide her toward the river, deep in thought again. What was she to do with this new role? Was she supposed to kill Sebastian and his pack? How? A skunk had its scent, a porcupine its quills, deer and elk their antlers and hooves, but her alchemized form had no claws or fangs. And her failure to shape-shift when Sebastian swept her into the forest had shaken her faith in her abilities. What if—

Almost as if she'd asked the question aloud, Tony began talking. "In case you decide to stay . . . Well, you'll find you have abilities you never suspected."

Lily looked up at him sharply.

"You will, honest," he said.

"How did you know what I was thinking?"

He tapped the side of his head and smiled mysteriously. A small smile to be sure, but it made Lily feel somewhat better. "Actually," he admitted, "it was a no-brainer. What else would you be thinking at a time like this?"

"You know I couldn't alchemize when Sebastian had me?"

"When you didn't, I figured as much." He paused, draped an arm over her shoulder, and turned to a path that went past the women's pool then on to the river. "But you were in the middle of the inquisition, which sapped your strength. And you have the crystal. Keep it with you. Use it."

"Something about it . . ." She felt bemused. "It almost has the same effects as holy water."

"Only when it's in your possession. For anyone else it's just a crystal."

She touched the stone. The now-familiar thrum emanated from its clear depths, but she still felt unarmed. So many people depended on her. How could she do it all? Again Tony seemed to read her thoughts.

"I'll be with you. And warriors will guard the tribespeople during the exodus. We'll only have to contend with the werewolves." He cleared his throat. "About the bear . . ."

He fidgeted, an uncharacteristic behavior for a shaman, and Lily looked up at him.

"Well, it . . . it was me."

"You're becoming quite the shape-shifter." She tried to sound light, but failed miserably.

"I don't know if I can do it again." He gave a bleak smile. "We sure can't count on it."

They exchanged wan expressions, then Lily glanced away, realizing they were finally alone. Now feeling fidgety herself, she asked the question heavy on her mind.

"Do the stories say you and Shala live in Quakahla?"

He stopped and brought her into the circle of his arms, the plastic capes rustling as their bodies touched. She rested her chin on his chest, waiting for his answer.

"There are . . . so many factors to consider. I'm a shaman and warrior, a leader in the tribe. Riva is Shala's grandmother, and Shala has her own destiny as a shaman. With Ravenheart lost, there aren't many among the young ones who have chosen the shaman's way. The Dawn People need me. They need Shala."

"You don't have to go?" She couldn't quell the excitement in her voice.

"I have free will."

"Then stay! I don't want you to leave, Tony. Shala doesn't want to go. Hasn't she told you that?"

He smiled grimly. "She is only now entering her seventh winter. That's too young to make such far-reaching decisions."

"What about *her* free will?"

He answered with a frown, and she let her gaze drift to the cattails swaying in the river. A new drizzle was starting. Drops collected on the leaves, falling into the river to ripple in every direction, merging with one another to create new patterns, just as her earlier acts had done. This decision facing her would cause ripples too.

"Is loving me one of the factors?"

"Oh yes, my darling, the biggest one, and it's tearing me apart."

He kissed her forehead, letting his lips linger, wanting to crush her to him and never let go. She trembled slightly, and he put a hand under her chin, lifting it to gaze into her dark slanted eyes. They shone with angry, distraught tears.

"Why can't I go too?" Her voice was husky.

So was his. "I don't really know. The stories only say that Wolf and Bear get separated in battle. After a futile search, Bear crosses alone. The Dawn People return to their true home and tell the White Wolf Woman legends each time the dark moon rises."

Lily let out an agonized cry. Jerking from his embrace, she planted her feet and slammed her fists on her hips.

"A stupid legend's going to decide our fate? A stupid legend?" She spun on her heels and paced along the river, spun again and paced back. "You and Star Dancer are mistaken. I'm not White Wolf Woman, I'm not! I don't want to be a legend! I just want to be Lily!" She tapped her breast rapidly several times. "Just Lily. An ordinary woman."

Suddenly she stopped and stared into Tony's eyes. He tried to prevent it, but she read his thoughts too quickly. "You *knew*! You knew we wouldn't be together even before we went to the sweat lodge!"

Flying at him, she beat her fist fiercely on his chest. "Damn you! Damn you! You had no right to keep it from me!"

"Shh . . . shh, shh . . ." Her anguish was tearing Tony apart. He wrapped his arms around her, bringing her so close she lost her leverage. She kept hitting him, but her blows grew weaker and more infrequent. Suddenly, her tears broke loose. She collapsed against his shoulder.

"I'm sorry, Lily," he rasped, his throat tightening. "I'm so sorry."

"Damn you." She sobbed and wrapped her fists in the folds of his plastic rain cape. "You had no right . . . You had no right."

"I know. I know."

Tony's eyes stung and he blinked hard, wondering if he should point out what Lily failed to notice. It seemed as cruel as dangling a carrot before a horse, but she deserved to know this part as much as the rest.

"I have a hope." He pressed her head more tightly to his shoulder, unwilling to meet her eyes. "It is not already done. There are many possible outcomes. Anything can happen."

A measure of tension left her body. She let go of his rain cape. "Does that mean I might enter Quakahla after all?"

Tony cleared his throat. "It's only a possibility. A small one. We have to be careful not to hope too much."

"I see." She stepped from his arms and dabbed at her tears with a piece of her own cape. "I've never been much for caution."

Dropping the cape, she jutted out her chin and met his eyes decisively. "I'm staying, Tony White Hawk. If there's any chance we can be together, I'm not turning away from it."

They spent the rest of that afternoon quietly with Shala. The entire village was subdued. To Kessa and her family's relief, the warriors found Frieda's remains, and the women of her family prepared for the funeral that would be held after the crossing.

Only half in jest, Tony had pointed to the place where Lily had climbed to the rim, with a remark that he wanted to be sure she hadn't forgotten where it was. She knew he was trying to get her to reconsider. But Star Dancer's guardedly jubilant response told Lily the High Shaman was more relieved than she was willing to let on. Lily suspected that if she had refused the challenge, not only would the People fail to pass into Quakahla, none would survive the werewolves' siege. This made her more determined to stay, and finally Tony gave up his attempts to change her mind.

Then the sun began to set, barely noticeable behind the relentless drizzle. Men, women, and children began filing into the longhouse, all in rain gear, carrying satchels with the remainder of their belongings. Tony and Lily passed out the last of the ammonia capsules and holy water to the warriors who would guard the people's passage. When the sun's meager light finally disappeared, Gerard closed the door.

Amid candles and incense and wafting herb wands, the villagers chanted and sang in their own language, holding hands in a circle and swaying rhythmically. Lily heard Quakahla mentioned several times, but other than that she didn't understand the words. She stood between Tony and Shala, and found the swaying movement eased her tension.

Finally Star Dancer broke the circle. The room grew hushed. Outside the storm picked up. Raindrops pounded the roof of the longhouse. Wind beat at the eaves. Thunder clapped faraway. Bleats and grunts arose in the animals' pens. Then the first howl rose. Soft at first, sounding almost like the wind, then piercingly louder, closer.

"The dark moon rises," Star Dancer said, shattering the stillness inside the room. "Quakahla awaits."

Gerard opened the door. Wind blew rain into the room, and the temperature dropped sharply. People moved from the circle, lining up in front of the door. Mothers held their babies tight and kept their other children close to their sides. Warriors stood behind their families. Grandmothers and grandfathers picked up their burdens. Then everyone turned their eyes to Lily and Tony.

"We must go out first, before the warriors," Tony told Lily. "It's our job to fend off the beasts. If we do it admirably, they'll pass through safely."

He bent to kiss Shala.

"I'll see you in Quakahla, Papa." Then she turned to receive Lily's kiss. "You too, Lily."

So Tony hadn't told her. The coward. But this night promised enough pain. If he'd held back to spare his daughter from any more, Lily couldn't truly blame him. And his lapse renewed her hope. Perhaps his faith that she'd make the crossing with them was stronger than hers.

Suddenly he looked up, his eyes growing distant, a sign he was projecting the hawk.

"Hurry," he said. "The werewolves are in the maze."

They exited into a wind-driven downpour, but even the clouds didn't hide the first movement of the eclipse across the moon. The warriors formed a protective line from the longhouse to the canyon that held the cave. Lily and Tony moved to a spot between their position and the maze. People began filing out the door toward Quakahla, moving behind the warriors' shield.

More howls sounded. Only yards away, blurred shapes took form in the curtain of rain. Then Sebastian appeared, his lips curled into a feral smile. Beryl, Philippe, and Ravenheart flanked him.

Behind Lily, the villagers calmly started their pilgrimage, giving the werewolves no attention. Beside her, Tony shifted form so rapidly she hardly had time to blink, becoming a bear of such enormous proportions his back almost reached her head. Magnificent, she thought, deeply relieved he'd shifted so effortlessly.

Breathing easier, she put a hand on his shoulder.

Alchemize.

She remained as she was. A second try also failed to produce results. Shocked, and suddenly terrified, her mind spun. What use was she here? How could she protect the Dawn People with only the knife Tony had belted around her waist? This was foolishness. No, craziness. Sebastian would steal her from the village and keep her captive for life. Tony would have to protect his people alone.

The satisfied gleam in Sebastian's eyes told her he'd read her thoughts and knew she was helpless. She struggled to pull herself together, to block her mind and make him believe she could still fight.

"The gemstone, Lily."

At Tony's words she reached inside her rain cape, finding the smooth hard edges of the crystal. She closed her hand around it and pulled it out.

The bear growled. In that same instant, Sebastian took a menacing step forward. "I see you have a new skill, Shaman," he said. "But that will not be enough to save Lily, nor stop Arlan from making a coat out of your dead hide."

Tony lunged at Sebastian. Using his werewolf agility, the King sidestepped. Propelled by his own momentum, Tony sped forward, crashing into Ravenheart, who leaped on his back, growling.

"Your time here is short, White Hawk." Ravenheart snarled, nipping and tearing at Tony's shaggy fur. "Soon all that was yours will be mine."

Roaring denial, Tony rolled, crushing Ravenheart beneath his weight. The werewolf whimpered, wrapped a clawed hand around Tony's ear, but Tony rolled again, landing on all fours, head lowered.

Philippe and Beryl alchemized to wolf form and flew at Tony. Sebastian closed in on Lily.

"This will be much easier than I anticipated, dear one." He moved a hand toward her shoulder.

Lily clutched the crystal tighter. It pulsed to life just as Sebastian grabbed her. A pained moan left his lips and he jerked back as though he'd received an electric shock. The smell of burning hair filled the air. Searching for the source of Sebastian's injury, Lily looked around wildly, her eyes coming to rest on her own body. It glowed with light, just as it had in her dream. But it hadn't been a dream. This was the weapon Tony had promised would come.

She had no time to wonder how. Sebastian was jabbing at her like someone trying to see if a coal was still hot. A finger grazed her hand. He moaned again, then dropped his arms and let out an enraged howl.

To her right Tony battled Ravenheart. Beryl and Philippe nipped at his flanks with their wolf-form teeth. Mud flew everywhere, and all of them struggled for footing on the slick ground.

Disregarding Sebastian for the moment, Lily rushed to Tony's side. Avoiding a kick from Beryl's hind leg, she enclosed the limb with her hand. He gave a high-pitched squeal, then cartwheeled and landed in the mud, panting as he scrambled to make another leap.

The loss of a foe gave Tony new strength. With a twist of his massive body, he jarred Philippe loose. Lily bent down and touched the omega wolf's back.

Screeching in pain, Philippe ran off to lick his wounds. Having lost the advantage given by the other wolves, Ravenheart strained to break free of Tony's hold, finally managing to rock to his feet. Then he saw Lily. His eyes widened and he backed away.

"Lord," he called, "we must devise another tack. The wolf woman has the power of the light. She is invincible."

Still rubbing his scorched hand, Sebastian inclined his head gravely. Then he gave a guttural order to Beryl and Philippe.

They streaked toward the villagers, who trudged quietly through the rain to the cave. The warriors guarding them threw ammonia capsules. Beryl and Philippe skidded to a stop almost simultaneously. Coughing and cursing, deforming hideously, they kicked the capsules beneath the mud. Several moments passed while the pair transformed to human shape.

A woman warrior moved forward, holding a vial of holy water. Lily saw her hesitate, knowing she'd been warned to use it sparingly. When the two resumed wolf shape, they charged again, and the woman sprinkled drops, some of which landed on Philippe. Philippe yowled and collapsed on the ground, writhing in the mud, trying to rid himself of the burning liquid.

Beryl leaped at the woman, who barely had a chance to scream before she slammed against the ground. Other warriors moved to take the fallen woman's place.

As instructed, the villagers ignored the battle and calmly continued toward Quakahla. Tony came to Lily's side and she again put her hand on his shoulder, watching the drama unfold and trying to choose her next move.

Philippe had resumed human form and was now groveling naked in the mud. Snarling and yelping, Beryl wove between the warriors, deftly avoiding the flying holy water. Sebastian grinned in satisfaction, which told Lily he had a plan.

Suddenly realization dawned like a punch to the belly. The rain was diluting the effects of the capsules and water. Already Philippe was back in wolf shape, scrambling to his feet. Beryl was through the line of warriors, almost upon the people. A boy of about ten walked behind a woman carrying a baby.

Sebastian barked an order in Lupinese. *Him,* Lily realized. Sebastian was sending the wolves after the boy, who she recognized as Gerard's grandson, exploiting her love for children.

"Lord," Ravenheart cried. "Your promise."

"It only bound me if the others did not fight," Sebastian snarled. "Be still now, and watch my plan take shape."

Beryl closed in on the boy, whose eyes were firmly affixed on his mother's back. Tony bellowed, racing forward to assist. Lily flew behind him, her sandaled feet barely touching the earth.

By the time she caught up, Tony was already standing protectively in front of the boy. Beryl crouched down, his muzzle curled back to reveal his fangs. But trapped between the warriors and Tony, he couldn't avoid their weapons. Coughing from the ammonia, singed by the holy water, and besieged by the warriors' spears, he jumped to safety.

The boy's mother grabbed his hand and they moved on with the rest of the villagers. Philippe cowered beside the fallen Beryl. Tony lumbered toward them, roaring angrily. Lily ran behind him.

Then the last of the pilgrims exited the longhouse. Star Dancer emerged, holding Shala's hand.

"Now!" she heard Sebastian cry.

Lily spun toward the sound and saw Ravenheart barreling toward the longhouse. In one ground-eating jump he landed by the door and ripped Shala from Star Dancer's grip.

Chapter Twenty-nine

Shala screamed. Helpless, Star Dancer stared in horror. Tony abandoned his attack on the smaller wolves and galloped forward.

"Back off, White Hawk"—Ravenheart snarled—"or I'll break the neck of this sniveling spawn of yours."

"What do you want?" Tony asked.

"My Lord wants the she-wolf. I want your life."

"Are you prepared for a fair fight?"

"Fair, bah? When the wolf woman possesses such powers? No. Enter the woods with me. Alone."

"No, Papa!" Shala cried.

Lily realized no one was paying attention to her. The rain made everything hard to see, even for the keen-eyed wolves. Carefully guarding her intention from psychic probes, she inched her way closer to Ravenheart.

"You will have your fight, Arlan." Tony growled. "Now let my daughter go."

Just as Lily neared Ravenheart's elbow, Shala came alive in his arms, kicking, screaming, creating the final diversion Lily needed. Leaping forward, she touched the young werewolf. His fur sizzled and he whimpered. Lily ripped Shala free and raced toward the forest.

"Get her!" she heard Sebastian shout, but knew his order fell on deaf ears. Beryl and Philippe were still licking their wounds, and Ravenheart clearly understood the futility of his lord's request.

"Papa, Papa!" Shala cried as they ran across the rain-drenched village. "Go back, Lily. Help him."

"I will, sweetheart," she rasped, almost too winded to talk. "As soon as you're out of danger."

"But, Papa . . ."

"He's a warrior. Trust him." And then they were in the trees and Lily thought of the ravine where she'd frequently taken her meals. Shala would be safe there.

Soon she settled the girl in the big sycamore. "Stay here until one of us comes for you or—" She hesitated. "If all grows silent in the village, watch the dark moon. Run for Quakahla before it passes."

"No, Lily. I want to help you save Papa."

"You can't, Shala, and you know that. You'll just get in the way." Lily tried hard not to speak sharply, but Tony . . . he was in such danger. "You must promise you'll do as I say. Please promise."

After a long pause, Shala replied weepily, "I promise."

Lily whirled for the village. The rainy night fell into total blackness. The eclipse was now complete and would start to move off. Time was running out.

Knowing Shala was safely with Lily, Tony's terror eased. He lowered his head, backing up, and drawing the werewolves from the door of the longhouse. Beryl and Philippe had shape-shifted and healed their injuries. Ravenheart had also recovered and now crept forward. Sebastian stood behind him, waiting.

Many of the warriors had fallen during the battle. Their comrades handed their injured or lifeless bodies over to the pilgrims, then regrouped. As instructed, none would abandon their post to come to Tony's aid.

Which is as it should be, he thought, as the four werewolves converged. Too many to beat, but he roared and rose on hind legs regardless, preparing to fend them off for as long as he could.

Beryl sprang at him first, his jaw poised to clamp on his throat. As Tony braced himself for the blow, the werewolf suddenly fell. Ravenheart stood over him, glowering.

"No, whelp," he snarled. "The shaman is mine!"

"Yours?" Beryl screamed, bouncing to his feet and towering over Ravenheart. "This is my rightful kill."

Ravenheart dipped his head, then surged upward, closing his teeth on Beryl's throat. Gurgling, Beryl drove his clawed hands into Ravenheart's head. Ravenheart grunted, then lifted a leg and jammed it into Beryl's tender underbelly.

"Desist!" Sebastian roared. "Cease!"

But the two werewolves were tearing at each other. Mud scattered under the force of their powerful claws. Fur flew; blood flowed. Philippe stood by the raging Sebastian, clearly stunned. Then Beryl fell and didn't get up.

Tony was forgotten for the moment. Though the rain beat down relentlessly, casting everything in gloom, Tony still saw the faint curve of light that signaled the dark moon was ebbing. Less than a dozen people were left in the village. The rest had passed into the canyon, and the warriors would soon follow.

He loped toward the forest. Lily and Shala were somewhere in there, and he'd bring them out and take them to Quakahla or die trying.

Then without warning, a massive weight landed on his back and he fell into the mud. Rolling, he came face-to-face with Ravenheart.

Already suffering from his first encounter with the werewolves, he wasn't certain he could prevail. But Ravenheart had his own share of battle scars. Blood trickled down his wolfish forehead from a ripped ear. A patch of missing fur on his shoulder oozed red.

Tony sank his teeth into the injured shoulder. Ravenheart quivered, then closed his own fangs into Tony's head, shaking it viciously, ripping flesh. Blood seeped into Tony's eyes, but garnering his strength, he twisted his hindquarters and sent the werewolf tumbling on the ground.

Then they were both on their feet—Tony on hind legs—circling each other, feinting, moving closer.

"After you die, White Hawk, I'll take out Star Dancer.

I was planning to kill your daughter too." He laughed cruelly, the sound resembling a hyena's cackle. "But I have decided she will make a fine servant when I finally rule Quakahla."

"You'd better hurry, traitor." Tony gestured his great white head to the sky. "The time for passing is nearly over."

With a howl, Ravenheart lunged. Tony let him gain speed, then swiveled just as the werewolf struck. Ravenheart fell to the earth, but quickly regained his footing. Crouching, he moved in on Tony. Then he was all over him, claws digging, teeth biting, and the blood pouring from Tony's wound was nearly blinding him. He aimed at Ravenheart's throat, but missed. A leg aimed at the belly fell short of its mark. When the werewolf flew at his own underside, he tried to swivel again, but his muscles had grown weak and clumsy.

Just as Ravenheart was about to rip into Tony's stomach, his weight was lifted up.

"You are too ambitious for your own good, wolfling." Sebastian held Ravenheart several inches off the ground by the scruff of the neck. "Rule Quakahla? Bah, you are not good enough to lick this shaman's feet. You are doomed to remain an omega wolf indefinitely."

Sebastian threw the younger werewolf toward the body of Beryl, where he landed on the lifeless form. With a shudder of revulsion, Ravenheart regained his footing and lifted his head, a deadly expression in his eyes. But the werewolf King took no notice as he turned his back and gazed down at Tony, "Philippe will deliver your coup de grâce, Shaman."

Tony saw Philippe covetously moving in on him, and saw Ravenheart crouch behind Sebastian's back. He was losing blood, losing it fast and too much of it, but he still had some strength left. He considered breaking the connection with the bear, but either way he was no match for two werewolves. Philippe, he could take care of. If luck held, Ravenheart would give Sebastian more than enough to deal with.

"You old fool!" Ravenheart roared, charging at Sebastian. He head-butted the older werewolf, but Sebastian recovered quickly and whirled, giving his attacker an open-handed blow that sent him reeling.

Philippe, taking no chances of losing his kill, dropped his head to take out Tony's entrails. Tony rolled, digging out a mound of mud and kicking it into Philippe's eyes.

Then a wild scream undulated through the night. Everyone froze, eyes turning toward the sound. Lily was careening across the village, slipping and sliding in the mud, silver hair streaming behind her and uttering a fierce cry.

Ravenheart forgot about Sebastian. Returning her enraged cries, he raced toward her. They met under the light of the half moon, Lily not skipping a beat as the werewolf put his hands on her. Though he shuddered horribly, though the stench of burning hair rose from him in waves, he held on, shaking Lily. Her head flopped back and forth. Her eyes fell closed.

Tony scrambled to his feet and broke into a run. But Sebastian was ahead of him. With a spray of mud and water, he vaulted through the air, landing just behind Ravenheart. In one quick movement, he grabbed Ravenheart's neck and wrung it.

The wolf sank to the ground, taking Lily with him. Disregarding his own safety, Tony broke his connection with the bear and knelt beside Lily in human form. Her face was white against the dark mud. The crystal at her neck had grown pale, as lifeless as she looked. Whipping out his knife, he pivoted to protect her from Sebastian.

But the werewolf king made no move. Ravenheart lay dead in his moonlit shadow, and he turned dully to take in the body of the fallen Beryl. Philippe alchemized to wolf shape and began slinking backward toward the maze.

Arching his neck, Sebastian let out a howl so mournful it chilled Tony's bones. Then Sebastian swept down, lifted Lily off the ground, and ran toward the forest.

Lily's outraged cries hit Tony's ears, alleviating his dread, but they faded into the darkness of the woods before he could get to his feet. Deathly stillness now cloaked the village. All the people had entered the cave. The animal pens were empty.

He sprinted into the forest, ducking here and there to avoid runoff from the trees. He ran with the quiet movements of a practiced warrior, but still heard no other sounds. It was as if Sebastian and Lily had disappeared, and though he knew Lily had taken Shala here, he had no idea where.

He heard a twig snap. Brandishing his knife, he spun toward the sound.

"Papa?"

And then Shala was running toward him, throwing herself into his waiting arms. "Oh, Papa, you're safe."

Tony held her close, his joy at finding her dimmed only by Lily's disappearance. Should he instruct Shala to stay here and continue searching? But the smaller werewolf was lurking about somewhere. Shala had no defenses against him, while Lily had many.

"Hang on, little one," he said, then broke into a run.

"Where's Lily, Papa?" Shala asked in alarm as they came upon the quiet village square. "Where is she?"

In the sky, the pale moon grew larger—less than a quarter of it remained in darkness—spilling light across the village that revealed the brutal wounds on Beryl's lifeless body. Tony pressed his daughter's head against his shoulder to shield her from the sight.

"She's at the gate," he told her, then took off for the cave, hoping against hope that Lily had escaped and was waiting for them there.

Riva was standing beside the gate, obviously waiting for them. "Hurry," she urged as Tony raced into the cave.

"Is Lily here?" he asked.

"Where's Lily?" Shala cried simultaneously.

Sadly, Riva shook her head. "The gate is closing, Tony. You can't wait much longer."

"We aren't leaving without Lily," Shala asserted, squirming out of Tony's arms. She ran to the mouth of the cave, peering out. "Where is she, Papa? You promised she'd be here."

He walked over to her, knelt, and brought her to his chest. "Not promised, little one. Just hoping."

His daughter raised her head. In the diminishing pulse from the gate, he saw her eyes were dry and her face full of determination. "Then we'll wait for her."

"Shala," Riva said softly from her place beside the gate, "the dark moon is waning. If we don't cross soon, it will be too late."

As if emphasizing her words, the pulse surged, then vanished. The cave was plunged into darkness.

"I don't want to go to Quakahla," Shala said, unmoved by the gate's disappearance. "I never did. And if Lily can't go with us, I truly don't want to live there."

Although loathing to speak the words he feared, Tony knew he still must say them. "She might not be alive, Shala."

"No, she isn't dead. I sense it, Papa, and that's why we must wait."

She ran back to Riva and looked up at her pleadingly. "Stay with us, Grandmother. We'll live here. This is a wonderful world too, and we could go outside. Lily might take us to the Disney lands."

Her eyes as sorrowful as they were the day Tajaya's battered body was carried into the village square, Riva bent over and kissed Shala's forehead. "I can't, Shala. The Dawn People need me. New shamans must be trained. Traditions must be passed along. There is no one else to do it."

"But I love you, Grandmother."

"And I love you, little one. But sometimes duty must win out over love."

The gate resumed pulsing. Tony looked at his determined daughter, then back to Riva.

"You've had your own doubts about Quakahla, Tony," she said. "The time for choosing has come."

Tony stood and met Riva's understanding eyes. This woman had been his teacher for close to a score of years, was the mother of his late wife and the grandmother of his daughter. Parting from her would leave a hole in their lives. But her warning brought back Quetzalcoatl's message during the Tribunal.

Yes, the time for choosing had come.

The moon was bright, undimmed by the thunderheads and pouring rain—a yellow harvest moon that looked as if someone had taken a perfectly curved nibble from its edge. Lily crept through the woods beneath its light.

The gemstone at her neck had come alive again, delivering toxic surges to Sebastian's body. He'd staggered several hundred yards before falling to his knees. Taking advantage of his weakness, Lily had ripped the knife from the sheath at her waist and driven it into his belly. Freed, she'd turned and fled.

While in Sebastian's grip, she'd heard Shala call her father's name, knew they were by now safely at the gate. She still could join them. The dark moon had not yet passed.

But . . .

Sebastian's injuries weren't fatal. She'd missed the vital spot. He'd shape-shift, heal, and come back to plague mankind. This was her last chance to stop him.

She hadn't fared too well herself. While reeling from his shock, his claws had shredded her plastic cape, leaving deep gashes on her arms. They stung and oozed blood, which the rain diluted and rushed down her hands. She ignored the cuts, knowing they would heal almost instantly. But nothing could heal the werewolf blight except her actions.

She listened intently. Between claps of thunder she heard the soft snap of twigs beneath a heavy weight. She followed the sounds, pausing when the sky roared again. Then a moan came. Holding her knife aloft, she moved stealthily forward.

The earth shook from thunder, the sky filled with a burst of light. Sebastian lay beneath a tree, half man, half wolf. His hands were over his stomach; blood seeped between his clawed fingers. His silver coat was singed and matted with mud and leaves.

"It seems your magic hinders my alchemizing, my dear," he croaked. "Have you come to finish your handiwork?"

Slowly moving closer, knees flexed, legs spread, she swung the knife before her. "You'll make no more monsters like me, Sebastian. Your rule has ended."

"Ah, Lily . . . how magnificent you are. As fierce in your mortal state as you were as a Lupine." He sighed. His pointed ears and facial hair disappeared. The man she'd met in Paris emerged, but now the ice blue eyes were faded and sad. "I have missed you,

Lily . . . none go to the opera with me since you have been gone."

She sensed his sincerity, but didn't trust it. His mood would change like mercury when his wounds were gone. She continued forward, keeping her eye on the small, vulnerable spot beneath his sternum. One sharp stab would slice his aorta. Death would come quickly.

"You brought elegance and grace to the Lupine race," he gasped. "A humanity, if you will. None can take your place."

A flood of yearning overcame Lily—Sebastian's yearning. A cry for enduring love, for kindness and gentleness, for integrity, for the humanity he spoke of. This was what he'd valued in her. Not her devotion to Lupine Law, not her ability to keep the betas and omegas in hand, but for the remnants of simple human emotions she'd somehow retained.

And she remembered the irresistible tug of the hunger, knew it drove Sebastian just as it had driven her. None had been able to withstand it except Morgan Wilder. None.

"I loved you, Lily." He sighed. His hands regained their human form. The flow of blood from the wound was easing. This was her last chance. She mustn't hesitate.

A tear spilled from his eye. "Even now I love you . . . fool that I am."

Waves of compassion assailed her. Fighting them off, she lifted the knife and moved closer, but each footstep she took seemed heavier than the one before.

Pausing, she watched in morbid fascination as the lone tear streaked down Sebastian's mud-smeared mortal face.

"Lily . . ." He spoke so softly she barely heard it.

She let out a choked cry, horrified to realize she was backing away, then spun and took off through the forest. Somewhere she lost a sandal. She let it fly and kept on running. Tears streamed down her face, clogging her breath, but still she ran. Out of the woods, through the village square, toward the cave, the gate of light that would take her to another better world. But, oh dear God, she'd left a monster alive in this one, and that omission would haunt her the rest of her days.

When she reached the sharp rocks inside the narrow canyon, she stopped running, but her sobs remained. Her shoulders shook badly, her foot ached, and she barely maintained her balance as she crossed the unsteady field of stone.

Only when she reached the mouth of the cave did she look at the sky. The rain had stopped. The clouds were moving off. And above—oh dear God—shone the moon, large and round, as bright as a globe-shaped lantern.

The dark moon was over.

Chapter Thirty

On the far wall of the cave a faint light pulsed, vanished, and pulsed again. An image only marginally brighter than the light appeared within the pulse.

"Star Dancer," Lily cried ecstatically.

"Call me Riva," the High Shaman replied. "You've done well, White Wolf Woman, and have earned that right."

Lily rushed forward. When she reached the wall the light was gone. The cave was plunged into darkness.

"Wait!"

"It's too late, Lily," Riva said thinly from the other side. "The dark moon has moved on."

"No, oh no!" Wrapping her arms around herself, Lily sank to the floor, too numb to weep or wail. Now and then a lightning flash came through the mouth of the cave, a cruel reminder of how she'd missed the only light she cherished, the one that would take her to her loved ones.

How would they fare in paradise? Would Shala be bereft that Lily had failed to join them? Would Tony be overcome with grief? Or would they forget about her in time? Except, of course, when the legends were told.

She'd never wanted to be a legend. Never wanted to be a werewolf queen. Since her earliest memories she'd yearned to be an ordinary person, with loving and ordinary parents. To marry an ordinary man and raise ordinary children. Why hadn't she remembered this before succumbing to Sebastian's seductive promises. Why hadn't she remembered before it was too late?

She lowered her head to her hands and rocked back and forth on the hard dirt floor in the darkness, trying to endure her pain.

Rocks shuffled near the mouth of the cave, but she paid them no heed. Her misery was far too great to wonder what was out there. Then something touched her shoulder. She brushed at it absently, thinking it was an insect, and her hand connected with warm flesh.

She jerked up her head.

Tony stood before her, with Shala in his arms. Lily stared at them, frozen in place for the time it took to take one long breath. Then she sprang to her feet. New tears flowing, she threw her arms around them, hugging them, kissing them. Tony pushed back the hood of her rain cape, stroked her hair. Shala hung on to her fiercely, also crying.

"How? Why?" she gulped between sobs. "I thought—"

"We've been searching all over for you, Lily," Tony said, his voice crackling with emotion. "We'd given up hope."

"You didn't even know if I was still alive! And you've come back too late to cross to Quakahla." Their sacrifice was almost more than she could bear.

"We couldn't leave without you."

Tony still stroked her hair, as if confirming she was truly in his arms again. Lily nestled deeper into his shoulder and ran a hand down Shala's arm, seeking the same confirmation. They stood like that in the shelter of the cave for a long time, not moving, not talking. The faint glow of moonlight came through the entrance of the cave. Only the drip-drip-drip of water from the stone walls kept the silence from being complete.

A clatter outside broke them apart. They listened warily. More rocks clattered.

"The wolf that ran away," Tony said.

Only then did Lily realize he thought she'd killed Sebastian. "No," she whispered, filled with shame. "I—I couldn't do it, Tony. Sebastian is still alive."

He put a hand under her chin, leveling his gaze at her as if trying to gauge her reason. Then he nodded in understanding and put Shala on the ground. Inching closer to the entrance, he gestured for the two of them to stay put. Lily paid him no attention. Telling Shala not to move, she scooted along the wall until she reached Tony's side. He made a hissing sound of disapproval, but took her hand anyway, and they both cautiously peered out of the cave.

Sebastian stood on the rocky ground, staring up at the moon, his silver coat rippling in the gentle post-rain breeze. Philippe cowered at his feet in wolf form. Raising his arms, Sebastian started shouting at the sky in the Lupine tongue. He cursed the moon, the dark forces, his every word heavy with outrage and sorrow.

"What is he saying?" Tony asked.

"He thinks I went to Quakahla."

"Then let's not clear up his misunderstanding."

He gave her a nudge and they slunk back to Shala. Lily saw him place a finger over Shala's lips, saw her nod. The mouth of the cave grew dimmer. The moon was sinking. Eventually Sebastian stopped bellowing. Soon after that, they again heard the rattle of disturbed stones.

"Let's wait till dawn," Lily said, "just to make sure they're gone."

Tony agreed. Shala fell asleep across Lily's lap, and as time passed, she felt sure enough Sebastian was gone that she dared speak.

"I should have killed him," she said regretfully.

"He was your kinsman, Lily. That couldn't be easy to forget."

"I won't fail the next time." Her words came out clipped and decisive.

Tony nodded, believing her.

"But what of you? You've missed a chance to live in paradise."

"The spirits have been guiding me on a different path," he replied, then told her of Quetzalcoatl's message during her inquisition. He ended by saying, "I've been ignoring my misgivings for some time, but when I thought you were lost, my choice became clear."

"You chose me over Quakahla?"

"Yes, Lily." He leaned forward and put a soft kiss on her lips. "Without you there'd be no life for me no matter where I was."

"Nor for me," she murmured. "Nor for me."

They awoke to sunlight spilling through the mouth of the cave. Birds were singing, the sun was shining, the air was cool and fresh. And when they stepped outside, Lily found a world so clean and pure, she was sure nothing evil could survive. With Tony and Shala she crossed the jagged path that led back to the village, moving slowly because of the missing sandal.

Then she spotted a tuft of silver fur caught between two rocks. She lingered, staring down at it. Shala continued to lithely leap across the rocky ground, but Tony stopped and squeezed her hand.

"Will you go after Sebastian?" he asked.

"In time, I suppose." She met his clear golden eyes, took in the gentle waves of his dark hair, then glanced at Shala. Everything she needed was right here. "In time."

"When that time comes, I'll be with you."

"I hoped you'd say that."

Then, leaving the hair and all the memories it evoked behind, they went on toward the village. A ghost town greeted them. The gates to the empty pens lay on the ground, ripped loose in the storm. The longhouse door was open, the building stripped of everything that mattered.

It seemed so sad to Lily. A tribe that lived here secretly for a thousand years was gone forever. Then she saw Beryl's body not far from the hearth where Kessa had cooked each morning. Tugging Tony's hand, she led him toward it.

Beryl was in human form, the gaping wounds he'd received from Ravenheart still very much in evidence, but the cruel sneer had left his face and he now seemed at peace. Not far away, Arlan Ravenheart also lay dead, his oddly cocked head the only evidence of his injury.

"We'll build a pyre for them before we leave," Tony said, "and scatter their ashes in the river."

A shaman's words, Lily thought. A shaman's deed. All creatures are one in the eyes of Quetzalcoatl.

She nodded. "Sebastian will leave now," she said. "There will be no more werewolves in Ebony Canyon." Then she had another thought. "What happened to White Wolf Woman, Tony, after she drove the wolves from the wild forest?"

Tony grinned. "She returned to the deer people, and lived the rest of her life as an ordinary doe respected by all."

Lily smiled brightly at the words she'd been longing to hear.

Then she turned and led Tony away from the fallen bodies toward his wickiup. He called for Shala, who came running quickly, and arm in arm the three of them walked across the village center.

"Will we go to the Disney lands now, Lily?" Shala asked.

"Yes, sweetheart. First thing after we get a bath and some new clothes."

For some reason they all thought that was funny and laughed in unison. Still feeling like laughing, Lily looked up at the blue, blue sky. Much remained the same. She still had the magic of White Wolf Woman, Tony was still a shaman, and shaman's blood still ran through Shala's veins. But a shining future lay ahead of them, one that promised the opportunity to live as ordinary people.

At least for the time being.

Dear Readers:

I hope you enjoyed *Shadow of the Wolf*. When I first conceived of Tony White Hawk in *Shadow on the Moon* it was love at first sight. But Lily? I wasn't so sure about *her*. The fallen heroine is somewhat unusual in romance novels, and redeeming her was not an easy task. Yet, somewhere between the first and last page, I came to understand, forgive, and love her, too. When Tony fell hard for her (and he did have so much to forgive), I felt in my heart that these two were meant for each other. If you also found yourself understanding, forgiving, and loving Lily, and cheering her during her struggle toward redemption, then I've done my job as a writer.

For my next book, *The Fire Opal*, I'll leave Ebony Canyon and send reunited childhood sweethearts deep into the swamps of Bayou Chatre. They encounter one eerie experience after another. Soon the toothpick structures they've built to explain away the superstitions of their Cajun heritage come unglued and feed the embers of their abandoned love until it burns so hot it cannot be denied. It is my wish that their journey has you on the edge of your seat until the very end.

With warm regards,

Connie Flynn